Here's what critics are saying about Jennifer Fi...

"It grabbed me by the hand ... until the very last page. Highly recommended."
—*Melody's Bookshelf*, on "Unbreakable Bond"

"Weaves mystery with laughs (and a few tears). This delightful tale is a definite read! I would read it again as well as the rest of the series."
—*Should You Read This Book?* Review Blog, on "Secret Bond"

"The characters are always so well written. They feel like they could pop off the page. I can't wait for the next book in the series!"
—*Wakela's World*, on "Secret Bond"

"I approached this book with the idea that it would be the light reading many of us look forward to enjoying in the summer. It turned out to be more than that and I couldn't put it down."
—*The Birch Bark*, on "Secret Bond"

BOOKS BY JENNIFER FISCHETTO

Gianna Mancini Mysteries:
Lipstick, Lies & Dead Guys
Christmas, Spies & Dead Guys (holiday short story)
Mini Skirts, Mai Tais & Dead Guys

Jamie Bond Mysteries:
Unbreakable Bond
Secret Bond
Lethal Bond
Dangerous Bond

Danger Cove Bakery Mysteries
Death by Scones

Disturbia Diaries:
I Spy Dead People

LIPSTICK, LIES & DEAD GUYS

a Gianna Mancini mystery

Jennifer Fischetto

Lipstick, Lies & Dead Guys
Copyright © 2014 by Jennifer Fischetto
Cover design by Yocla Designs

Published by Gemma Halliday Publishing
All Rights Reserved. Except for use in any review, the reproduction or utilization of this work in whole or in part in any form by any electronic, mechanical, or other means, now known or hereafter invented, including xerography, photocopying and recording, or in any information storage and retrieval system is forbidden without the written permission of the publisher, Gemma Halliday.

This is a work of fiction. Names, characters, places, and incidents are either the product of the author's imagination or are used fictitiously, and any resemblance to actual persons, living or dead, business establishments, or events or locales is entirely coincidental.

To Mom, Aunt Connie, Aunt Marie, Linda, and Vicki—for making that night at Aunt Marie's house the best scare ever! And for all the awesome memories.

CHAPTER ONE

I drop my purse on the hardwood floor and giggle like a teenage girl at her first boy band concert. The apartment is small, the bathroom so tiny there's only room for a shower stall, not a tub, and the toilet is close enough to the sink that I think they're married. The bedroom closet won't hold my growing boot collection or all of my handbags. I may have a slight addiction.

But despite the apartment's limitations, it's all mine. I don't have to share one single square foot. I can paint over the current off-white walls, fill the front windows with plants, and buy an excessive amount of cute pastel throw pillows.

I half-twerk, half-chicken dance across my new space. Yes, it's as bizarre as it sounds, but I only do it in private. And not very well.

Having my own place is a first for me. Of my twenty-six years, I spent the first twenty-three living at home. Then I moved to Connecticut and lived with my chatty, somewhat self-absorbed cousin for two years. She got married, and what did I do? I moved in with the super hot, super new boyfriend, Julian, hereafter known as Douche Nozzle. I should've immediately known we weren't soul mates. Who finds true love and moves in with them after one week?

I moved back home to South Shore Beach, New York four days ago, and it's been awesome. I forgot how entertaining it is listening to Ma sing show tunes while she cooks and cleans. This week's theme is *My Fair Lady*, and yes, Ma, it would've been lovely if I could've danced all night in the rain in Spain. The only down part about being back home is my sister and niece are staying with my folks, too, and I've had to endure sleeping on their lumpy couch. But I've missed my family tremendously, and being home simply feels so right. And the cream cheese icing on the pumpkin cupcake—I'm craving sweets—is that the folks handed over the keys to the apartment above the family deli. The one my parents lived in when they first married. The one my siblings and I were conceived in. Despite the pungent stench of salami and Pine-Sol, and what an eye-watering combination that is, I choose to believe this twist of fate, this full circle, is the universe's way of pushing me down the right path. Hopefully I'm correct, and the universe isn't mocking me.

    I open my arms wide and take in a long, deep breath. Then immediately gag, sputter, and choke like a dying car. Dear God, my brother lived here for five years. How did he stand it? Silly question. This is the same person who left a pepperoni and Swiss cheese sandwich in his backpack in the trunk of the car during a camping weekend with Pop. In June. Not only does he have seriously odd taste buds, but he could live in a can of sardines and not be bothered.

    I rush forward and open each of the three windows facing the street out front. I press my nose to the middle screen and breathe in lungfuls of clean air until I'm lightheaded and almost pass out. That would be one way to not notice the smell.

    My phone plays Cyndi Lauper's "Girls Just Want to Have Fun," which means it's my sister. I swipe the green flashing circle while making a mental note to use the rest of my credit balance on cases of Glade PlugIns.

    "Izzie, I shouldn't be much longer," I say. She and I have a night of drink, dance, and darts ahead of us. This will be our first night out since I've been back. I'm just waiting for my bed to arrive.

    "Why are my husband and his buddy hauling a mattress out of his truck?" Her words are garbled, as if her mouth is directly pressed against the phone.

    The answer seems pretty obvious to me. "Where are you?" I ask, and spot her car parked down the street by Park Place Bakery.

    "In the deli. Pop's cleaning the front counters, and I'm in back."

    No doubt peering through the peephole in the door. I don't know what's wrong with her marriage. When Ma and I pressed her on it, she said something about lonely nights and cabana boys. She gets muddled when upset. This was two days ago. I figure a pitcher of margaritas, a few hip thrusts to the latest bebop, and she'll be spilling her guts.

Ma gave me explicit instructions to report all findings back to her pronto, but I won't betray Izzie's trust. Ma knows this. All those times Ma tried bribing me with ice cream or cookies so I'd spill about Izzie's latest crush or whether she really went to the library after school. Not once did I tell what I knew, and I knew tons. Izzie was not a reader. Despite her being five years older than me, she's my sister, and I'm not a tattler. Besides, Izzie knows a wild shopping cart didn't dent Pop's car when I was in twelfth grade. I accidentally inhaled some secondhand marijuana smoke—that's my story anyway—and got slightly high. Then I volunteered to go on a munchies run. I didn't see the Return Carts Here sign when backing out of the space. I only tapped it. Nine years isn't long enough though for that truth to come out. Not that Pop is violent or easily angered. I just don't want to see the disappointment on his face. He restored and adored that car.

"You couldn't ask someone other than Paulie to help you move?" Izzie's voice penetrates my memories.

Heavy boots clamor up the back steps.

"Pop asked him. I couldn't very well say no. Ma and Pop aren't bringing the rest of the furniture until tomorrow after Sunday dinner. As appealing as it sounds, sleeping in the shower stall is out of the question."

I turn to let Paulie and his buddy in and spot an unfamiliar guy standing by the breakfast bar. I scream and freeze, because that will save my life.

The phone slips from my hand as I remind my heart to beat.

"What is it?" Izzie shrieks from beside my shoe.

Something hard hits the door. "Gianna?" Paulie calls through it. He sounds concerned. Good brother-in-law. No matter what's going on between him and my sister, he has a lifelong duty to help me move, kill spiders, and protect me from murdering, raping, stealing home intruders.

Technically the guy doesn't look threatening, but I read that Ted Bundy didn't either. How did this guy sneak up behind me? The downstairs entrance has a dim light bulb, but it's only two walls and a narrow staircase. How didn't I hear him?

He's wearing khaki shorts, a light blue polo shirt, and beige flip-flops. He holds his skull. "Whoa, dude, you can see me?" He looks barely legal and sounds like he's spent one too many hours surfing waves.

What is he talking about? Of course I can see him. Did he accidentally inhale secondhand weed smoke?

Paulie manages to open the door without letting go of the mattress and knocking his buddy down the stairs.

Izzie still calls my name. If she was a loving sister, she'd run up with Pop's cleaver, regardless of the fact that her husband is making his way in.

"Are you okay?" Paulie asks as he turns the corner. His sweaty face is pink, and his eyes are wide. He stares wildly around the room, which is really one half stretch of the neck, and looks straight through Surfer Dude.

Oh crap. I take a step closer and realize Surfer Dude isn't standing but hovering. Well isn't this interesting? My brand new apartment comes equipped with its very own ghost. How many have I seen in my lifetime now? Close to a thousand? What is he doing up here? And does he do windows? That's the worst chore in the world.

"Gianna?" Paulie asks again, dragging the mattress farther in and allowing me to catch a glimpse of his buddy—six feet, bleached blond, light green eyes, and a back so broad he won't need shoulder pads when they come back into fashion. All the weird things do.

I instantly blush, already knowing the fantasy I'll have tonight on that very mattress. "Um, yeah, sorry. It was just a spider."

I snatch up the phone, say, "I'm fine. See you in a bit," and disconnect the call.

Paulie nods. "This is one of the paramedics, Harry. And this is my sister-in-law, Gianna Mancini."

I hold out my hand, anticipating his warm flesh against mine, and practically purr, "You can call me Sally."

Harry and I exchange smiles bright enough to put the sun out of work. While he checks me out from head to toe with a slow, smoldering gaze that almost singes my black mini dress to ash, I do my best not to lick my lips. It may have only been two weeks since Douche Nozzle and I officially broke up, but it's been four months since I got freaky. That's not very long, but since that time has been filled with a *hide-in-your-bed, sobbing, snotting, Ben & Jerry* emotional meltdown and an out-of-state move, it feels like a stint in a nunnery.

Paulie smirks. "So, uh, bedroom?" He tugs the mattress forward, almost pulling it from Harry's grip.

As soon as they're out of earshot, I wave Surfer Dude over and whisper, "You know the freezer's downstairs, right?"

"Yeah, I know, but I don't need it now."

I do my best *what'chu talkin' 'bout, Willis?* pout. "But you're dead, and all good dead beings leave this world through the freezer." For some reason our deli freezer is the portal to the other side. I don't know why this is, and none of the ghosts I've ever encountered know either. I've often wondered if there was something special about our freezer or if there were freezers all over the country acting as rotating doors to the great beyond. Whatever that is.

He shrugs. "I'm not ready to go yet. Is there a deadline? The freezer's not disappearing, right?"

I cock my head and frown. "Exactly how does a freezer disappear?"

He shrugs. "I don't know. I haven't exactly died before. But you can see ghosts, so anything's possible."

He has a point. "No. Leave when you're ready, but I didn't sign up for a roommate." I don't mean to sound stingy, but a plus-size girl with an adequately big butt shouldn't chicken dance in front of people.

He flashes a smile that would put the Cheshire cat to shame. "You won't even know I'm here."

I roll my eyes. I doubt that.

Paulie and Harry step back into the living area. "We'll get the box spring and set it up."

As much as I want to drool over Harry, I don't have time. Izzie's known for her impatience, and I need to get downstairs before Izzie explodes and Pop has to clean up bits of her off the back door. "Don't bother. Just prop it up against the wall, and I'll do it later."

"Are you sure?" Paulie asks. He chews his bottom lip, which means he wants to talk to me—probably about Izzie. I wish I could pat him on the head, rub his belly, toss him a treat, whatever will make him feel better, but when I gotta go, I gotta go.

"Absolutely."

They head out, and I turn to Surfer Dude. "What's your name?" I ask.

"Billy."

"How old are you?"

"Nineteen."

I close my eyes for a second, and a chill runs through me. That's way too young. "How'd you die?"

He shoves his hands into his pockets and hangs his head. "According to my folks it was alcohol poisoning."

I attempt to slap him on the shoulder for sheer stupidity, but my hand goes through him. Wait, he's seen his folks. So he's been around for a bit, at least. "When did you die?"

"Spring break."

That's March for the college crowd. "Six months ago?"

He shrugs. "I guess. Time is kinda irrelevant now. So what's with the freezer? Why is it the portal?"

"Beats me. How do you know about the freezer? Does it have a beacon or some kind of alarm only the dearly departed can hear?" It's a question I've asked many times to many different deadies.

He shakes his head. "Nah, some dead guy by the beach mentioned it's the way to pass over, but he didn't say why."

That's the same sort of answer I always get. I guess we're the talk of death-central. Maybe we should add that to our advertising. Mancini Deli—Fresh Sandwiches, Salads, and Portal to the Other Side.

As far as I know, the deli has always been a hub of paranormal activity. When I was eight I went into the walk-in freezer to steal a Good Humor Chocolate Eclair. Ma and Pop were up front dealing with customers, and Izzie and our brother,

Enzo, were arguing over whom Ma told to sweep by the sinks. It was totally Enzo, but he'd do anything to get out of chores, even make Izzie think she'd gone crazy.

The boxes of ice cream were on the third shelf, and I had to climb to reach them. I slipped and hit my head on the floor, knocking myself out. By time they realized I was inside, I was a human Popsicle. There's irony there too. Thank goodness 'cause it slowed down the dying process. According to the paramedics, I flatlined in the ambulance for one minute and thirty-two seconds.

I don't remember much—just falling, and some guy with white hair and shocking blue eyes grabbed my hand and tried to pull me to him. I later realized he was dead, too, a ghost who wanted me to cross over. You'd think there was a more tactful way of welcoming the recently deceased. Yanking is so tacky.

Thankfully, either the paramedics were skilled, or I couldn't fathom a future without grilled cheese. Miss all that ooey-gooey goodness? I think not.

It was after this that I started communicating with ghosts while awake and conscious. I could suddenly see them everywhere. Graveyards and hospitals are the worst. For some unknown reason they pass over to the other side through the deli freezer. The first time I saw it happen I thought the little old lady was looking for the Chocolate Éclairs. Really, who can resist them?

One day I asked one of them, and the guy said it was their way over. It seemed weird, but who am I to say how a dead person should cross? I don't make the rules.

Paulie and Harry walk through the living room with the box spring. Preoccupied with the past, I barely notice Harry's lecherous grin. When they're done, Paulie's steps seem to slow down, as if he wants to hang and chat and brew tea. We can't have that. I practically feel Izzie's negative energy float through the floorboards, and I don't want her to get too annoyed to go out. We both need tonight.

"Okay, well, I need to go." I make crazy eyes at Billy, hoping he'll think I'm a bit unhinged and find a new place to hover. He seems like a nice kid, but I want to be able to walk around in the buff, leave the bathroom door open when I pee, and not have to hold in gas until pain shoots into my belly. I don't think I'm asking for too much.

I run down, knock three times on the deli's back door, and stick out my tongue when Izzie's deep brown eyes appear in the glass. She unlatches it, and I hurry in with a glance to Paulie's black truck. He's watching us through his side view mirror.

I shut the door. "You ready?"

She looks awesome. She's wearing black pants and the pumpkin-colored, silk blouse I bought her for Christmas last year. Even though we both have an olive complexion, she looks good in the color. I wouldn't be seen dead in any shades of orange, brown, or gold. They make me look so washed out. Maybe it has to do with her hair being a milk chocolate shade of brown, and everyone thinks mine is black.

Izzie's arms are crossed over her chest. Her foot's tapping a groove into the tile. "You're not supposed to be nice to him if I hate him. That's the sister rule. What did he say about me?"

Whoa, paranoid much? There's some serious discord between these two. Weren't they happy five months ago? She sent me a photo from their anniversary, and they were both smiling.

"Nothing. I didn't give him the chance."

Her foot stops. A half smile appears on her face. Hurricane Isabella has redirected itself. "Good. I'll go get my purse."

Her three-inch heels click-clack as she heads up front, and I'm reminded of her weird height issue. She's five-four and insists on never standing below five-five. I don't think she's owned a pair of flats since junior high. Meanwhile I'm five-two and won't wear any shoe attached to a long, narrow spoke. Stilettos and pumps are evil, gorgeous torture devices. They trap you with their sexiness and leave you in pain. Give me wedges or chunky heels, even flats, any day.

I walk to the freezer, in my chunky-heeled, thigh-high boots, which are comfortable yet still rockin', and stare at the stainless steel. It's shiny, and it almost looks brand new. Ma knows how to sweet talk with a bottle of cleaner. I tug the handle and jerk the door. It opens with a soft whoosh. I shut one eye, anticipating a freezer full of walking stiffs. Nope. Nothing but trays of Ma's lasagna and eggplant parm. Not a single dead person. Ma will be happy. Not that I plan to tell her though. The family knows I've seen ghosts walk around the deli, but at around age fourteen I stopped sharing. No sense in freaking out their dreams as well. As open-minded as the family is, I don't think Ma would like to know that grumpy, old dead lady from church has been yelling at her every time she's muttered damn all week.

I shut the door and sigh. I'm not sure if no deadies is a good or bad thing. Living above ghost plaza could get disruptive, but then again, I've been kinda hoping to put my skills to use, to help. I like the idea of having "Ghost Whisperer" (in a Jennifer Love Hewitt way) engraved on my tombstone when I die. Although, "Master of Deliciousness Between Bread" will be okay too.

Someone has to invent the next greatest sandwich.

"Gianna, you're staring at the freezer," says Izzie. She should work for the CIA.

I shut the door and turn to her. "Ready? I can really use that one drink."

"We need to make a quick stop first."

I groan. "Does this have to do with Paulie?"

She pushes me toward the back door and shouts, "Bye, Pop. We're leaving." To me she says, "Nope. It has to do with our annoying brother."

"Uh-oh. What'd he do?" I offered to be the designated driver tonight, so we walk across the gravel to my old silver Kia Rio.

"He snuck into the house last weekend, went into the basement while Alice and I were watching a movie, tripped the circuit breaker, and screamed like he was being gutted by a serial killer."

I fasten my seatbelt and try not to laugh. I love her imagination. Knowing my sister, she screamed as well. Knowing my thirteen-year-old niece, she did not. That girl is so like me. My earlier reaction to Surfer Dude Billy doesn't count.

"And what are we going to do?" I pull out of the corner lot and head east on Park Place.

"I went by his house this morning and unlocked the window in his spare room. We're going to sneak in and pay him back."

Oooh, a good old-fashioned Mancini scare. I've missed them. I'm so glad I'm home.

CHAPTER TWO

I was ten when I realized other families don't hide in closets and jump out at their siblings. It's something we've always done, even our parents. Ma says she did it with her sisters, but while Aunt Angela didn't mind, Aunt Stella hated it. Maybe that's why they never got along and Ma didn't want to go to her own sister's funeral.

I turn onto Enzo's street and switch off the headlights. It's quiet. Most of the homes are dark. There are no dogs barking or traffic zooming by. It's a great location. Enzo bought his first home a couple of months ago. He's the responsible one who makes plans and follows through. He decided to join the police force when he was eleven. When he graduated high school, he enrolled in college, got his bachelor's in criminal justice, and then started at the academy.

That's not to say that Izzie and I are irresponsible. Just that our plans don't always work out as we hope. Izzie got pregnant her senior year of high school and never went to college. I majored in psychology with no concrete plans for afterwards, and it shows. I've had one dead end job after another. If the ghost whisperer and sandwich maker gigs go south, I could be a professional babysitter or dog walker.

I park three houses before Enzo's, and we're careful not to slam the doors.

"What if he locked the window?" she asks, sounding worried. Luckily this is a one-story home, 'cause I'm not climbing trees and swinging on vines ever, but especially not in a mini dress. No one needs to know my love for cotton Hello Kitty drawers.

"We'll figure something else out," I say.

I take the lead, bend at the waist, and run along the side of the house in true *Mission Impossible* style. Enzo has no fence or bushes, nothing to block the front from the back. His neighbor to the right has a six-foot, white picket fence along the sides of their property, so we're slightly hidden from prying eyes. Suddenly the tune of Hall and Oates' "Private Eyes" fills my head. Ma's a huge music fan. I know the lyrics of songs released before I was born more than what's currently on the radio.

We get to the last window at the side of the house, and I take a deep breath and hold it. I push the window up. It doesn't budge. What if Izzie's right? How the heck will we pull this off? Then the wood around the glass gives, and the window rides up. I'm so excited that I almost laugh. I lift the pane as high as it will go and freeze. The nearest street lamp casts enough light into the room for me to see there's a lump under the covers on the bed.

I crouch down and exhale slowly. Shoot.

Izzie's by my side. "What is it?"

"Enzo's in there."

"Why is he sleeping in the spare room?" Her whisper becomes shrill.

I shrug. "Because he can? Maybe he christens each room by sleeping in it. Maybe he's role-playing and he's Goldilocks. Who knows? Now what?"

We're silent for a second, and she says, "He's a heavy sleeper. He won't hear us."

Is she crazy? I'd hear someone climbing through my window.

"Remember the time he slept through the smoke detector?"

That's right. I was in junior high and they were in high school when Ma burned bacon on the stove. It was an early Saturday morning, and the darn thing rang for ten full minutes before it turned itself off. Enzo didn't stir the entire time. Izzie and I stood in the doorway to his room, watching him sleep and waiting for Ma to air out the kitchen by beating the smoke with a towel. It became a running joke—how the house would burn down around him and we'd all be outside watching the flames.

We have a weird sense of humor.

"Okay, let's do it." I stand, plant my palms flat on the sill, and hoist myself up at the same time Izzie grabs my butt and pushes me forward.

I knock my forehead into the bottom edge of the window, and it takes all my will not to yelp.

"Sorry," she whispers.

Thankfully, Enzo doesn't have a lot of furniture yet, and this room only holds a bed. I lean forward and tumble toward the carpet. I give a quick prayer that I don't snap my neck and remember to tuck in my head. I land sprawled out in a very unladylike pose, exposing Kitty, and I freeze, listening for signs that we woke him.

Izzie perches halfway in and halfway out of the window in some delicate dancer-type pose. She took ballet as a child. I colored with my box of 96 Crayolas. I don't think Burnt Sienna could've helped with my landing.

We both hold our breath. A door slams in the next house. A car horn honks in the distance. I return to breathing, and Izzie climbs inside, *sans* the awkward finale.

I get to my feet and take a step toward the bed.

Enzo's on his back with covers over his head and one arm dangling over the side, although I can't make it out due to the blankets. In that position though, it has to be his arm. He was never one to worry about the monsters under the bed. Izzie and I liked our limbs tucked beneath our magical blankets, 'cause we knew that nothing could harm us under them.

Izzie whispers in my ear, "I'll find the fuse box."

She leaves the room, and I just stand there waiting.

And waiting.

This is the part of the plan that makes no sense. How is she going to find a small metal box without turning on a light? Granted, Enzo will probably sleep through that too. Some cop he makes. Although I'll forget to tell him that.

I think a carefully laid plan would be great if we were stealing the Hope diamond, but surprise is always best with a scare. Hasn't Izzie learned that by now? She's always been an eye-for-an-eye kinda girl though.

I, however, want to...

Without a second thought, I charge toward the bed, leap as high as I can, and let out a war cry that would make Spartacus proud, especially if I had one of those nifty little loincloth-type outfits.

This time I land with precision—hands on both sides of his head, legs straddled across his thighs.

Enzo doesn't flinch, but I know I surprised him. He had to wake up to that.

"I got you, Enzo," I say and pull the cover off his head.

I gasp. It's not him.

A pasty-faced plastic chick with painted-on blonde hair, brown eyes, and a huge red open mouth stares up at me. Hey, that's just like my lipstick shade—Bossy from ColourPop. It's an online store for lips, eyes, and cheeks that's super affordable and has the most pigmented products ever. I'm an uberfan.

Izzie's voice and Enzo's laughter comes from the hallway. When they reach the spare room, Enzo flips a switch, and the bedside lamp zaps away all the shadows. And I'm left straddling a blow-up doll.

Darn brothers.

"Gianna meet Dolly." Enzo holds his stomach as he leans against the door, chuckling like an idiot. It takes him a few seconds to control himself. "There was a retirement party for one of the Sergeants. He shoved Dolly into my car after. He didn't want his wife seeing it."

Izzie curses under her breath while I detach myself from an embarrassing picture-worthy moment. Thank goodness Enzo isn't clutching his phone.

I don't blame him. It is funny, but Izzie isn't amused, and I'm spending the next few hours with her, so I hold back my laughter.

"You're such a jerk," Izzie says and not-so-playfully slugs him in the arm.

It makes him laugh harder. "You think you're cool coming over this morning wanting another look around because you love this house so much. I'm not dumb, sis. I knew exactly what you were up to when I opened the door."

Izzie can be pretty obvious. She didn't inherit the sneaky gene.

"You'll never get me back," Enzo says. "I'll always be waiting for you."

I grab Dolly and give her a hard smooch on her cheek. Yep, the shades match.

* * *

I pull down the visor at a stoplight just before Lindy's Bar on Atlantic Avenue. I touch up my lipstick, flip one of my dark brown curls to the other side of my side part, and wipe a black mascara dot from under my eye. I pull another strand of hair from the right, dangling, silver, filigree earring and then glance at Izzie. She's still seething about Enzo. Is it really that big a deal?

"We're going to get him," she snaps. Since she's the oldest, she believes she should be in control and win every time. I was never one for the competitiveness. That was her and Enzo. I was just happy talking to the dead.

I pull into the parking lot and toss my lipstick back into my purse. "I know. But you have to admit that was clever." I wait for her to implode on me for taking his side.

But instead she lets out a deep breath. "Maybe."

Wow, she didn't take my head off. I can't imagine her annoyance is solely directed at Enzo. I'm sure seeing Paulie started her snarkitude.

"Let's go. I want to unwind with a drink. It's been a long day." And since I only get one for the whole night, I'm anticipating delicious magic in a glass.

"This will be fun." She plasters a smile on her face. I can't tell if it's genuine or falsely creepy.

We get out of the car and walk across the parking lot. In college this was my favorite place to hang. Admittance for ages eighteen and up, cheap drinks, no cover charge before eight, a small dance floor, and free darts. What else could a living-at-home, nineteen-year-old with a part-time job in a deli want? Besides a photographic memory for acing tests and a loyal, devoted boyfriend who looks like The Rock.

I yank open the heavy wooden door as some guy rushes out. I see a blur of plaid and denim charge toward me, and I freeze. I'd be great in a disaster. Luckily he stops before plowing me down, and we do that weird, embarrassing sidestepping dance together.

I smirk at the awkwardness and look up into his face, but his Yankees' cap is down too low, so I can't make out his eyes.

He grips my shoulders hard to pin me down and runs around me. As he lets go, I wince and watch him head across the street.

"How rude," Izzie says. "Wonder where his fire is."

"Who cares? Come on," I say and make my way inside.

The place is relatively empty and quiet. Since when? It's Saturday night. We have our pick of seats at the bar, and there are even several available tables. I'm a bit dumbfounded. I've never seen it like this. A lot changes in a few years.

We take seats at the wraparound bar and only have to wait three seconds before the cute bartender sets cocktail napkins in front of us. "What can I get you?" he asks. He can't be older than me, with a shot of thick brown hair and light blue eyes. He smiles, and a couple dimples appear. He's gotta be a heartbreaker. I have a couple of dimples too, but I bet I rarely look *that* adorable.

I glance at Izzie. Has she changed too? "A couple of margaritas on the rocks, please." When she doesn't ask for a different drink, I sigh in relief. Nice to know some things stay the same.

When he sets the drinks in front of us, I ask, "Why is it practically empty in here?"

He shrugs. "Everyone's probably at Mitch's Tavern."

I stir the red straw in my glass. "That dive in the East End?"

He nods. "They have live music now." A customer calls him over, and he walks off.

"That's where Paulie likes to hang." The only reason I think Izzie says it without choking on venom is because she's already sipped a quarter of her drink.

"Because of the music?" I ask.

She shakes her head, and her long, wavy hair sways against her shoulders. "Because it's a dive. He fits right in."

Ah, there's the venom. Right on schedule.

I take a sip of my 'rita for liquid courage and go in, praying I come back out with all my limbs. "So what's going on with you and Paulie? Why are you and Alice staying at Ma and Pop's?"

She glares at me in her peripheral, and I hold my breath. Maybe I should've waited until she was on her second or third drink. "He's cheating on me."

Whoa.

My body and mind stop moving for a moment. I never expected her to say those words. Not Paulie. He's one of the good guys. They've been married for four years. Alice was nine when they met, and he loves her as if she was his own. Alice's biological douche walked out on them when Izzie was still pregnant—immediately following high school graduation. So Paulie stepping up and making sure Alice was okay with him gave him huge points in my book.

"How do you know?" I ask, hoping she didn't walk in on him. That has to be fifty shades of disgusting.

She shrugs and takes another sip, more like a gulp. "I just know."

I lay my hand on her arm. "Wait. You don't have proof? Maybe it's not true then."

"We've only had sex twice in the past month," she says and signals the bartender for another. "And when he comes home, he's always tired and immediately wants a shower. A wife knows."

I roll my eyes. That's it? "Maybe he's tired from work, and I'd certainly want to bathe after dealing with the sick and dying all day."

I get another glare. We keep this up, and I'll need to invest in some protective gear. She downs the remains of her drink. "What are your plans now that you're back?"

I guess that's the end of that conversation. Now onto one almost as stomach turning. "I'm not sure. Live in the apartment, work at the deli, spend time with the family."

"Oh yeah, that's a great plan." She winks at the bartender when he places down her second drink.

"What's wrong with it? It's solid."

"And boring. What happened to the girl with dreams of being a doctor, a lawyer, a teacher?"

"I wanted to be a lot of things as a kid, like a spy and a professional candy taster too. None realistic."

"A doctor, lawyer, and teacher are realistic."

"Yeah, if I want to spend another ten years in school, spend my days buried in briefs and law journals, or be underpaid. Besides, I don't want to be those things anymore."

She pokes an ice cube in her glass with her finger. "Okay, then what do you want to be when you grow up?"

I sigh. I've thought of this a hundred times, and I always end up back at the beginning. I don't know. I majored in psychology because I had to pick something. I've worked in various jobs to see what I like and to pay the bills. None of them I want to return to. On the other hand, I don't get the rush to have my entire future mapped out right now. "Do I have to grow up?"

"You'll figure it out one day," Izzie says, trying to be reassuring.

I think it bothers my family more than me that I'm not working toward some specific career. I don't mind waffling in the wind. I'll figure it out eventually.

"If nothing pans out, I have a future in sandwich inventing."

Izzie laughs. She either fondly remembers my BLT abilities, or she's starting to loosen up. And a loose Izzie means some hip-thrusting action is near. I love dancing, letting go and feeling free. In the last year I've only danced once, not counting the twerking and chicken dancing in Douche Nozzle's apartment when he wasn't home. Other than at my Cousin Claudia's wedding, he and I never went out dancing. His job as an investigator for a law firm kept him busy most of the time.

The door opens, and several people walk in. First a tall, slender, tanned couple who look like they stepped off the New York Fashion Week runway. I stare hard at the woman's light blue sheath dress. It's simple yet gorgeous. I wonder if it would look right on me.

Behind them are a couple of middle-aged guys dressed in skinny jeans, V-neck tops, and loafers. This place is not only dead, but there's no one to flirt with either.

The final person is a single guy. He's looking down at his phone, so I can't see his face. Instead I check out the bod. Dark jeans, a light gray tee, and a black leather jacket. There's something familiar about him. I know that jacket.

He looks up, and our gazes lock.

Crap. My entire body tenses.

Douche Nozzle.

CHAPTER THREE

It feels like I've been staring at him for an eternity. My brain is stuck in reverse, and all I keep thinking about is how he said he needed space. Yet here he is, in my bar, in my hometown. Why?

I grab my drink and down the rest of it in one choking gulp, and when I glance back, he's already by our side. "What are you doing here?" I whisper, still a bit shell-shocked.

Izzie looks at me in question then notices him, and her eyes widen even more.

Douche Nozzle glances to her and smiles in that deliciously charming way of his. "Hello, Izzie."

"Hi," she says, all full of sunshine and rainbows. The hypocrite. What happened to the sister rule?

Julian glances around. "I thought this place would be jumping. You always spoke so highly of it."

My chest tightens at the memories of spooning with him in bed while watching the moon and stars through the large paned windows of his apartment. We'd talk about our pasts and share our dreams. There was something so magical about those moments. No matter what the next day brought, the harsh realities, the annoyances of bumper-to-bumper traffic, spilled coffee on a white blouse, it was all easier knowing we would curl up again that night.

He stares at me. I hate his face. His chiseled chin, scruffiness of a ten o'clock shadow, his tanned complexion, tousled dark hair, and those chameleon eyes that lighten or deepen from icy to charcoal, depending on his emotion. Okay, so maybe "hate" is too strong of a word. How about I wish it didn't remind me of laughing at episodes of *Modern Family* while eating Chinese food every Wednesday night? When his job didn't call him away.

I can't believe this is happening. He shouldn't be here. He shouldn't look so calm and beautiful. He also shouldn't smell like coconut and musk. And he certainly shouldn't look so unaffected, just standing here as if I hadn't crushed his heart and soul when I walked out on us two short weeks ago.

The nerve of him. Is he made of steel?

"I just moved here."

His words are like a bucket of ice cold water dumped on my head. What? My body starts to convulse. At least that's how it feels as my mind races with this information.

"Excuse me?" Maybe I didn't hear him correctly. The music is loud, plus tunnel vision sets in.

"Since when?" Izzie places a hand on my arm.

He runs a hand along the top of his hair. "I arrived yesterday. A new job. I start on Monday." His words aren't coming out as smoothly as usual.

His nervousness makes my stomach spasm. If I could be honest with myself right now, I think I'd admit I'm far from over him. I didn't want to break up, but when I left his apartment and stayed with my cousin, he never called or visited. For an entire week he stayed away. It took us a week to fall in love and a week to fall out. Except I'm still very much someplace in the middle.

I suddenly can't sit here any longer. I toss several bills on the bar, not really caring if I'm giving a five- or a fifty-dollar tip, and say to Izzie, "Let's go."

I step off my stool, and my knees feel like jelly. I step around D.N. He doesn't seem to notice my wobbling.

He moves in front of me and tries to prevent me from walking away. I can't allow my hurt feelings to take over again. That week-long self-pity party I had at my cousin's was enough. He had a chance to make things right. He had a chance to say something, but he ignored me.

The pain ignites anger, and I glare. I can't say I glared much in our ten months together. I'm a talker. Had a bad day at the evil day job? Rant about it with friends. Pissed Douche Nozzle left the toilet seat up for the eighteenth time in a week?

Leave neon Post-It notes with instructions written in black Sharpie. Writing…talking, it's all still words.

My glare must work, though, because he takes a step back. "Can we talk in private?"

I scoff. Too late, buddy. "No!" I stomp to my car.

Before I can open the driver's side door, Izzie slides up to me and yanks the keys from my hand.

"Let me drive."

She has more alcohol in her system than I do, but I'd bet her heartbeat isn't in her ears and throat simultaneously.

As she pulls from the parking lot, I try my damnedest not to watch him in the side mirror. My feelings keep jumping from wanting to cry to wanting to lash out at something.

"How can he be here? How can he have a job here? It doesn't make sense. Is he following me around? Stalking me?"

Izzie's been circling the same four-block rectangle for ten minutes.

"Where are we going?" I finally ask.

"I figure you need to blow off steam, so we're doing that."

I punch the door. "I mean, what right does he have to show up out of nowhere? This town isn't big enough for the both of us." Yeah, I heard what I said.

Izzie stifles that giggle. "Maybe he misses you and wants you back."

I cross my arms over my chest and huff. "Well, he should've thought about that while I was still in Connecticut, not after I leave. He had plenty of time to ask me to stay, to talk things through."

Izzie scrunches up her face in that weird annoying way of hers. She obviously doesn't agree with something I said.

"What?" I ask.

Unlike me, she holds everything in. It's like her mouth is constipated. It's no surprise she and Paulie are having problems.

"First, you didn't give him much time. A week isn't very long. And second, you have a habit of walking away when things get too tough. Actually, you run."

Wow, she blurted that out easily. Has she wanted to say it for a long time, or has she changed while I've been gone? Either way... "That's not true."

"Um, what about when Craig died? That's the reason you hightailed it out of here and moved to Connecticut."

I shake my head and press my lips firmly together. She's wrong. I think.

I met Craig Nixon at Lindy's after I graduated college. We hit it off immediately, dated for a while, and fell in love. He didn't care that I hid parts of myself from him. He never asked why he'd sometimes catch me talking to the air. Five months into our relationship his car broke down on the way home after work. I was at his place cooking us dinner. He chose to walk the seven blocks and was hit by a car. The driver was high on coke. Craig was killed instantly, but I didn't realize it when he arrived home. Told him he had enough time to shower before the chicken Marsala was ready. That's when he learned my secret. And I learned he was dead.

Izzie pulls into the parking lot of Mitch's Tavern.

"Why here? I thought you hated this place," I say.

"I didn't say 'hate.' I said it's a dive, and Paulie likes it here."

She circles the parking lot looking for an empty space. At least they're packed. Maybe I can drown myself in a pitcher of margaritas and not care that I'm sitting on cracked barstools or that the guy next to me smells like a distillery. Screw designated driver, too. We can call a cab.

Izzie strikes the steering wheel with her palm.

"What?" I follow her gaze straight ahead. Parked two spaces ahead is Paulie's black truck.

"I am not going in there if he's here."

What the heck is going on tonight? It's the night of the exes. I'm not too sure that's better than the living dead.

"We could go to that place on Vermont Avenue." Her tone is hopeful, so I hate to shatter it, but I suddenly want today to end.

I lay my head in my hand. "I'd rather go home. It's been a long day. And I'm not willing to risk running into another jerk from our pasts."

"Yeah, but how many times do we get to hang out?"

I wish she wouldn't push. "I'm back in town now. We can hang out any time we want."

"But I'm a mom. And I don't have time for myself," she whines.

I don't point out that Alice is thirteen and no longer in need of her constant attention.

"What is that?" she asks.

I look up and see movement in the front seat of Paulie's truck. She inches my car closer and puts on the brights. It's hard to make out, but it almost looks like something neon blue weaving and bobbing. She puts the car into park, opens her door, and steps out.

For reasons I'm not sure of, I follow her. My stomach is in knots. I'm not sure if it's from my encounter with D.N. or whatever is going on in the truck, but I have a really bad feeling.

As we reach the driver's side window, I realize Paulie's in there. His seat is all the way back, and his face is contorted in a look I never wanted to see, but I'm sure Izzie knows intimately. And the movement is some woman's face in his lap.

Izzie gasps and covers her mouth with her hand.

With all of today's activity, including seeing D.N., I do the only thing a sister can. I curl my hand into a fist, bang on the window, and shout, "Hey."

The woman—at least I think it's a woman in a neon blue wig or oddly shaped hat—looks up as Paulie opens his eyes.

Crap! I stagger back.

Her face is covered in white paint with pink, round circles on her cheeks, drawn-on long lashes, and a painted mouth even bigger than Dolly's.

Paulie's getting blown by a clown.

CHAPTER FOUR

It takes a second for our mental hamsters to pick up their slack jaws and jump back onto their wheels.

A clown? Balloon animals, teeny car, squirting flower clown? Seriously? I'm momentarily struck with how hilarious this is, but if I laugh, Izzie's sure to slug me. Plus, I'm not insensitive. Usually.

Paulie's the first to move, swatting at the clown to get up. His windows are rolled up, and a drum solo in the bar makes it impossible to hear him, but he mouths "wife" to the clown, who wobbles on her knees. You'd think she'd bolt out the door and make her escape, but she just kneels there. She must be drunk.

Izzie moves next. But instead of ripping open the door with super human strength and wrenching each of them from the vinyl interior, she steps around me and climbs up into the bed of the truck. When she jumps out, she's holding an aluminum baseball bat.

Oh no.

Paulie jerks open his door and stumbles out, zippering up his pants. Dude, can't you do that in the truck?

Something falls off his pants and rolls toward my feet. It's round and red. I pick it up and realize it's the clown's nose. Oh no! I shove it into my purse before Izzy can see it.

"I can explain," is the first idiotic thing out of Paulie's mouth. "Just listen," is the second. And with each syllable, Izzie tightens her grip on the bat.

I step in between them. Maybe not the brightest move, but I won't spend the night at the police station waiting for Pop to bring bail. Plus, under normal circumstances I like Paulie, and he has a nice face. That won't last once a bat messes it up.

"I'd stay out of her way," I say as a warning.

Two couples leave the bar and turn our way to get to their cars. I'm pretty certain catching a crazed woman growl in the headlights of a truck is pretty shocking. They stop and watch because an audience is exactly what we need right now.

The clown manages to stumble out of the car. She falls onto her knees, and I pray Izzie isn't paying attention. I consider doing my twerk-slash-chicken dance. No one can stay mad watching me make a fool out of myself. But it needs some serious work before I perform it in public. I figure it'll be ready in never. And mostly, I don't want to make light of this serious situation.

Instead I shout, "Izzie, don't do this."

She either doesn't hear me with the music blaring or doesn't care. I'm laying bets on the latter. She grips the bat with both hands, swings high, and shatters Paulie's left taillight.

Paulie backs away, pressing into the chain link fence that separates this parking lot from Golden Express, the Chinese place next door. Who, BTW, makes *the* best pot stickers in the entire world.

"For three years I've cooked and cleaned and have given him a great home," Izzie shouts.

I stand a couple of feet from her, not wanting to get hit by flying plastic shards. I should do the sisterly thing and stop her. Somehow. But I figure letting her kill her husband's car rather than her husband *is* the sisterly thing.

She aims for the right taillight and glances at me, bat way above her head. "Do you know the things I've done for him because he enjoyed it?"

Oh God, I don't want to hear this.

"Foot massages. He spends eight-hour work shifts in thick socks. Oral sex. You know how strong my gag reflex is."

Yep. In sixth grade her class went on a field trip to a museum, and when she reached into her mouth to unstick a piece of taffy from a back tooth, she touched the roof and puked all over the kid seated next to her. The other kids called her Pukey for a long time.

"And the icing on the cake," she says, "I applied the ointment when he had anal fissures."

I frown, unsure what she's talking about, although anything that has the word *anal* it in should be a telltale sign that I don't want to know. Just the same, I say, "Huh?"

"Hemorrhoids."

Oh crap. No pun intended. In that case I take a step back and allow her to swing to her heart's content.

And she does. The right taillight pops out, and Paulie's groan is unmistakable.

From the corner of my eye, I see the clown stagger off farther into the back of the parking lot. There's no way to get out by car, but if Mr. Wong hasn't fixed the fence, she may be able to squeeze through the broken links.

I'm grateful the clown is gone. Izzie loves Paulie, so while she may smack him or want to, I know deep down she doesn't want to hurt him. I can't say the same for the woman doing the one thing Izzie only performs out of duty.

"And how does he repay me? By screwing a clown?"

Technically they weren't having sex, at least not in the traditional sense, but I keep my mouth shut.

"Lots of men cheat. I know this. But usually it's with the temptress secretary or friendly coworker. Sometimes it's even more scandalous and with the wife's best friend or sister."

I raise a brow, waiting for her to glance my way, but she doesn't. She better not. That would be gross. He's practically my brother.

"But no. He had to pick *It*'s sister."

I smirk. I can't help it. At least I'm not chuckling. That would be totally inappropriate.

She swings again but this time striking his back window. It's one thing to break a couple of taillights. It's another to try to shatter an entire window.

"Whoa, Iz. That's enough."

She looks into my eyes, and fear strikes me. To say she looks crazy is an understatement, and for a second I wonder if she'll come after me with the bat. But I remind myself this is Izzie—the girl who threatened to kick Alfred Shaw in the balls when he called me a dyke 'cause Ma cut my hair too short in middle school. And Izzie's the one who virtually held my hand and let me cry in her ear for two hours when I walked out on

Douche Nozzle. Just because I did the breaking up doesn't mean it didn't hurt like bacon grease splattering on bare skin.

Izzie beats the back panel, causing it to dent some. Paulie's going to have one heck of a bill when she's done. It's not like he can file an insurance claim.

"Tell me, Paulie, what attracted you to her the most? Was it the big mouth? Do I not wear enough makeup for you?"

I bite my lip and suppress a snort on that one. She has a point. How could he look past the costume, or does he have a clown fetish no one knows about? Is that even a thing?

"I knew it. I knew it. I knew it," she says through clenched teeth. "Oh, not that you'd humiliate me with Chuckles, but that you're a coward and a bastard."

I glance over at Paulie who's decided to squat by the fence. His weight pushes into it. His head is bent toward his lap, and his fingers are in his hair. He's not even watching anymore.

A wave of sympathy washes over me. I know I probably shouldn't feel this way. Izzie would kick my butt if she knew. But Paulie's been a cool brother-in-law, and up until this point, I thought he was a great husband.

"All I asked for in return was your love and trust." She walks to the driver's side door and practices hitting the window, like a golfer lining up his shot on the greens.

By now a bigger crowd has emerged. There are whispers, but everyone is pretty quiet all things considered.

"I didn't expect candlelight dinners every weekend or luxury vacations. Heck, except for our three-day honeymoon in Atlantic City, we never even had a vacation. But I deserved more than finding you doing the one thing you swore you weren't doing. In public!"

She swings, hits the glass, and it shatters. Broken shards fly onto the seat. Startled by it, I flinch, Paulie shouts, "Come on," and Izzie dances on her toes. She laughs and acts as if she just won a championship.

Heading to the front of the car, Izzie knocks out a headlight. Then the other. She strikes the windshield, but luckily it's as thick as the back and doesn't shatter on contact. She hits it again and again until a crack forms and spreads. She's clearly going over the deep end. What's next? Slashing his tires and keying his doors? Maybe carving her name into his pleather seats?

A tall but scrawny guy with blond, spiky hair turns the corner. He's wearing a blue, half-apron and has a small white towel slung over his shoulder like he's about to burp a baby. He must be the bartender, which means someone went back inside to alert him. What a tattler! No way he heard us over the music. "Hey, what's going on?" he asks.

Izzie doesn't care. She doesn't stop. Has she already leaped over the edge, arms outspread, hoping to fly?

"If you don't get out of here right now, I'm calling the cops," the bartender shouts.

Soft-spoken chatter floats among the crowd and out to us, like whispery tendrils.

Paulie gets to his feet and steps off the fence. "Izzie. Stop!"

She looks up and locks eyes with him. Her pupils are wide. She takes another swing, and the bartender hurries inside, muttering under his breath.

I step forward, fearful of getting hit but more fearful of calling our parents to ask for bail money. Every time I've had to ask them for money, they've reminded me I'm an adult, even though I don't feel like I've grown up. And technically the money wouldn't be for me, but still.

I step between her and the car and keep my voice even. "The cops are coming. Think of Alice. She can't have her mother in jail."

She flinches, hesitates, and lowers the bat a few inches.

I take that as a sign and grab the head of her lethal weapon. "Let's go. Now."

She allows me to take it from her and turn her toward my car. Just in case she gets riled up again, I toss the bat into the back of Paulie's truck and climb into my driver's seat. Izzie and I are playing musical chairs tonight, all due to a couple of guys.

I don't get it. We're just a couple of regular girls who love to accessorize, appreciate a really good red wine, and eat our weight in carbs. When did our lives become so insane?

As I pull out of the lot, my headlights display people staring, pointing, and gawking. And the guy from Lindy's, the one in plaid and a Yankees' cap, with whom I'd danced at the front door. He turns and walks toward the back of the parking lot.

I take a last glance at Paulie. He's climbed back into his truck and is just sitting there. What the heck was he thinking?

* * *

There's no way I can take Izzie to Ma and Pop's. She's likely to wake them with her seething. Besides, who can sleep after this? So I plan a mini adventure. First I head to the closest liquor store and buy a bottle of raspberry flavored Smirnoff. Then I drive to the gas station for a couple of cups of ice, and finally I head to Lincoln Park. Yes, the streets in this town are named after the Monopoly game, as well as dead presidents. I think the original founder was really into money.

Growing up, my then best friend, Hilary, lived across the street from the park in an apartment with her mom. Whenever I visited her we'd come here. Even when we were too old for the teeter-totter, we'd either sit on the swings or be up on the boardwalk, just chilling with our feet dangling over the side. That's exactly my plan now. To get Izzie to a state where she's too calm or too drunk to wake anyone.

I park my car, grab the bag of booze, and head across the street. But the park isn't how I remember. The slide, the swings—all of it is for little kids and is way too small for us. I distinctly remember a metal slide. When did it change? Everything feels like I've been gone so much longer than three years.

"There's no place for us to sit," I say.

"I'd rather not be under a street lamp anyway." Her mouth is turned downward, and I can't tell if she's still angry or about to start crying. I hope it's the former. Once she starts blubbering it'll take her a while to stop, and I didn't bring tissues. I might have a T-shirt in my trunk.

I take her hand and walk up the ramp to the boardwalk. There are benches, but I don't want to get arrested for public drinking. I shove the bag into her hands, unzip and pull off my boots, toss them over the railing to the sand below, and climb over the metal bars. I haven't jumped off the boardwalk in years. The ramp down is only a block away, but this is faster.

I forget to bend my knees when I land, and pain shoots through my shins. I groan and reach up.

Izzie drops the bag into my grip and jumps over, still in her heels. Never under five-five.

I peel off my socks and pick up my boots, and we walk to the water. A gentle wave splashes up to my toes. The water is freezing. I take a few steps back, sit down, and fill our cups. I hand one to her.

"You know—I knew it. He kept denying it, but I knew. A wife always does." She plops onto the sand.

I don't respond because I know she doesn't want to hear me say how sorry I am or that it'll be okay. She needs to vent, so I need to keep my lips shut.

"How can he do this to me, to us? And with a clown? Seriously?"

I reimagine the car scene and shiver. It's worse than Stephen King's *It* on so many levels. I'm gonna have nightmares for weeks. I take another swig of my drink.

"And just wait until I find her," she screams. "I'm going to kill her."

CHAPTER FIVE

———

It's so cold, I'm shivering, and I can actually hear my teeth chatter. Condensation billows out from my mouth. Fog surrounds me. No matter how far I walk or in what direction, it's thick and never ending. Fear crawls up my back until it's wrapped around my throat and makes breathing difficult.

An old man appears before me. He's hunched over and looks to be in pain. But when I get closer, he straightens and smiles widely and creepily. His skin stretches so tightly across his bones that it looks like his face is made out of putty. Piercing blue eyes stare at me, and a familiar shock of white hair sits atop his head. He reaches out his hand, wanting me to take it, to pull me over to his side.

I know this, I fear this, yet I extend my arm just the same. No matter how much I don't want to touch him, I can't stop my arm from rising.

Cold radiates from his fingertips as they brush mine. Just before we touch he fades away.

* * *

Gosh, it's cold. And why is my new bed so lumpy…and sandy?

I open my eyes and stare at the dusty blue sky. What the…? I sit up and wipe the drool from the corner of my mouth and end up covering my lips in sand. Izzie is sleeping beside me. Waves crash to my left. The sun peeks at the horizon. We fell asleep on the beach?

I push Izzie's arm. "Iz, wake up."

What time is it? I pat myself down. I left my phone in my purse under my seat in the car. Shoot. What did I do that for?

Because I knew I wouldn't need it while I listened to my sister whine, and deservingly so, about her marriage.

My head pounds. I get to my feet and shove Izzie again. "Get up. It's light out."

Her eyelids flicker, and she bolts up. "Crap. What time is it?"

I pick up my glass and the empty bottle of vodka. "I don't know. Let's get out of here."

"I hope Alice isn't awake yet."

I frown at her. What teen wakes at the crack of dawn on a weekend? "I'm sure she's still asleep."

She grabs her cup, and we head to the nearest ramp.

Once we're back in my Kia, I feel a bit calmer. Waking up outside leaves me feeling disoriented and exposed. One of the reasons I never went camping with Enzo and Pop. Another is bugs, dirt, and more bugs. Eww!

I flip on the interior light, pull out my purse, and dig for my phone. It's almost six- fifteen. I toss them both onto the floor behind the passenger seat then stare at Izzie's rumpled skirt and blouse. It was white last night, and this morning it looks almost cream colored with several small red spots.

After Izzie had cursed the clown and Paulie about thirty times each, I'd lost track of time and the conversation. I hadn't eaten much yesterday, so the vodka went straight to my head. The last thing I remember is Izzie slurring her words. Something about implants and the inadequate size of Paulie's penis. I thought she was considering bigger boobs, but now I realize she meant a penile implant.

"What are you staring at?" she snaps, giving me the stink eye. She's a cranky morning person.

"The stain on your shirt. Do I look as bad as you?"

She looks down to the row of buttons. "Yes, and that's blood."

My heartbeat jumps. Is she hurt? "From what?"

She holds up her left hand. There's a cut next to her palm, beneath her thumb. It's so small I barely see anything. "It's from the glass last night. It's not a big deal. Can we go, please?"

"Sure." I back out of the space and head to Ma's.

* * *

I pull up in front of the two-story, part brick and part Stucco house I grew up in and glance at my sister. "Will you be alright? I need a shower and a nap before I deal with this afternoon."

Sunday dinner is so important to Ma and Pop that they actually close the deli for the day. Most people think they're crazy, me included, but it makes them happy, and they've always done it. They start the day with church then cooking, eating, and sharing with family. It matters more than an extra day's income. As a kid it meant the world, even if I didn't fully understand it. As an adult, I could really use the work hours. Egyptian cotton sheets and Kitchen Aid mixers won't appear out of nothing.

"It's fine. I plan on doing the same." Izzie opens the door and gets out. She doesn't bother waving back, just lets herself into the two-story house and shuts the door.

I drive to my apartment and stagger up the back stairs. The first order of business, after peeing and coffee, is a scalding shower and assembling my bed. Then that nap. With my dress hiked to my waist, I run to the toilet and relieve my angry bladder. I peel off my sandy clothes and jump into the shower. The chill both from that weird dream and from sleeping on the beach is still inside my marrow. I can't seem to make the water hot enough to warm up. I try to take my mind off it, but thinking of last night is worse, and it's really hard not to think of the horribleness. I can't believe Paulie did this. I can't believe Izzie has to deal with this crap. And I can't believe D.N. is in town permanently. I need a day of puppies and rainbows.

I scrub my skin until it tingles, but as soon as I step out, I'm cold again. What the chicken club! And for some reason the salami scent is stronger when the temps are down. I run to the thermostat to check the heat. I bump it up a few degrees and rub the goose bumps on my arms. Coffee. That's what I need. Intravenously if possible.

I dress in a long sleeve, pink tee, white sweatpants with Betty Boop on the thigh, and thick socks. What can I say? I like big-headed, animated chicks. I go to the unopened, brand new Mr. Coffee on the kitchen counter and notice Surfer Dude Billy in my peripheral. I pretend I don't see him. Too bad ghosts don't sleep.

"You look hungover. I hope your kitty got lucky," he says in a happy, upbeat tone that wouldn't annoy me if I'd slept in an actual bed last night. I don't mind mornings as long as I'm allowed to move at a tortoise's pace and there is silence, something having my own space is supposed to offer.

"Did you just make a crack about my vajayjay?" I try to tear into the coffeemaker box with my back to him, but I chewed my fingernails off last week, and the leftover stumps aren't long enough to help yet.

"Hello Kitty. Your underwear. Get it?" He roars with laughter. "Man, you're either a grouch, or you didn't get laid. And that's a shame 'cause you got that thick, curvy thing going, and you're kinda hot."

"Kinda? If you're going to live in my apartment, you can at least butter me up."

"Will that be on white or wheat?" He cackles.

I smirk. A corny ghost. That's better than my grumpy ghost-aunt in Connecticut. I use my teeth to gnaw at the tape holding the box flaps together. Ma packed a small box of kitchen gadgets, extras from her drawers, but I'm not sure if I even own a knife or where they are.

"Um, have you noticed your new guest?" Billy asks.

"Dude, you and I met last night. What's wrong with you?" Is he amnesiac or something? Maybe he died from a hit on the head while drunk. When I find the time, I need to check out his *who, what, when, where, and why* status. And speaking of *why,* why the ricotta pie am I so cold? I hope I'm not getting sick from sleeping on the beach.

"Not me. Her."

Her? Her who? What is he talking about? I turn, corner of the coffee maker box still in my mouth, and follow his stare.

Standing over by the windows is the neon-blue-haired clown. Yep, *that* home-wrecking clown!

"I'm dead, aren't I?" she asks.

The box slips through my hands. It lands right beside my left foot, nicking the corner of my big toe. Ow! That's gonna bruise. "Why are *you* here?"

Billy raises his brows. "You know her?"

"Considering she just screwed my very married brother-in-law last night, not well but more than enough."

"We didn't have sex. I don't think." She looks bewildered, as far as I can tell. That painted-on smile is making my head spin. I need to find my Tylenol. It's in one of my boxes.

I push the coffeemaker out of my way with my foot. "Oral still counts as adultery."

"Do I know you?" she asks.

"Oh, come on. I may be dressed a little less hoochie right now but… Wait, you're dead?"

"You're swift," Billy says with a scoff.

I give him a look of disdain then focus on the clown. "How? When?"

She shakes her head. "I don't know. I don't remember."

I lean on the breakfast bar beside Billy. "Puhleeze. How is that possible?"

She shrugs.

This isn't happening. While I want to know why she decided to come up here, my stomach churns with nervousness. How did she die? And can't she just pass through the freezer without a formal good-bye?

I grab my phone from my purse and dial Izzie. It goes straight to voicemail, which means her cell is off. Great. She probably passed out as soon as she hit our old room, but she may be in the shower or planning Paulie's murder. I need her to hear this from me and not the TV. Ma should be up. She's one of those cheery, early morning people. I dial their landline next. Yes, they're the only couple on the planet that still owns a landline and rarely use their emergency-only cells.

"What's wrong?" she asks after two rings.

I smile and roll my eyes. She's so dramatic. "I'm fine, Ma. I was wondering if Izzie is up."

"Didn't you just drop her off? Did she spend the night at your place or at home with her husband where she belongs?" Water runs in the background. She must be making coffee. She loves it more than I do.

"Um, yeah about a half hour ago." I ignore the second question. She'll have to learn about last night from Izzie. That's her place to tell. "Never mind. I'll talk to her later."

"Okay, remember, we eat at two."

That hasn't changed all my life. "I know."

I hang up and call Enzo. It rings four times before his voicemail picks up. "Hey Enz, it's me. I'm wondering if you guys found any dead bodies this morning. Give me a call."

When I hang up, I lightly kick the coffeemaker box and go in search of the Tylenol.

* * *

I'm running a comb through my wet curls when my phone buzzes. I hurry into the living room and spot the clown and Billy seated on the floor where a couch would go if I had one. There's no way they're both staying here.

"Tell her about the freezer," I say to Billy.

While he fills her in about portals, I grab my phone. It's Enzo. "Hey, thanks for calling back so fast."

"I'm downstairs," he says.

My chest tightens. Something's up. Otherwise he'd call rather than make an impromptu visit. "I'll be right there." I hang up, yank on sneakers, and slip the phone into my bra. Where else can it go? It's not like fashion designers make women's clothing with adequate pockets. Besides, if the pink Felina is good enough to hold my double Ds, it can also support the electronic device that is my existence.

I grab my keys and run down. Neither of my ghosts seem to notice. Some houseguests they are.

A thin cloud blocks the sun, but it's still bright out. A light breeze makes me glad I'm wearing long sleeves, but it's much warmer outside than in. Double the ghosts must mean double the chill. Another reason to help them move on ASAP.

Enzo leans out the window of his red truck. "Why'd you ask about a dead body?"

I nod toward the building. "Why you think? There are two ghosts in my apartment, and one died last night."

He scratches his chin. "There was a body found a bit ago. I'm on my way there now."

"Officially?"

He glances away. "Not exactly."

Enzo aches to be a homicide detective. It's all he's talked about most of his life. He's taken the exam and now is waiting for a spot. Since the force isn't that big, he's basically waiting for someone to retire or die. Not something he likes to say out loud.

"Is it a woman?" I ask.

"Yeah, a clown on the beach."

Goosebumps pop up onto my arms. "Crap."

I don't need to say anything more. He nods. "Get in."

* * *

As soon as I jump into Enzo's truck, the clown appears in the back seat. I'm used to ghosts popping up whenever they want. In my shower, in the cart at the grocery store. Weird stuff. But this is my first dead clown, and she's seriously creeping me out.

"What's your name?" I ask her, figuring calling her "the clown" only adds to the creep factor.

"Emma Tinsdale, but my clown name is Cupcake."

Of course. "You mean was."

She averts her gaze, and sadness seeps into her eyes.

Normally, I'd feel awful, but she helped screw up Izzie's marriage. Can't say I'm feeling the love right now.

"What'd she say?" Enzo asks, searching the back seat through the rearview. Like he's going to see her. Silly guy. Tricks are for resuscitated sisters.

I fill him in on all I know so far, including why Cupcake's lipstick is smeared.

He gives me that look, the one that wonders if Izzie's the reason we're racing to a crime scene.

I shake my head. "Of course not. I was with her the whole night." Except for when I passed out and slept soundly outside on the beach. I must've been exhausted and sauced because I used to have trouble falling asleep to Pop's snoring from the next room. But I could've been in a coma, and I know Izzie wouldn't kill a person. Just cars.

Enzo pulls up behind a police cruiser on Broadway. The area is flooded with emergency vehicles, which makes driving nearly impossible. He puts his truck into park and turns off the ignition. "My badge will only get us so far. I'm not a detective, and I have no right being here."

I don't expect to be able to walk up to the body and start poking around. This isn't my first crime scene. When I realized the Craig in his apartment wasn't of flesh and bones and would no longer enjoy the dinner I cooked, I raced to where the accident had taken place. I don't recall much before the tunnel vision set in, other than a cop holding me back, the very one I've always shared a hate-hate relationship with.

"This is it? Where I died?" Cupcake makes a noise that sounds like she's sucking in a breath, but ghosts don't breathe. As for sucking... Never mind.

My stomach flips, even though I'm not supposed to care. I follow Enzo out of his truck and onto the boardwalk. The crowd is massive—people practically glued together in one long and wide parade. I grab the back of Enzo's jacket as if I'm a kid, and we push our way through. Luckily, his badge gets most people moving out of the way. I step on a few toes of the ones who don't. Hey, you gotta move 'em or lose 'em.

We make it to the ramp leading to the beach. Enzo doesn't need to flash his badge to the officer who's pretending he's one of the Buckingham Palace guards, making sure no one unauthorized goes down. Enzo points to me. "Hey, Arnold. This is my sister."

Arnold is huge well over six feet, broad as a quarterback with padding, and a crew cut that shows off his square head well. "I can't let her go down. Sorry."

"Let her stay up here, close to you."

"Sure." He steps aside for Enzo to go down and points to a spot right beside him and away from the main crowd for me to stand. It gives me a perfect view of the beach, too.

Yellow police tape sections off a large portion of the sand, and at water's edge is a body. The wig is missing—she's a redhead—but the rest of the outfit matches. I visually search the water for a blotch of neon blue, but I don't see it. A couple of plain-clothes detectives inspect the sand around her.

"That's me." Cupcake hovers beside me.

I don't glance her way. I can't take my eyes off the scene ahead. This is only four blocks from where Izzie and I spent the night. That can't be a coincidence, can it? But if it's not, what does it mean?

Enzo approaches the detectives. One of them turns toward him, and I get a good look of his ugly mug. Kevin Burton. Of course.

I must make a disgusted sound because Cupcake asks, "What?"

I shake my head. She doesn't need to know my business, and it's not like I can tell her with a cop pressed against my spine. He'll haul me off to an asylum, and I'll miss Ma's manicotti later today.

Kevin went to school with Izzie. He was best friends with Alice's father. Before the pregnancy, the three of them hung out at our house frequently. Which made it easy for Kevin to leer at me. I was only thirteen, so some of his innuendoes went over my head. It was never physical. Not then. But Enzo overheard him once and nearly knocked the jerk's front teeth out.

When I was in college Kevin tried again, but this time he used his hands. Let's just say I kneed him so hard I bet his left nut aches whenever he sees me approaching. And because his itsy-bitsy feelings were hurt, he has it in for me.

When my boyfriend Craig died, Kevin tried to blame the accident on me. As if I stole a car and hit Craig on purpose because he forgot Parmesan cheese at the store. But even without a motive, Kevin tried busting my butt for a week straight. He'd park outside Ma's and watch the house. Finally Pop called his supervisor, and Kevin stormed away, madder than before.

He started dating my ex-best friend Hilary right before I moved to Connecticut. I know it was to get at me, but at that point I didn't care. I was itching to get off this island, away from all the pain, and Hilary and I had stopped talking senior year of high school anyway. Shoot, maybe Izzie's right. Do I run?

The only reason Enzo deals with Kevin now is because they work for the same police station. Kevin was promoted to detective earlier this year. Enzo won't admit it, but he hates that. I will admit it. So do I.

Now, Kevin glances up at me. His eyes narrow, and his mouth twists into a snarl.

I consider offering a half smile or flipping him the bird, but he's not worth the exercise.

"You sure you want to be here?" I whisper to Cupcake.

Arnold shifts his weight. I keep looking straight ahead, whistle half a bar of "My Little Sunshine," and pretend I haven't said a word.

I glance to Cupcake as she disappears. Gee, rude much? How about a good-bye? A see-ya-later? Or even a thank you for finding her corpse? Guess she couldn't hack it. Who am I kidding? I would've freaked as soon as I realized there's no more bacon in my future. Does she really not remember what happened to her? I think back to last night and how she wobbled and seemed out of it. She must've drunk a lot not to recall anything. Or she's lying.

With all my time chilling with the afterlife, I still don't know if ghosts can be trusted. Other than dear, dead Aunt Stella in Connecticut, who doesn't really like me, and D.N.'s grandmother, I've never spent more than an hour with one. They usually move on quickly. I have a feeling Billy's going to be a handful. Cupcake, too.

Several cops search under the boardwalk. I can't imagine anything important being that far away from her body, but what do I know? I spread mayo on toasted bread for a living. The only rules for sandwich making is don't slice off a finger or sneeze on the order.

An officer shouts, "Over here. Get me a baggie."

Kevin and an older detective rush over. Enzo follows but stays several feet behind.

I lean over the railing as do many on the boardwalk, but I can't see a thing.

They seem to hem and haw below for an eternity. I glance at Arnold, who raises his brows, also curious as to what they found.

Eventually, they come back out, and one of them is holding a giant evidence bag with an aluminum baseball bat inside. Is that Paulie's? No, it can't be.

The sun glints off the bag, and I spot blood along the tip of the bat. Cupcake's blood? As in she was hit with the bat? Was she murdered? My mind flies to the drops of blood on Izzie's shirt.

This can't be happening.

CHAPTER SIX

It takes Paulie six minutes, two knocks, three doorbell rings, and one very loud fist-pounding-slash-kicking before he opens his front door. His eyes look like he poured gasoline on them and lit a match. He wears light blue pajama pants and a white tank, and there's a small, red stain the size of a blood droplet on the right strap that I'm hoping is from shaving and not beating bodies. What's with my family and bloodstains? I suddenly feel like a character in a vampire novel.

He squints, shielding his eyes from the sunlight. "What are you doing here, Gianna? I don't need a lecture."

"Do I look like a schoolmarm? I'm not giving one."

When Enzo dropped me off at my apartment, I ran up determined to get the truth from Cupcake, but she wasn't there. Neither was Billy. You'd think a couple of unemployed dead people would have no place to go and no one to see. Yesterday, I begged for an empty apartment. Today, it's suffocating. I need answers. So I jumped in my Kia and drove straight here.

Paulie rubs his face hard with his hand. "Then what?"

Normally, I'd be a bit miffed that he's not inviting me in for tea and crumpets, but under the circumstances, I'll let it go. This time.

"What happened after Izzie and I left last night?"

"What do you think?"

I sigh dramatically. "I don't know, Sherlock. That's why I'm asking?"

"I came home." He exhales loudly.

If he thinks he can win in a sighing contest, he's sadly mistaken. I have experience as a teenage girl. He does not. My sighs and eye rolls are an art form.

"You didn't see the clown again, after we left?"

He frowns. "You think I'm gonna hook back up with her after my wife kills my car?"

That wasn't what I had in mind, but it's interesting how it's his first thought.

"So what about the bat?"

He rubs the back of his neck. "What about it?"

"Where is it?"

He shrugs. "In the back of my truck where you tossed it."

I can't tell if his demeanor is flippant because he's an emotional wreck and can't be bothered, or because he's purposely trying to avert suspicion. I realize I'm being super paranoid. I don't actually believe Paulie is capable of killing a woman over an affair. Over anything. But I still need to make sure.

I turn and walk to the driveway where his truck is crookedly parked.

He follows me, steps on a pebble, and winces. The big baby. "What are you doing?"

"Checking on the bat."

He scoffs. "You think I'm lying? First your sister accuses me for months of cheating. Months."

I look into the truck's bed. Nothing. I lift a light blue tarp. It's empty. "You did cheat." I remind him.

"Yes, one time, last night."

I face him and place a hand on my hip. "And you don't think that counts?"

"Of course it does, but I wasn't cheating all those times she accused me. I was working late, trying to make money so we could live in this house. I am a good husband."

I get his point. Izzie's badgering was uncalled for, but he's starting to piss me off. "No matter how misguided or wrong Izzie was, you still chose to cheat. You don't get to blame that on anyone but yourself."

He opens his mouth to say something, but I'm tired of listening. Plus, the temps have risen, and I'm starting to sweat. Perspiration is as horrendous as the DMV line and taxes.

I start walking off and tap him on the chest twice. "By the way, you have more to worry about than Izzie leaving you."

He sucks in a breath as if surprised, like he hasn't realized that's even a possibility.

"The clown's body was found this morning. She was beaten to death with a baseball bat."

He turns a dumbfounded look to his truck.

"And yours is missing."

* * *

I drive nine blocks east and park in front of Ma and Pop's. I let myself in through the front door and instantly smile at the aromas of coffee and tomato sauce. It's great to know the deliciousness hasn't changed.

The living room is empty. Clanking sounds come from the kitchen, and the shower is on upstairs. I walk toward the sounds of pots and pans, and find Ma stirring a spoon in her tall, dented silver pot. She cooks all her pasta in it. That thing is probably older than me.

She's dressed in a navy blue dress and black heels, but her hair is still in curlers. She still uses the old kind that you stick bobby pins in. And she's humming "Tomorrow" from *Annie*. We must be on a new week. "Lorenzo, did you grab my purse."

I set mine on the table. "Ma, it's me."

She halfway turns, brows up. She looks me up and down. "Why aren't you dressed?"

"I'm not staying. I need to talk to Izzie, and I'll be back later."

She nods and turns back to her pot. "I think she's in the shower. There's time for both of you to join us for church."

I roll my eyes. Every Sunday since high school graduation, she asks or states the same thing. When is she going to accept that church isn't for us?

"No thanks." I grab a mug and pour coffee into it. While I add sugar and half-and-half, Ma watches me from the corner of her eye.

"Are you going to tell me what's going on between the two of you?" she asks. "This feels like when you were in high school. All the secrets, the whispering…"

She drops the wooden spoon inside the pot and turns fully. "You're not pregnant, are you?"

I snicker. "Hardly." I'd have to be having sex for that to happen. My eggs are single and fancy free.

She pulls out the spoon, rinses it off, and places it on a ceramic spoon holder. "Fine. I won't press, but you know I'm here for you if you need to talk, right? And there won't be any judgment."

I smile, lean into her, and give a one arm hug, still holding strong to my cup of coffee. "I know, Ma. This isn't my story to tell though. I love you."

She pulls back just enough to push one of my erratic curls behind my ear and kiss my cheek. "I love you too. You're a good sister and daughter, Gianna. I wish my older sister and I got along like you and Izzie."

Oooh, did she just give me a segue into their discord? "Yeah, tell me again what happened between you and Aunt Stella."

She narrows her eyes and smiles. "Nice try. It was nothing."

But that can't be true. If it was, she'd spill. One day I'll get it out of her. Hopefully it'll be half as juicy as the things I've imagined.

She pats my arm. "Come downstairs. I want to show you my latest collection piece." She flips the basement light switch, and we walk down.

The front half of the room is lined with metal shelving that holds the crazy trinkets Ma's collected over the years, an antique locket, a blood-tipped switchblade, a stuffed bear with a missing eye. And so much more. This is Ma's murder room. So to speak.

It started simply enough when Aunt Stella, Ma's oldest sister, was found dead in her bathtub. The cause of death was drowning, but for a week there was suspicion of foul play, due to blood on the candleholder and shoddy police work. During that time, Ma got it in her head that someone snuck into the old house she and her sisters grew up in and killed her. Aunt Stella wasn't the nicest person, always barking at people, so it wasn't too farfetched. It turned out she didn't pull the drain plug before standing up and slipping into her robe. She slipped, hit her head first on a metal candle holder, and then on the side of the tub before going underwater.

After the truth was discovered and the candleholder returned from the police, Ma took it and put it on her dresser. She never explained why it became so important to her. I think it has something to do with them never getting along. Like maybe this was Ma's way of finally being close to her sister.

It spurred a compulsion for Ma to collect murderabilia, but for years the only item she owned was the candleholder. Then Pop bought a computer, opening up a world of murders for her. She began blogging, and before long followers started sending her murder items they acquired. She must own nearly a hundred now.

We're pretty sure most of them are fakes, but they make Ma happy. It's not that she enjoys death. She doesn't want people to die, but it's pretty inevitable, and acquiring an object from a case that makes the news gives her some kind of thrill. She takes precautions too. Like getting a PO Box from the post office and using a fake name. The online community knows her as Clarice. Yeah, she totally borrowed the name from *Silence of the Lambs*.

Except for our immediate family and one of Ma's close friends, people in her real life don't know about her murder shrine. We're perfectly aware that our hobbies and interests aren't exactly normal. We, as a family, spend our free time concocting the best ways to scare the crap out of each other. I communicate with the dead. Enzo's a cop, wanting to investigate the dead. And Ma collects items that once belonged to the dead. We should have our own reality TV show—The Deadly Deli—but I think you need to have a special sense of humor to appreciate it all. Some people don't get that scaring one another, that jolt of adrenaline is super fun.

Ma picks up one of those square, silver lighters with the lids and hands it to me. It's in a baggie. Everything is. Ma wants to preserve the items.

"Please don't tell me this was a weapon used in burning someone," I say.

"No," Ma says. "It did belong to a man accused of killing his neighbor in Portland."

I flip it over, see the initials JHP carved into it, and hand it to her. "What did the neighbor do?"

She places it back on the shelf. "He played his music too loud night after night."

"Gosh, some people are so testy. Did this JHP guy ever think of calling the cops instead of murder?"

Ma laughs lightly. "I thought the same thing. They discovered the murderer is schizophrenic and his hallucinations told him to kill."

"That's sad," I say.

We head back upstairs.

"For the murderer or the victim?" Ma asks and turns off the light.

"Both."

Pop is in the kitchen, putting two slices of rye bread into the toaster. He gives me a hug and a kiss and nods to the table for Ma. Her purse sits beside mine. "Why is your purse so urgent when you still have to go up to finish your hair?"

"I feel naked without my lipstick." She rummages through it and pulls out a tube.

Pop shakes his head. He never understands us girls.

Footsteps sound on the stairs. As Izzie rounds the corner, I wonder if I should tell her about Cupcake in front of our parents. What if she doesn't want them to…?

Oh my goodness. My jaw drops at the sight of her hair. This morning, it was waist length, and now it's just below her chin and very uneven.

"What'd you do?" I ask.

Ma and Pop stare, mouths open, too.

Izzie self-consciously runs her hand down the back. "Is it that bad?"

Actually, it's super cute and accentuates her face. I tell her so. She doesn't seem too happy though. Not unexpected. I doubt a compliment will stop her feeling like her world has caved in.

"I thought a change was in order." She reaches for the coffee.

I go over to her, crowd her at the counter, and whisper, "How are you?"

She waves her hand and takes a sip. I don't know how she drinks the stuff black. "I don't want to talk about me. Why are you here so early? I figured you'd be sleeping."

"I wish, but I've had a very eventful morning. An uninvited guest showed up."

She wiggles her brows. "Julian? How does he know where you live?"

"No. It wasn't Douche...er...*him*. It was the clown."

Color floods her cheeks. She sets her mug down with a bang. Somehow it doesn't crack.

Ma gasps. Pop, who's in the fridge, turns around. "What's wrong?"

We ignore them.

Izzie clenches her fists, but before her head explodes, I quickly add, "She's a ghost."

This takes the scream out of her sail. "What?"

"She's dead, Izzie. I called Enzo. They found her body this morning."

"Who's dead?" Ma's eyes gleam with joy. Yes, we're all a bit warped.

Izzie glances their way and says, "Last night, we caught Paulie with another woman."

Ma gasps. Pop slams the fridge door. A stack of aluminum plans on top rattles. "I'll kill him."

Ma groans. "Oh don't be so dramatic, Lorenzo."

Yep, Ma's the pot, and Pop's the kettle.

"This is our baby girl, Rosa. No one hurts our baby." Pop's usually a laid-back, quiet guy, so hearing this makes my heart swell.

Ma scoffs. "I know that. I'm just saying it may not be that bad."

Now it's mine and Izzie's turn to scoff. Is she serious?

Ma opens her mouth again. "I just mean..."

But before she ends up digging herself deeper, Izzie storms past them.

I follow, stopping her by the front door.

"Wait. There's more. They found her on the beach, only a few blocks from where we were last night. She was bludgeoned, and they found a bloody baseball bat."

Izzie wobbles and leans against the wall. Since she's already shaky, I may as well go in for the kill.

"And since the bat is missing from the back of Paulie's truck—I checked—I'm assuming it's the same one with our fingerprints all over it."

She blinks twice. "You went to Paulie's?"

Did she hear me?

I nod. "Yes, and he looks like crap." That should make her happy.

One corner of her mouth lifts. I know her so well. "Good. I hope he killed her. Then he can spend the rest of his pathetic life in jail." She runs upstairs.

I go back into the kitchen for my purse and remember the thing in it. I hand Ma the clown nose. Who knew, when I picked it up last night, it would become a part of our lives? Maybe I should turn it over to the cops, but it's not like I found it on the beach near the crime scene. And it would give a lot of pleasure to the woman who raised me and who loves me. Seems like a clear-cut decision.

She stares at the red blob. "What's this?"

"It belonged to Emma Tinsdale. The woman Paulie was with. The one who was murdered last night."

Ma squeals, kisses my cheek, and rushes down to her shrine.

CHAPTER SEVEN

When I pull up to Ma and Pop's for the third time today, I immediately spot D.N.'s black SUV parked across the narrow street. You've got to be kidding me. I consider leaving and going back to the apartment, but Ma will kill me if I miss a Sunday dinner. They're practically holy—up there with baptisms and 50% off sales at Macy's. And since I've already been here today, I can't feign malaria.

After leaving earlier I went back to a quiet apartment, put together my bed, and crashed for a couple of hours. When I woke up, Billy and Cupcake were still gone. I seriously need to invent a supernatural pager.

As soon as I open my door, D.N. does the same. I can't get away now even if I want to. He'd probably follow me.

"This has to stop," I say, slamming my door harder than necessary.

He's by my side in three long strides, and my breath catches in my chest. One of the things I love about him is the confident way he moves, which of course leads me to think of his bedroom moves and the way he uses his tongue to…

"We didn't get a chance to talk last night," he says.

I look away so he won't see the lust in my eyes. "That's because I don't want to talk to you. What part of that do you not understand?"

Just because I want to tear his clothes off doesn't mean we have anything to say to one another.

The front door opens, and Ma looks out. Darn. There's no way she's going to let me push him away. She has a compulsion to feed people. I think it's an Italian thing. They can be complete strangers, and it doesn't matter. She wants to feed the world. I guess that's why she and Pop opened the deli.

She hurries down the steps and over to my car. "Julian, is that you? You've been sitting out here for almost an hour. Why didn't you knock, hon?"

Hon? Seriously? She's only met him twice—once when I first moved in with him and then for my birthday last spring. She and Pop drove up to Connecticut to make sure I wasn't shacking up with a serial killer. Little did I know he'd slay my heart.

"Hello, Mrs. Mancini. I've been waiting for Gianna. I didn't want to intrude." He kisses her cheek.

She swats the air. "Nonsense, dear. You're always welcome. Now come in, and join us for dinner."

I toss a glare her way. She puts up her mother-knows-best face, and my glare bounces off her. She's like a superhero with special maternal powers.

I brush past both of them. "And one day when I'm married and have kids, you'll still be inviting him inside." It's a stupid comment, but I'm annoyed and a tad hurt that she doesn't ask me first. Don't my feelings count? She birthed me, not him.

I head through the living room, stopping only long enough to kiss Pop on the top of his head. The TV blares, so he doesn't hear my hello. He's too busy watching *Jaws* eat someone. I find Izzie in the kitchen pouring a huge glass of red wine. She's dressed in yoga pants and an oversized, stained tee she wore when pregnant with Alice. She still owns that thing?

I glance down at my blue wrap dress and the black suede, chunky heeled boots. A large silver owl hangs from a long matching chain that nestles just below my chest. He's cute. Totally costume but cherished. So while I'm comfortable, I'd rather be in leggings and an oversized tee.

She looks my way. "Want some?"

Ma and Julian enter the house.

I nod. "Oh yes. And why doesn't the dress code apply to you?"

She grabs another goblet and pours me half a glass. "Because my husband is a no good, cheating bastard. Do you have one of those around?"

Pop greets Julian with sheer jubilation in his voice.

"I have a bastard. Does that count?"

Izzie shrugs and slurps her wine.

* * *

The seven of us are seated in the formal dining room, stuffing ourselves. Well, Pop and Enzo are stuffing. Enzo acts as if he only eats once a week—Sunday feast—but he used to stop here for dinner nightly, and I doubt that's changed. Izzie's having a liquid lunch, Ma's talking nonstop with D.N., and Alice is pushing her food around on her plate. She's texting beneath the tablecloth and trying to go unnoticed.

My niece looks up, and I give her a quick smile. She and I used to be close. I was her age when she was born. Izzie got pregnant on Valentine's Day, on some cheesy date Joey planned—McDonald's and wine coolers in the back of his father's van. Izzie still winces when it's mentioned. I wince for her. Not that we mention it often. Alice has no idea the circumstances around her conception, and if it's up to Izzie, she never will. After graduation Joey moved away to college and never came back. Alice was born a week before Thanksgiving. I helped Izzie look after her and on occasion pretended she was mine. She was cute. All pink and squishy.

Now, she's still cute but ornery. She inherited it from me. She's all kinds of awesome.

I'm sandwiched in between D.N. and Izzie, staring at Paulie's empty seat across from me. Every time D.N. raises his fork or reaches for his glass, his arm brushes against mine. Why couldn't my dress have long sleeves?

"How's school, Alice?" I ask, hoping to steer the conversation to something that's not personal. At least not for me.

Alice shrugs and shoves a wedge of lettuce in her mouth, probably so she won't have to talk. I should be ashamed to put the kid in the spotlight.

An awkward silence rides over us, and I want to go home, but I need to wait if I want furniture. Ma and Pop have a garage full of old pieces from the past, purchased from garage sales but never used, given to them by dead or dying relatives. It's not my first choice. I prefer new things that don't have other people's juju, but I can't be picky right now. My job at the deli is part-time and doesn't pay much. I'm glad Ma and Pop aren't charging me full rent.

"The manicotti is delicious, Mrs. Mancini," D.N. says.

If she tells him to call her Ma, I'll stab myself in the eye with my fork.

"Thank you. So how is it that you were offered a job here in town so soon after Gianna returned?" Ma asks.

Yes, I'd like to hear that answer.

He glances my way before answering. "I applied for the job months ago."

He did?

Ma stares at me with that goofy grin on her face. When I told her, on the phone, we had broken up, she was almost as upset as I was. I don't know why she likes him so much. Or why she almost defended Paulie earlier. She does the same thing with Enzo—gives him a free pass on stupid stuff like breaking up with his last girlfriend via text message. The man is twenty-eight years old. He knows better.

D.N. keeps his attention on me. "I wanted to keep it a secret until I knew I had the job. Then my grandmother died, and everything…well, it got crazy."

He means we started arguing. A lot.

His grandmother's ghost appeared in his apartment shortly after her death. I was just coming out of the shower, and she got full frontal nudity. I knew exactly who she was. We'd met before, and she adored me. And after I screamed and slipped into one of D.N.'s shirts, he raced into the room, much like with Billy in my apartment yesterday, and I had to pretend I didn't know his beloved grandmother was dead.

She didn't want to pass over that day or the next week. Not until she spent more time with her grandson and made me promise to give him a message. She then moved on, and the arguing over her letter began.

Before D.N. can finish his story, which I'm suddenly very curious about, there's a knock on the door. Pop gets up to answer it, and Kevin, also known as the jerk with a badge, and his partner walk in.

Crap.

I quirk an eyebrow at Izzie, who stiffens and tells Alice to go upstairs if she's done. The teen doesn't have to be told twice. She charges up mid-text. I'm totally impressed she doesn't smack into a wall.

Enzo rises and greets his coworkers. "How can we help you?"

"So sorry to interrupt your meal," says Kevin's partner. "I am Detective Sanchez, and this is my partner, Detective Burton. We need to speak with Gianna Mancini and Isabella Donato."

Ma looks at us, worried. I see her feelings and raise her a *freaking out.*

Pop asks, "What's this about?"

"It's about last night, sir. It's just routine questions."

I highly doubt that.

"About what though?" He knows full well why they're here. But he won't let them talk to us until they state their reasons. He, unlike Ma, always takes our side. Maybe it's an opposite sex thing. Pop sides with us girls while Ma sides with the boys. I vow to not do that with my kids.

"A murdered woman was found on the beach," Kevin blurts out.

I'm glad Alice isn't in the room.

Pop stands his ground. "And what does this have to do with my daughters?"

"They were with the deceased last night," says Kevin. "Sources say she and Paulie were screwing around."

His partner gives him a disgusted look. I bet he hates Kevin as much as the rest of us. "Like I said, it's just routine."

D.N. catches my eye and gets up. "Excuse me," he says and walks into the kitchen.

Detective Sanchez takes a step ahead of Kevin. "We'd like to talk to you individually. Mrs. Donato, perhaps you and I can speak in the living room?"

Izzie softly whimpers.

She sets her wine glass down and is about to stand when I shake my head.

"I'm not talking to him," I say and jut my chin toward Kevin.

Sanchez looks from me to his partner then back. "Is there a problem?"

"No," Kevin says. "It's fine." He rubs his right arm, and I notice the wedding band on his finger. Who in their right mind married him?

"Bull," I say and jump to my feet. "We have history, and I will not speak to him."

Kevin's neck turns pink, and soon the color rises up into his face. He narrows his eyes.

I don't care how pissed off I make him. I won't give him the satisfaction of questioning me.

"If Mrs. Donato doesn't mind, my partner can talk to her, and I can sit with you, Miss Mancini."

I can't very well argue against that, but I try anyway. "No, that won't work either. He's not welcome in this house."

"Gianna," Mom whispers.

"Not after assaulting me." I don't know why I blurt that out. The idea of him questioning Izzie or me about another death, this time an actual murder, I can't deal with. Not after how he treated me when Craig died. I don't know if I can ever forgive him for that, especially since he spent so much time in this house as a teen. I never considered him family, but the betrayal feels as deep.

Everyone stares from me to him.

I catch movement from the corner of my eye.

D.N. stands in the doorway. How much of that did he hear?

Sanchez clears his throat. "If you have an accusation, Miss Mancini…"

I shake my head. "It was a long time ago. He's just not welcome in this house."

Kevin's lips are pressed firmly together. The blush is gone, and in its place is a paleness that makes me think he may snap. But he just stands there not looking at any of us directly.

Sanchez rubs his chin. "I guess you and your sister will have to come down to the precinct."

Great. Now I made it worse. I don't exactly want to spend my Sunday afternoon at the police station.

D.N. holds up his phone. "Actually, I spoke with my boss, Mr. Hamilton at Carter, Hamilton & Levine. He doesn't want either of you talking to the police without him."

A lawyer?

Izzie and I look at one another.

Sanchez scratches his head. "There's no reason to involve…"

Kevin steps forward, knocking into Sanchez's arm. "Do they have something to hide?"

Sanchez visibly scowls at his partner. I'd love to be the fly on the windshield in their car on the way back to the station.

Izzie starts to protest, but D.N. cuts her off. "They'll meet you at the precinct tomorrow at noon."

"Fine," Kevin says. "But they need to bring in the clothes they wore last night."

My stomach twists, and I glance at D.N.

He looks at me, and I'm suddenly not so upset he's here.

* * *

After we choke down cheesecake, Pop, Enzo, and D.N. follow me to my apartment with several carloads of old furniture and stuff Ma was only too eager to get rid of. It looks like a garage sale vomited in my living room. At least I have a couch, but now D.N. knows where I live. I guess the upside is he won't be stalking Ma's anymore, and she won't be inviting him to look at baby pictures and plot an evil plan to get us back together.

For some reason, D.N. doesn't try to hang around when Pop and Enzo leave. In fact, he gives a curt goodbye and walks down with Enzo, discussing baseball. So now I have him living in my town and getting close to Ma and my brother. Maybe I should move back to Connecticut.

And maybe a small part of me, like one single atom, is disappointed he doesn't try to stay.

An hour later, I've changed into baby blue leggings adorned with lambs and a tee and am unpacking. When coffee is dripping from the new maker, Billy and Cupcake decide to join me. He jumps on the sofa and does his best Tom Cruise impression.

"Where have you guys been all day?" I ask and immediately hear my mother in me. "Never mind. We need to talk." I eye the pot and watch it fill with gorgeous brown liquid. Halfway there.

"Who? Me?" Billy asks, eyes wide and innocent looking.

"Yes, but I'll deal with you later. For now, this one needs to spill." I point to the clown. Why couldn't she die after she'd showered and changed?

She tries the innocent expression too, but it doesn't work for her. I had a front row seat to her behaving far from innocent.

"First off, is this the only look you have?" I ask her for the heck of it.

She glances down at herself. "This is the one you know."

"So you can do more?" Suddenly, I'm intrigued.

She squeezes her eyes shut, and her appearance changes. The multicolored skirt and top, the oversized shoes, and the polka dot tights remain the same, but the makeup and wig are gone. She has shoulder-length auburn hair and bright green eyes. And because all ensembles lately aren't complete without blood, the side of her head is smashed in. Blood and hair are all matted together.

I grimace. "That's not better."

"No, that's cool," Billy says and walks to her side and stares into her wounds. "I didn't know I could change."

He scrunches up his face, looks constipated, and wills himself to change but nothing happens. He opens his eyes and looks down. "Hey, what gives? Why didn't it work?"

"Because you didn't get mangled in death. You drank too much, dude," I say.

He pouts. "Shouldn't there at least be some vomit?"

"Just be thankful there's not. I am." Turning back to Cupcake, I ask, "Can you do anything else? I really don't want to talk to this either."

She tries again, and this time she appears normal. Jeans, sneakers, a light yellow tee. This must be her everyday look. "Better."

"Nah, I like the oozing blood one," Billy says and goes back to couch jumping. How old is he again?

The coffeemaker has stopped doing its thing, and I grab a mug. "So tell me everything you remember about last night. But leave out the parts with my brother-in-law."

"It was a regular day. I worked a party for the agency," Cupcake says.

I grab a notepad I borrowed from Ma before leaving the house. It has two apples at the top and says *An Apple a Day*. I knew I'd be grilling Cupcake. I dig a pen out of my purse, brush crumbs off of it, and start jotting. "What agency?"

"Jolly Time. It's on Park Place, in the west end."

"It's a company of clowns? Isn't that the name of popcorn or something?" I'm a bit surprised. I can't say I've ever seen clowns roaming the streets. "What kind of party? Who, where, when?"

"It was a birthday party for a four-year-old in the next town. Not around here."

It's unlikely a preschooler killed her, unless... "Did you sleep with anyone there?"

She narrows her gaze. "No."

Billy finally stops jumping and tries to grab the remote. I try not to laugh as his hand goes through it on each attempt.

"What time was the party?" I ask.

"From six to eight."

"What did you do after that?"

Billy gets up and flies into the television. It shakes, and I fear it'll crash to the floor. It's an old set my parents had in their bedroom. Pop wasn't keen about giving it up, but Ma was thrilled. I'm pretty sure Pop will replace it this week, and the new one will probably be bigger.

"I went to a bar."

The TV goes on, and Billy flies back out of it and onto the couch. He leans against the back cushions and crosses his legs. The only thing the dead can manipulate is electronics. I'm not sure why, something to do with the currents, but if it's plugged in, they can control it. I once had a ghost who loved the refrigerator. Every time I opened it, he was there, just like the light. It was quite unnerving, especially in the middle of the night when I wanted something to drink.

"Mitch's Tavern." I say.

She shakes her head. "No, first I went to Lindy's."

My full attention centers on her. "You were there? Why'd you leave?"

"It was dead. There were hardly any people and absolutely no cute guys."

She's right, but I purse my lips into a snarl. Every time she mentions men, my stomach seizes, and I think of my poor sister.

"Do you normally go out to pick up guys dressed as a clown?" Maybe it's a new trend I haven't heard of yet.

She gives a half smile. "No, but I hadn't eaten since breakfast, and I was starved. Lindy's has awesome wings, although I didn't get a chance to eat them. I ordered them and a beer, got a bit creeped out by some guy watching me, and left. I don't usually care for some mild leering, but he was staring hard. Plus, like I said, it was practically empty."

"What guy?"

Another shrug. "I don't know. Plaid. Baseball cap."

Him! She must've left right before Izzie and I got there, and Plaid Guy almost ran me down following her out. But why?

"You didn't recognize him?" I ask.

She chews her bottom lip. "No. Is he important?"

I reach for the half-and-half in the fridge. "I don't know. Yet. So what happened at Mitch's? Did you see the plaid guy?" I know he was there.

"No, but it was crowded, and I don't remember much. I don't think I saw him." She sits on a stool at the breakfast bar.

It amazes me how a dead person can sit but not actually feel it. It's like they go through the motions because they're used to them.

"And you were there all night until Paulie showed up?"

She frowns. "Who's Paulie?"

I dump two teaspoons of sugar into my mug. "My brother-in-law."

Her eyes widen. "Oh. Yeah, but it wasn't long after I got there."

She doesn't know his name? At least that means he was telling the truth and this hasn't been an ongoing affair.

"Was there anyone else at the bar that you knew? Maybe an ex or someone who hates you?" Assuming the bat used to kill her is Paulie's, someone had to take it from his truck. It's highly unlikely this killer randomly found it while the truck was parked in Paulie's driveway. Someone at the bar saw the fight and the shattering glass and took the bat on purpose. Someone who wanted to blame the murder on an adulterous husband and an angry wife. Someone like Plaid Guy.

Cupcake shakes her head. "I don't remember."

"Well, try. This is really important."

She keeps shaking her head.

"You're not trying," I snap. I should finish unpacking, not play detective.

Billy looks over with a scowl.

Cupcake looks like she's gonna cry, not that she has that emotion anymore. And now I feel a bit like crap. Just a smidgen.

"You don't get it. It's all blank. Like I blacked out or something."

"Is that common?" Billy asks. "'Cause I used to get blackouts from drinking too much, and look where that got me."

I don't point out there's no sense in warning a dead person about dying.

"Okay, let's start over. What did you do when you first got to Mitch's Tavern? Start at the beginning, and tell as much as you remember," I say.

"I arrived and got a seat at the bar. Their food will tear your stomach up, so instead of ordering I pulled over a bowl of pretzels."

Because an open bowl everyone had their hands in won't also cause intestinal discomfort.

"Then a guy sat beside me. He looked down, so I started chatting." She stops talking and looks me straight in the eye. "More like flirting. And it was Paulie."

I expect to get annoyed, but her honesty takes me by surprise. It's nice.

"We chatted for a bit, and I ate the jam and crackers."

I stop writing mid-word. "What jam and crackers?"

"Oh, they were in my purse," she says matter-of-factly.

"Do you always carry jam and crackers in your purse?"

She shyly smiles. "No. They were at my apartment door when I left for the party that night."

I raised a brow as my suspicion rose. "A random jar of jam is left at your door, and you eat it?"

She widens her eyes. "It was in a box. I order free samples all the time. I must've sent for it."

My cousin loved getting samples in the mail too. "Okay, then what?"

"I ate and drank some beer while we chatted."

She means flirted, and I appreciate the subtlety.

"Then it gets hazy, and I remember pieces. Being in his truck, hearing knocking on the window, and that's it."

I hold up a hand. "Okay, wait. Let's stick with the bar for a sec. Do you go there every Saturday night? Is it routine?"

She nods. "Either Lindy's or Mitch's. It used to just be Lindy's, but they aren't what they used to be."

Tell me about it. But now we're onto something. Anyone from her life could've been there waiting.

"Okay, so who wants you dead?" Of course, there were other questions. Like how did she drink so much so fast that she doesn't remember anything, but I'm more interested in finding suspects who aren't related to me.

"I don't know. There have been some other angry wives."

Billy giggles.

I take a deep breath. "So screwing married men is a pastime?"

She doesn't respond.

"Okay, well how many? Who are they?" I get my pen ready to scribble.

Her eyes widen. "I don't remember them all."

Billy giggles incessantly.

I blow a raspberry. "How about the recent ones?"

"There are three wives since I moved to South Shore Beach. Plus, my landlord hates me because I'm always late with rent."

I doubt her landlord bashed her skull in on late rent. That isn't very business practical. "Who are the wives?"

"Um, Naomi Anderson, Stacey Anne Ingles, and Fawn Stewart. They all live here in South Shore Beach. And their husbands are very friendly."

I bet.

"There are also the accidents."

The hairs on the back of my neck stand up. "What accidents?"

"Last week, I was almost run over while walking to the store near my apartment."

This is a very dangerous town for pedestrians.

"Then I tumbled halfway down the escalator at Roosevelt Mall the week before."

Ouch. Falling is one thing, but almost being hit by a car is another.

"I'm accident prone," she says with a giggle.

Or someone really wanted her dead.

CHAPTER EIGHT

I tap my foot on the tile as I set a new ringtone for Izzie on my cell. "Girls Just Wanna Have Fun" doesn't cut it anymore. She's inside Interview Room Two. What kind of name is that? Does the South Shore Beach PD really think a serial killer will see that little sign and think, "Oh, they're going to ask me some questions about my job experience"? Why not call it what it is? An interrogation room.

My tapping grows faster. Izzie's been in there with Kevin, Sanchez, and the attorney, Mr. Hamilton, for thirty minutes. Kevin and Sanchez. I smile at my name choices. It's very *Law & Order* of me to call a detective by his last name. Kevin doesn't deserve that. I still think he cheated somehow at getting his promotion. No way he's smart enough to pass the test. I distinctly recall him and Alice's father joking around about how they were failing math and might not graduate high school.

A couple of female uniformed officers pass me, headed to the elevator bay. Their voices are low, and whatever they're discussing makes them laugh. They remind me of Izzie and me. I sigh.

When I picked her up, we didn't speak about what we were going to say. We rode to the station in silence, except for Izzie relaying a message from Ma about her stopping by my apartment with groceries. Which is also a way for Ma to snoop. Luckily, I haven't unpacked my personal items yet. I hope she doesn't dig through my suitcase and find my stash of glow-in-the-dark condoms. It was an impulsive buy the night before D.N.'s grandmother passed away.

Speaking of him, I was disappointed D.N. didn't tag along when Mr. Hamilton arrived. But just for a second and I was over it. Yep, completely unbothered.

The interrogation room door opens, and Izzie walks out wide-eyed, like she saw something unspeakable. She's rubbing her palm. In the same spot where she'd cut herself the other night. I want to ask her what happened, but Sanchez calls me straight in. I grab the plastic grocery bag I threw my dress in, and as Izzie and I swap seats, I think how we should've compared stories in the car. Is there something I shouldn't say? Did she twist any truth to make it sound less incriminating?

Mr. Hamilton is roughly Pop's age but more distinguished looking. A Smith Brothers suit instead of a greasy, capicola-stained apron will do that to a man.

As Sanchez turns on a recorder in the center of the table, Kevin folds his arms over his chest and narrows his eyes at me.

I roll mine, displaying how childish I can be. Yay, me. I toss my bag of clothes at him, take a seat, and try not to fidget with the hem of my top. So I clasp my hands together on top of the table and give my fingers a stern glare so they'll stay still.

"Ms. Mancini, you recently returned to town, yes?" Sanchez asks. Now that I'm closer to him and more focused, I see that Sanchez looks slightly younger than I initially thought. He's dressed in a white button-down and a brown and silver striped tie; a beige jacket lies over the back of his chair.

"Yes. Tuesday, last week."

"Where have you been living?"

"In Connecticut."

"Were you living there alone?" asks Sanchez.

Kevin remains unmoved, like he's frozen. Too bad he's not. I could find a dog outside to pee on him.

"At first with my cousin and then with my boyfriend."

Kevin flinches, and I feel a bit triumphant. The creep doesn't still have feelings for me, right? I mean—that would be disturbing. Plus, he's married.

"Did your boyfriend move to South Shore Beach with you?" Sanchez asks.

I glance to Hamilton, who nods, as if I'm looking for approval to answer this question. "Not exactly. We broke up, but he does live here now."

Sanchez smiles. "Okay, let's move on. What did you do this past Saturday evening?"

"My sister—"

"That's Isabella Donato, correct?" he interrupts.

"Yes. She picked me up from our family deli, and we went to our brother's house."

"The family deli being Mancini Deli over on Park Place? And can you state your brother's name, please?"

"Yes and Officer Lorenzo Mancini, Junior."

Sanchez nods. "Continue."

"We went to Enzo's house to scare him, but—"

Sanchez holds up a hand. "Wait, I'm sorry. You went to scare him?"

I smile. "It's this thing we do, ever since we were kids. We'd jump out of closets at each other. Hide under beds and grab my sister's ankle. Stuff like that."

Hamilton holds back a laugh.

Kevin narrows his eyes. "Aren't you a little old to still behave like children?"

"I don't know. Aren't you a bit too old to still be pissed I didn't date you in college?"

His face reddens, and I can't help but smile. Okay, so maybe I can help it, but I don't want to. He makes it so easy. He's like a big, walking bull's-eye.

"After Enzo's, Izzie and I went to Lindy's over on Atlantic Avenue."

"Around what time was that?"

I shrug. "Maybe nine."

"And how long did you stay there?"

"Maybe thirty minutes."

"Why did you leave so fast?"

"I ran into my ex."

"And what's his name?"

"Dou…um, Julian Reed." I glance at Hamilton from the corner of my eye. He doesn't react at all. Great lawyer skills. "I didn't feel like talking to him, so we left and went to Mitch's Tavern."

"What happened when you got there?" Sanchez asks.

I fill him in on the night. I don't lie, but I don't emphasize the anger Izzie displayed. For instance, Izzie *struck* his windshield with the bat, rather than *beat it within an inch of its life*. Just a little turn of phrase. No lies. I make sure to mention I touched the bat, too. I want it on record for whenever they find an extra set of fingerprints. And I may have exaggerated Paulie's reaction to it all. Like when he told the clown Izzie's his wife, I add that he seemed annoyed he'd been caught. Irked. Even *positively angry*. What? The real events make Izzie look homicidal. I need to say something to save my sister.

"Did you see where the clown went after she left the car?"

I shake my head. "She got out of the truck and headed toward the back of the parking lot. I didn't see her again after that."

"Did you see anyone else in the area? Maybe someone stopped to help her or give her a ride?"

"There was a man dressed in plaid, jeans, and a Yankees' cap. He was coming out of Lindy's in a rush when we arrived. And when we were leaving Mitch's, I saw him again, staring at us." Okay, so the staring at us part is a bit of a fib, but it's just a teeny lie. He could've been staring at us. I want the police to take this guy seriously, and I can't very well tell them that Cupcake said he leered at her.

"What happened when you left the parking lot?" Sanchez asks.

"Izzie and I went to the liquor store and the beach."

"Do you normally drink on the beach?" Sanchez asks.

My shoulders grow tired, filled with anxiety, so I lower my hands into my lap. "No, but we don't normally find my brother-in-law getting a blow job from a clown either."

Kevin snickers.

I send another death glare. I'm getting really good at them.

"How long were you on the beach?"

I don't mean to sigh, but I do. It's a small one. This is just crap. They've obviously asked Izzie all the same questions, so why do I need to reiterate? "All night. We fell asleep."

Kevin leans forward. "You mean, passed out?"

Mr. Hamilton taps the table. "Don't answer that."

Sanchez clears his throat. I have a feeling he does that a lot due to his partner. It must get sore. When this is all over, I should buy him a pack of lozenges. "How much did you each have to drink?"

"We finished a bottle of vodka. I don't know individually."

"And what did you do?"

I stare at him, unsure what he means. "Do? We sat on the sand and trash-talked Paulie, Izzie's husband. We also discussed how most men in general suck and how the planet would be calmer and not as crowded without them. We also talked about—"

"He asked what you did," Kevin snaps.

I clench my hands into fists. Gosh, what I'd give for the freedom to slide over this table and slap him across the face. The joy, the glee, the sheer enthusiasm. But I'd be arrested for assaulting an officer, and no one needs that. But it would fill my happy card for the rest of my life.

"Nothing. We talked."

"What time did you leave?" Sanchez asks.

"A little after six a.m."

"And where did you go?"

"I dropped Izzie off at our parents'. She and her daughter are staying there. And I went home to my apartment." Before he asks, I add, "Which is above the deli."

"While you were on the beach, did you see anyone?" Kevin asks.

What a stupid question. How many people does he think hang out on the beach all night? "Nope."

"So you don't have an alibi." Kevin says.

Hamilton lays a hand on my arm, telling me to shut up. Gladly. "Ms. Mancini said she was with her sister all night. Now, I believe she has answered all of your questions. If that's all?"

Sanchez stares at me for a moment and nods. "That's all for now. If we have any more, we'll call you."

Mr. Hamilton cups my elbow and rises, guiding me to do the same. He places a business card on the table. "If you have any more questions, call me."

* * *

Afterward, I drop Izzie off at home and head to my shift at the deli. I grab an apron off a hook inside the kitchen and tie it around my waist.

"How'd it go?" Ma asks. She has her gloved hands deep inside a bin of tortellini salad, mixing it.

I shrug, not really sure. "We're not in handcuffs."

Ma clicks her tongue. She may approve and even laugh at how we scare one another, but when it comes to the safety of her kids, she's all mama bear. "Can you grab a lasagna from the walk-in and stick it in the oven?"

"Yep." I yank on the freezer door and step inside. As the door softly shuts behind me, I'm reminded of that almost fatal day. I always am. And it doesn't matter that the memories are vague, more like feelings. I can't even reach for ice cubes without them.

Everything in here is encased in aluminum foil, with labeling written on masking tape. Luckily, it's also stocked in alphabetical order. My parents—the OCD deli owners. I find a pan of lasagna near the back and grab it.

I'm about to walk out when something catches my eye. And as if the giant cube wasn't cold enough, a gust of freezing wind blows my hair off my neck. Oh, this can't be good.

Hoping the freezer is only going berserk, I turn and stare at the back wall. A swirling tunnel appears. Because that happens every day.

I should run out before whatever it is sucks me in, but I'm way too curious to simply walk away. I reach out one finger, like ET, until I almost touch it. It's so cold I can't feel the tip of my finger anymore. This is crazy, even for me. I start to pull back, and a bony hand snaps out of the tunnel at me.

It tries to grab my wrist, brushes up against my skin, and I'm instantly chilled from the inside out.

I step back, too fast for whatever it is.

Laughter echoes through the ice box—deep and maniacal.

The tunnel starts to fade, but before it's gone, I can make out a face. Old, wrinkly, electric blue eyes, a shock of white hair, and a menacing grin.

It's the ghost from my dream. The one that tried to pull me to his side when I died. It's been eighteen years. Why is he still sticking around? And why does he still want me?

When I step out of the freezer, I set the lasagna in the oven then go to the sink. I blast the hot water with a trickle of cold and hold my hands under it. They don't take long to heat back up, except for the tip of my right index finger. It looks like normal skin, but it tingles and still feels cold.

"What are you doing?" Ma asks as she walks past.

I shake my head, not wanting to scare her. "Just washing up. I'll be out front in a minute."

* * *

Two hours later, my finger still tingles, but I barely notice it during the lunch crowd. Salads, heroes, paninis…it's easy to get lost in the work. I'm wiping down the counter as the rush slows, and the bell above the door jingles. I look up, cheesy smile on my face, and spot Hilary Porter.

Crap.

Other than Kevin, she's the last person I want to see today. We became super close in fourth grade and stayed that way through eleventh grade. Just before twelfth the world imploded, and my sweet, gentle friend turned into a raging witch. Okay, so maybe I had a hand in it, but she started it.

Micky Sheridan, my kindergarten husband, hit puberty late but hit it like a land mine. Six feet, with long, brown bangs that he constantly pushed out of his blue eyes, he was all lopsided smile, and he stared at you from beneath his lashes as if he was too shy to look you straight on. It was incredibly adorable, and several girls had the hots for him. But he only talked to me. He really was shy. Hey, we shared grape juice, chocolate cupcakes, and a bouquet of dandelions at our wedding. That's a bond you can't break.

So when Hilary kissed him behind the shed at my house during a Fourth of July cookout, I lost it. And that was the beginning of the end. Fake wedding or not, she knew I still crushed on him, always had, and she only noticed him because of his growth spurt. Then she took it one step further and told him my secret. The one that took me three years to confide in her. The one that helped her move on when her grandfather died. She stabbed me so deep in the back, I still feel the wound when it rains.

Micky and I spoke a couple more times, and luckily he didn't believe Hilary about my being able to communicate with ghosts, but it was never the same again. Suffice it to say, what was supposed to be the best year of our lives ended up sucking like a pound of lemons. Hilary and I didn't keep in touch. The last I knew, after her brief stint dating Kevin in college, she moved to New Jersey.

And here she was, standing before me, grinning as if we're long lost friends.

"Gianna, I heard you're back. You look great."

"Thanks." I'm bitter enough not to repeat the compliment, even though she does look good. Her dark blond hair is pulled back into a bun, a minimal amount of makeup accentuates her naturally high cheekbones, and she's dressed in burgundy trousers with a cream-colored wrap top. "Can I get you something?"

That *is* why she's here, right? She didn't show up thinking we're going to pick up where we left off. No, she's intelligent. Straight *A*'s and *B*'s in school. She knows better. But when she doesn't say anything, just stares at me, I can't help but wonder if the years killed some brain cells.

Her gaze flickers up to the menu behind me on the wall. "Um, can I get a pound of Boar's Head Ham, thinly sliced, and a pound of tortellini salad?"

"Sure." I turn my back on her immediately and try to take a deep breath, but it's hitched in my chest, and all I want to do is cry or scream or burp. Something that will take away the pressure. I give Pop the ham order because I need a moment to remember how to breathe and because I hate the slicer. It's scarier than the freezer ghost. Well, almost.

I sprint into the back and see Ma grab her purse from beneath a back table. She's about to go out the back door when she notices me practicing my guppy routine.

She hurries over. "What is it?"

"H-Hil—" I can't form words, so I point to the kitchen door. Oh sure, this has me stuttering like Forrest Gump, but Freezer Dude didn't even accelerate my heart rate. What's wrong with me?

Ma looks through the window in the door and raises her brows. "Oh wow. I haven't seen her in years."

There goes the theory that Hilary's in here all the time and this isn't planned.

Ma squeezes my arm. "Come on. It'll be fine. She screwed you over, but she only has power over you if you let her."

I whip my head up and stare into her dark eyes. "Who *are* you?"

She frowns. "What are you talking about?"

"Yesterday, you practically offered D…Julian to move in with you and Pop, and today, a seven-year friend can be swept into the gutter?"

She sticks a finger in my face. "I never said that. But I remember all the crying you did over that girl, and she was wrong. She hurt you. Julian didn't. You two had a misunderstanding because you're keeping secrets from him."

"Yeah, well, she let my secret out. I think I have reason to be concerned."

"She was a child. Julian is a man who moved to another state to be closer to you."

Gosh, I hate when she makes a valid point.

"Come on." She pushes the door open, and we walk through as Pop is wrapping up the ham.

I head to the salads, grab a plastic cup, and start filling it.

"Hilary, I haven't seen you in ages. How is your mother?" Ma asks.

"She's good. She's living in Freeport now."

"Good for her." Ma's using her small talk voice. The one that says she's only being nice because it's not good for business or her entrance into Heaven to be rude.

This makes me grin. I hand the container to Pop to ring up.

"And you're back in South Shore Beach?" Ma asks.

I cross my fingers, including the weird tingling one, and hope she says no.

"Yes."

Darn.

Hilary gives Pop her bankcard and turns her hand around for us to see a diamond studded wedding band.

"You're married," I say.

Her smile is huge. "Yes, Friday. It was unexpected. He asked. I said yes. And we ran to the courthouse. We're taking a honeymoon next month."

"Love and romance is exciting," Ma says after giving me a look that says I could have the same if I tell D.N. the truth.

I use all my willpower not to roll my eyes. I'm not in a rush for marriage and kids. Eventually. But right now I'd like to find a career I love that doesn't have me running home to shower off the stench of meat.

"So, you're no longer Hilary Porter," Ma says.

"No. Now it's Burton."

My face drops. Not my actual face because that would be disgusting. And painful. But my expression metaphorically falls to the sticky linoleum. "I'm sorry. What did you say?"

"I married Kevin Burton."

And this day keeps getting better.

CHAPTER NINE

The rest of my shift goes well. Ma leaves, and it's Pop and me making sandwiches, putting together an order for a last-minute office party, and getting a small crowd of people who all think shopping between three and four will have them beat rush hour. I'd like to remind them this is a deli and not the highway, but it's busy. And filling orders beats standing around doing nothing.

When I get off work I take a quick shower, place a Band-Aid on my mildly tingling finger for the heck of it, and head over to Jolly Time Agency.

It's a one-story, brick building nestled between a barber shop and a used bookstore. From the outside it looks like another store. But when I step inside, the interior explodes with color. The walls are painted in a wave of bright yellow above candy apple red. The carpet is blue, and there are framed photos hung along one wall of various clowns at birthday parties. Their portfolio, I assume.

Cupcake is by my side. She and Billy were yakking about something when I got out of the shower. I told her where I was going, hoping she'd tag along. She's been silent the whole way over.

"May I help you?" A woman behind a glass desk greets me. Her smile is warm, and even though she's maybe a few years older than me, she sports two very high ponytails. She's dressed in regular clothes—a block maxi skirt in navy, beige, and cream with an off-white peasant top—and not clown garb. She has a very heavy hand when applying makeup though. Yikes, she should check out some YouTube tutorials for natural application and not theatrical.

"Hi, I'm…Gianna." I suddenly don't know what to say. Do I admit I know Cupcake from the bar, or do I make up some lie? "I, uh, met an employee of yours, and she said wonderful things about your company."

The woman's smile brightens. "Are you a clown, too?"

"Yes." It flies out of my mouth. Maybe if she thinks I'm one of them, she'll open up to me?

Cupcake raises a brow at me but doesn't respond. This is the quietest I've seen her.

But before we get a chance to continue, a door at the back of the room opens, and a big, burly man stomps over to the woman. He's dressed in full clown getup, all yellow, red, and blue. A perfect match to the lobby. His feet are covered in oversized, yellow and red shoes, and he's wearing a small red top hat with tufts of neon blue frizz coming out from beneath and covering his ears and the back of his neck. He's concentrating hard on a sheet of paper in his hands, and his furrowed brow almost makes it look like he has no eyes. He doesn't notice me.

Cupcake rushes over to him, like she's expecting him to turn and give her a hug. She must remember that he can't see her because her stature slumps, and she sighs.

"Danielle, call the Simmons to… Did it suddenly get cold in here?" He glances around and notices me. "Who are you?"

Danielle jumps to her feet. She's tall, naturally slender. "This is Gianna. She's looking for a job."

Whoa! I never said that. I'm not a clown. I can't do this.

Cupcake glances at me and laughs—a sign she's at least awake and not clown walking.

The man stares me up and down. "This isn't a good time." He starts to walk away, and Danielle steps in front of him.

She lowers her voice, but she's still loud enough for me to hear. "We could use another body for the Conroy party."

He turns his head to speak over his shoulder but doesn't actually look at me. "Do you have experience?"

"Yes," I lie. What else can I do? If I tell the truth, I'm outta here. If I can cozy up to them, maybe someone knows more than what Cupcake's telling me. Of course, I haven't a clue as to what to do, but I've been to the circus before. How hard can acting like an overgrown child be?

"I worked in Connecticut." Hopefully he won't ask for references.

The man nods. "We'll give you a trial run. Danielle will get you set up."

Danielle grins, Cupcake giggles, and the man walks back through the door. What the hell just happened?

"I'll be right back," Danielle says and hurries through the same door.

"I can't do this," I whisper.

"Then why'd you lie?" Cupcake asks with a mischievous grin.

"Because I have to in order to help you move on."

"Aww, that's sweet."

"Save it. I want you out of my apartment and my life."

The corner of her mouth twitches, and she looks away.

Great. Now I've insulted a ghost. That's a new one for me. I feel awful.

"Sorry, it's just I'm not over seeing you with Paulie."

She nods. "I'm sorry for that."

And there's our white flag in the sand.

"Since you're helping me move on, I'll teach you how to perform."

I smile. "Deal."

Danielle reenters holding a box with a manila folder on top. She sets it on her desk and opens the folder. "Here are some forms you'll need to fill out for tax and employment purposes. You can take them home and bring them back."

I take them, fold them in half, and stick them in my purse. "Was that man the boss?"

"Yes, Timothy. He owns and runs Jolly Time. He's normally more social, but things have been difficult lately."

"Because of the death?"

She looks up, wide-eyed. "You read about it in the paper?"

"Actually, the clown I met that told me about the agency was Cupcake."

A small gasp escapes her lips.

Cupcake slides up to Danielle. "She really looks upset. I thought she couldn't stand me. Oh, and only address a clown by their clown name while working. Otherwise, it's unprofessional."

Right. Clown rules.

"I'm sorry for your loss. I didn't know her well, but Emma seemed..." I have no idea how to finish that because my mind wanders. What if Danielle puts two and two together and realizes that I am one of the women in Mitch's parking lot that night?

"She will be missed." Danielle opens the box, changing the subject. "These are extras. You'll have to buy your own costume, but you can use whatever's in here until you do."

I peek into the box and inwardly groan at the bright, neon explosion. "Thanks," I say very unenthusiastically.

I take a step away, wanting to get as far away from the box as possible, and Danielle frowns.

"You'll need to pick something for the Conroy birthday party."

"Oh, right. How old is the birthday person?"

She glances at her computer monitor. "Little Jasper Conroy has just turned five."

Mine and Micky's wedding pops to mind. "Cute age."

"Yes. You may want to hurry. You only have about twenty minutes."

It's my turn to be confused. "Until what?"

"Until you have to leave for the party."

"That's tonight?"

"Yeah, is that a problem?"

I glance at Cup...Emma, who's grinning like an idiot. "Uh, no, that's fine. I wasn't expecting it."

The phone rings. As Danielle reaches to grab it, she points to the mysterious door everyone's been using. "There's a bathroom through there. Second door on the right. You can change in there."

"Right." I lift the box into my arms as she answers the phone.

"Jolly Time, how may I help you?"

I glare at Emma and nod at her to follow. It's her fault I'm in this mess, and she's my ticket to finding a way out. First, she's going to help me figure out what to wear. One party. I can quit after. How hard can this be?

* * *

After I'm dressed in black and white polka dot shorts with a bright pink and lime green striped, ruffled blouse, white knee-high socks, a silky straight, purple wig, and bright makeup, with white face, I'm ready. I feel incredibly foolish, but it gives me a great idea on how to scare Enzo.

Since I don't have proper shoes, Timothy Jenkins, a.k.a. Bobo, allows me to go in my black high-top Converse sneakers. 'Cause that's a pretty picture. He also offers to give me a ride, so I leave my car at the agency.

We arrive at the location, and I notice another car pull in and park behind Timothy. Sure enough, a man dressed as a clown gets out. Timothy introduces me to Wesley Vaughn, also known as Rooster, and he explains it's just the three of us tonight.

"If you get unsure or nervous, follow our lead." He looks skeptical as to whether or not I'll be able to pull this off. He's not the only one. Hopefully, I won't shame him so badly he'll have to close up shop.

I'm not feeling very confident, so it could happen. Luckily Cupcake's by my side. As long as she doesn't see a cute guy, I should be fine.

"What's your name?" Rooster asks me.

"It's Gianna."

He smiles, and despite the eerie makeup, it makes him look endearing. "No, your clown name."

Oh, I hadn't thought of that. I look around the area trying to get inspired, but all I see is gravel, the side of the fortress the Convoy's call a house, and a patch of grass with dandelions.

A thought comes to mind. "Um, Daisy."

The guys nod.

"Let's go," Bobo says and directs his oversized shoes toward the house.

"Why Daisy?" Cupcake asks.

I slow my pace and whisper, "'Cause I'm like pushing up daisies."

She laughs, and I suddenly feel like she's on my side. Maybe this evening won't be as embarrassing as I think.

We walk along the side of the huge rectangular house to the backyard. Timothy opens the side gate, and I see what the privileged live like. The enormous backyard has been transformed with a huge bouncy house, a multicolored tent, tables for food, and train tracks that circle the yard and make pit stops at each of the main areas.

Jasper Conroy's fifth birthday party is like nothing I've ever seen. In my family a backyard birthday means Pin the Tail on the Donkey, balloons scotch-taped to the house, and Ma worrying that there's not enough food even though she spent two days making tray after tray of Italian delights.

Bobo speaks with Mrs. Conroy, a petite blond with severely angular features, and I wander over to the tent, curious what's inside. The children haven't arrived yet. The only sounds are slight chatter from several people dressed in khaki pants and red polo shirts who are decorating the yard.

I peek into the tent and see a woman setting up paints and brushes at a table. Face painting. I should've had her do my makeup because I'm pretty sure my mouth is crooked.

Within ten minutes, the guests arrive, and every child that's ever been born has been invited. Surely Timothy doesn't think only three clowns is enough. But I spot the pony and a magician, and I'm able to breathe easier.

While Timothy creates balloon animals, I act silly. Whatever the heck that means. I think back to six. I liked to be scared. I envision myself throwing up my hands, curling my fingers, and growling. I giggle, but the small group of kids gathered around me do not. I guess scaring the munchkins won't help the business.

Cupcake starts doing cartwheels.

I haven't done gymnastics since elementary school, so that's not happening.

"Hey, do you do anything?" a little girl asks.

Startled and suddenly scared the kids will gang up on the lonely clown, I say, "Watch this." Screw it. What's a few broken bones?

I copy Cupcake but not nearly as gracefully, and I'm pretty sure my legs aren't straight when in the air, but at least I don't land on my head. And the kids start laughing, so score.

I spend the rest of the afternoon copying Cupcake—chicken dances. Now that's up my alley, minus the twerking—spinning around until I'm dizzy, sloppy cartwheels, and off-key singing, which isn't pretend. At one point, I have most of the kids watching. Me.

When it's time for cake, our job is done. Timothy finds me behind the tent catching my breath.

"I am so happy I hired you. You're a natural." He holds out a bottle of water, but he's frowning at me.

"Is something wrong?" I ask.

"You remind me of someone."

Yikes. Perhaps I copied Cupcake too well.

While he goes off to speak with Mrs. Conroy, I find a private spot in the yard to speak to my ghostly friend.

"So spill. Have you slept with your coworker and boss too?"

If ghosts still had emotions, I'd swear she's blushing. "Timothy, yes, but not Wesley. He and I are good friends." She scrunches up her nose.

"What?"

"I think I was at his house the night I died."

"You went there after the bar?" I ask.

She shrugs. "I'm not sure. My memory is so hazy. Maybe I'm thinking of another night."

Or maybe not. "And you're just friends?"

She nods. "Wesley's been good to me. Like a big brother. He listens to me. Plus, he's engaged to Danielle."

I raise one brow and stare at her. "The Jolly Time receptionist?"

Cupcake nods. "She also works as a clown."

"Okay, but since when does being attached mean you keep your hands off them?"

"Fine. But Wesley and I aren't like that."

I have no reason to think she's lying. She's been up-front so far. If she was at Wesley's house that night, then surely he knows something. I'll need to get him away from Timothy to question him though.

"Does Timothy have a significant other?"

"No. He's single."

Well that's something.

Timothy and Wesley gather around me. Timothy gives me a half grin. "Why don't you stop by the agency, and we'll see about getting you more gigs."

And I really thought I'd only have to suffer through the one. I'm about to decline but Izzie's face comes to mind. I need to do this for her. "Cool."

I turn to Wesley. "Would you mind giving me a ride back to the agency to get my car?"

"Sure. Let's go." No one seems to question why I'm playing musical cars.

Cupcake, however, decides to climb into Timothy's passenger seat. She gives me a wink before they take off.

During the ride, I try to steer the conversation around to Cupcake, but something keeps holding me back. Wesley seems so nice, and I don't want to upset him. And if he and Cupcake are as close as she says, he must be going through hell. Part of me is skeptical though, so I want to test it out.

"I'm sorry about the loss in the agency. I'd met her shortly before her death."

He nods, keeping his eyes on the road. "Emma was one of those lost souls. She jumped around trying to find herself, but deep down she was very generous and passionate about life. I'm going to miss her."

He sounds genuine. Is it possible they were just friends? But if she had been at his place that night, a nice guy would've told the cops. Would they still have questioned Izzie and me? Probably. So I don't know if they did or didn't.

As Wesley turns onto the agency's street, I come up with a plan. I slip my phone out of my purse and allow it to fall from my fingers between the door and seat. Maybe not my brightest move. Being without my phone will be like cutting off a limb, but it's better than leaving behind my wallet. And I don't think misplacing a stick of gum will be important enough for me to retrieve right away.

He pulls up next to my car. "You did great tonight. It's nice to be working with you."

"Thanks. I'll see you soon." *Sooner than you realize.* I get out, and as I shut his door, I notice the tip of my cell peeking out from beneath the seat.

I get into my car, turn the ignition, and drive home. How long do I have to wait until I get my baby back?

CHAPTER TEN

When I get home I go upstairs to a quiet apartment. I'm alone. No Billy. No Cupcake…Emma. Just me and the obnoxious stench. Normally that would be an occasion to celebrate, but I'm too anxious about my phone. Yes, I am clearly a product of my generation. I pace a good ten, maybe eight, minutes and run downstairs to the deli.

It's a couple of hours until closing and not very busy. Pop works these last hours alone, and when I enter through the back, the kitchen is empty.

I walk to the kitchen door and peek through the glass panel. Pop is handing change to a young woman in biker shorts and a sports bra. As the woman leaves, Pop leans over the counter to watch her go.

No! That's not what I want to see. Ma would never let him hear the end of it if she caught him checking out some babe's butt.

He takes a rag and wipes down the counter. The rest of the store is empty. Perfect.

I stand on my tiptoes, press my palms against the door's solid wood frame, and align my face in the round window. Careful not to lean on the door and make it swing out, I wait. Hopefully, he'll turn around before my calf muscles cramp up and give me a charley horse.

I sing "Tomorrow" in my head, the first song that pops up. Can't imagine why. And just when "the sun will come up," Pop turns.

His eyes widen, and he flinches. Hard. Then he yells profanity.

I laugh and push open the door. "Pop, you never curse." Especially not the f-bomb.

"I've never seen my daughter dressed as Pennywise. Aren't I too old to scare?" He lays a hand over his chest, and I panic.

Oh no, is he sick? Is his ticker weak? I am a horrible daughter.

I notice the smirk lifting one corner of his mouth and realize he's messing with me. I snatch the towel from the counter and snap it against the deli case.

"Pop, you can't scare me like that."

He raises his brows. "Gotcha!"

I groan. "Gosh, you're as terrible as your son. Wonder where he gets it from."

Pop's laughter follows me back into the kitchen, to the cramped closet they call an office. I pick up the landline, which is one of those old-fashioned phones with the push buttons. Ma says we should be grateful it doesn't have a dial.

I punch in the numbers to the agency and pray Danielle is still there. It feels weird asking her for her fiancé's phone number, but it has to be done. I need my phone back.

It rings four times before a male voice answers. "Jolly Time."

I'm thrown for a second and say, "Timothy? It's Gianna. I'm hoping you can help me. I left my phone in Wesley's car on the way back from the party. Can you give me his number?"

"Sure." He doesn't hesitate, just searches and rattles off the digits.

I thank him, hang up, and call Wesley.

"Hello?"

"Hey, Wesley, this is Gianna. I think I lost my phone in your car. Either that or at the party. I hope it's in your car." I'm rambling. I ramble when I'm nervous. And lying makes me nervous.

"Hang on. Let me check."

A door opens and shuts, and footsteps are heavy against…gravel? The ding of a car door sounds.

"Yeah, I found it," he says.

"Oh great. Would you mind if I swung by now to pick it up? I'm lost without it."

"No problem."

I grab a chewed up pencil, tear off a scrap of paper from a pad, and scribble down his address. "Great, thanks. I'll be right there."

I hang up, scream "'Night" to Pop, and hurry out to my car.

Wesley lives on the other side of town. The side where the cramped, two-story homes turn into oversized, modern sculptures of architecture. His sprawling glass and concrete McMansion, which is modest compared to several others in the area, is up on a hill. I pull into a gravel-filled driveway right behind his car and get out.

Between his house and the unattached garage, I catch a glimpse of the sun setting low in the horizon, but before I get a chance to step forward and get a better look, the front door opens, and Wesley steps out. He's changed into a smoking jacket, loose-fitting pants, and slippers. All he needs is a pipe. He's holding my phone. Shoot, I was hoping for a look inside. Not to be rushed away.

"This is a gorgeous house. Do you live here alone?"

His smile is bright. "Yes. My family has done very well for themselves. They live in Greenwich, Connecticut."

I nearly choke on my spit. Now that neighborhood makes this one look like the slums.

"And you play clown?"

He grins. "I'm a history teacher at the high school. But I enjoy making people laugh, and while others are scared of clowns, they always made me smile. I figure I should pass that on, right?"

Wow, he's so sweet I'm getting a toothache. "Absolutely. So thanks for letting me get the phone now. I hope I'm not interrupting plans or anything." *Hint, hint, invite me inside.*

"No, I'm waiting for my fiancée. You must've met her. Danielle. We're going to grill some steaks and stay in tonight."

I don't respond. I stare at his house and do my best to lick my chops without actually licking them. I must be pulling off the dazed yet eager look because he finally says, "Would you like to come in and have a tour?"

I'm sure my eyes light up. Honestly. "I'd love to. Thanks."

He leads the way through the front door, and I step into another world. Two-story ceiling with windows just as tall. I'd hate to be the one having to clean them. A low-hanging chandelier illuminates the delicate swirl patter in the light gray floor tile, and a semicircular staircase takes up most of the foyer. We step down into the living room where a black baby grand piano sits by a white stone fireplace.

On the mantle are three photographs. One is of Wesley and Danielle. They're smiling brightly into the camera. The wind blows Danielle's long brown hair into her face, and they're both squinting. The picture is so alive and captures their happiness. It's no wonder why he chose that one to display. It's vivid and beautiful. The second is of a family of five—two parents and three children. I assume one of the kids is Wesley as a child. And the final photograph is of Wesley as a man with an older gentleman that is his spitting image. Probably his father.

There's an open floor plan to the rest of the house that allows me to see the dark mahogany table and chairs in the dining room and the gleaming steel appliances, cherry wood, and granite counters in the kitchen.

The walls are mostly glass, and every view is breathtaking, even the front one that looks onto his quiet street. But the one out back displays a strip of sand below, and where the ocean meets the sky, they seem to meld together.

"This is beautiful," I say. I bet most other teachers-slash-clowns don't live this way.

"I'm very lucky," he says, as if reading my mind.

The front door opens, and I whirl around to see Danielle. She's holding a green canvas bag, and there's a loaf of French bread and what looks like a bottle of wine poking out the top.

She smiles at me. "Hi, Gianna. I was wondering whose car is parked in the driveway. It looks familiar, but I've been so scattered today I couldn't remember if I saw it parked at the agency, the grocery store, or the restaurant."

Wesley walks over to her and gives her a firm kiss on the lips. "Too many engagement details?"

She pouts. "Exactly." She pulls from his embrace and speaks to me. "I'm finalizing the plans for our engagement party.

Wesley feels we should still go ahead with it in two weeks, even though…with Emma being gone…" Her voice trails off.

Wesley wraps an arm around Danielle's shoulders. "Emma would want us to be happy. She was always about partying and having fun."

We have five seconds of silence, and I ask, "Oh, are you recently engaged?"

They both smile. Danielle's wattage could set off a car alarm. She holds up her hand and shows off a square-cut diamond so huge it must add five pounds to her weight. "A week and a half ago. During dinner. He surprised me."

I try not to think of Hilary and Kevin.

"Have you set a date yet?"

Wesley raises his brows. "She's holding out."

Danielle playfully swats his chest. "I want to enjoy my engagement. I've fantasized about this my entire life. All girls do, right?"

I smile. If she's looking for support there, I'm the wrong girl. I fantasized about being able to openly speak to ghosts without being labeled as a freak or crazy. Poufy white dresses weren't at the forefront of that dream.

"Why are you here?" she asks.

I hold up my phone. "Wesley gave me a ride home from the party, and I left this in his car. It's my lifeline. I had to get it back immediately."

She smiles. "I know exactly what you mean. If I leave my apartment without my phone, I have to go back to get it."

They definitely don't live together.

"I'm going to grab a quick shower before we start cooking, okay?" she says to Wesley and hands him the bag.

"Of course." He kisses her forehead. In flats, she's only a couple of inches shorter than him, and he's a good five-eleven.

"Timothy mentioned how you'll be stopping by for more parties, right?" she asks me.

"Yes. Soon."

"Great. I'll see you then."

After she walks off, I turn to Wesley. "Do you mind if I bring up Cup…Emma?"

Sadness shadows his eyes instantly.

"Timothy mentioned how you and she were very close," I say. Someday my lies are going to come up and strangle me. But until then...

He nods. "She was a good friend. I already miss her so much." He doesn't lower his voice or look over his shoulder to see if Danielle is listening like he would if he was hiding something. So maybe they were just friends after all.

"She was troubled," he adds.

"How so?" I ask.

"She had a rough childhood, and I suspect she didn't deem herself worthy of much good. She had a way of destroying the best things in her life and taking what wasn't hers. Mostly relationships."

"She had you."

He smiles. "Yes, she did. And I hope she knew that."

Oh, she does.

"Did you see her the night she died?"

He frowns.

"I mean, were you able to see her right before she died? Obviously, you didn't know she'd pass and couldn't say bye, but maybe if you had a good last time together it's almost like that." There goes the rambling again.

"That's a lovely thought, but I hadn't seen or talked to her since Wednesday."

I search his face for a sign he's lying, but I don't know him well enough to be able to tell. Plus, he's looking off past me, not at me. Are Emma's memories real? Was she here that night? And if so, is he covering up her murder?

* * *

When I leave Wesley's, I decide to swing by Ma's. It is Meatloaf Monday after all. When we were kids, with Ma and Pop working hard at the deli, it left little time for Ma to create inspired, varied family dinners. She'd give the days of the week cute names so we'd think it was special. Super Sunday, Meatloaf Monday, Taco Tuesday, Wing Wednesday, Tomato Thursday—which is just spaghetti with sauce—and Fish Friday.

Saturdays, when we were old enough to heat up leftovers or cook for ourselves, became Snack Saturdays. Izzie, Enzo, and I would buy a bunch of foods Ma and Pop didn't allow us to eat, like Doritos, soda, Hostess Cupcakes, and frozen pizzas, and we'd gorge ourselves. Sometimes, I still miss those nights.

I'm almost there when Emma appears in my car. I glance at her and scoff. "You know I've been calling you. There really needs to be a way to reach ghosts, like a supernatural pager."

Her eyes twinkle. "What's up, roomie?"

"Wesley said he last spoke to you Wednesday."

"You spoke to him?"

"I was just at his place. He didn't say you were there the night you died. But you remember it. Is it possible he killed you?"

She gasps like a strangled chicken, not that I know what a strangled chicken sounds like. "No way. Wesley and I are…were friends. He'd never. Plus, he's such a gentle guy. He won't even kill bugs, just cups them and sets them free outside. It drives Danielle crazy."

She laughs and suddenly stops. Moisture wells in her eyes. "I can't believe we'll never hang out again."

Darn. I hate the weepy ghosts. It's not like they have a chance to make amends or say good-bye properly. It's all so sad.

"I told you I'm not sure if the memory is from that night."

"But you think it is." I turn onto Ma and Pop's street.

She shrugs. "If he says I wasn't there, then…"

"He could be lying," I interrupt. Everyone lies. Even the small ones.

"Wesley would never kill me." She presses her lips together as if to say that's the end of the subject.

Fine. I'll let it go. For the moment.

"Tell me about him and Danielle. Is he the cheating type?"

Emma laughs. "He's rather religious. They've never even had sex. Saving it for marriage and all. I believe he's a virgin."

I stare at her and almost drive into a parked car. I swerve out of the way. "Get out! He's like, what, in his thirties?"

"Thirty-four. But this is his life and his choice. It's not like it's some bad joke like in that movie with the dweeby forty-year-old."

I laugh at her reference. "Okay, so he's faithful."

"Yep. I'm not so sure if she is though."

"Why do you say that?"

"That night the party I worked at was with Danielle and Timothy. Afterwards, I went to the bathroom. The lock was broken. I didn't know anyone was in there, so I walked in. Danielle was finishing up, and her purse was on the counter. Right on top, kinda sticking out, were birth control pills."

"Are you sure?"

"Absolutely. I saw the white and purple box. I take, or took, the same ones. Altavera."

"So why would she need them if they're abstaining?"

"Exactly. But also, she told Wesley she can't have kids."

"Maybe they're not for pregnancy but some hormonal thing. Some women use them for acne."

"I hope so. I don't want Wesley to get hurt," she says.

I pull up to the house and go inside, still thinking about all Emma said. She follows me in, and when I spot Izzie sitting at the kitchen table, I'm real glad I'm the only one who can see my little clown.

Izzie looks up, and horror masks her face.

Clown. Shoot, I'm still dressed as a clown.

She chucks a banana at my head. "What the hell are you doing? Are you mocking my life?"

I duck the flying fruit. The corner of it nearly hits my temple. Wow she has good aim. My stomach rumbles at the thought of her with the bat.

"Whoa, sorry. I forgot I still have it on."

Ma, who's at the stove, steps over. She bites her lower lip, obviously wanting to laugh, but doesn't due to her oversensitive eldest. Does Izzie actually think I'm poking fun at her misery? What kind of sister does she think I am?

I explain why I'm dressed like this, including the second job.

"You're trying to help her?" Izzie screeches.

Emma flits over to the stove and peeks into a pot. "I really wish I could still taste food. This looks delicious."

I ignore her and concentrate on my sister. "I'm trying to help us by figuring out the truth. I don't want to be called back into the police station."

This seems to calm Izzie down a bit, but she still glares at me. She folds her arms over her chest. "Is she here now?"

"Maybe."

Izzie scoffs so hard I can smell her coffee drenched breath from where I'm standing. She stomps upstairs as if she's three.

I smile at Ma. "At least she didn't throw an apple."

"Are you sure this is a good idea?" Ma asks.

I can't tell if she disapproves or not. "I think so."

She nods. "Be safe. Someone killed that clown. It could be a coworker."

Maybe, but my bet is on Plaid Guy.

The front door opens, and Enzo walks in. If he thinks I look strange, he doesn't say anything or even give me a second glance. Just a nod and straight to the stove as Ma pulls the meatloaf out of the oven. He's like a dog.

"I've been keeping it warm for you," she says after kissing his cheek. Then to me, "Are you hungry, Gianna?"

My stomach rumbles in response. That last thing I ate was half a cup of tortellini salad and a pack of Saltine crackers right before I left work this afternoon. "I can eat."

Ma sets the food on the table while I grab plates and silverware and Enzo fills two glasses with ice and water. Then we sit and feast. The pot Emma stared into contains mashed potatoes, and the smaller one in the back has carrots. By time Enzo and I…mostly Enzo…are done, I doubt there will be leftovers.

Emma sits beside Enzo, staring at every ridge of his pecs, and tries squeezing them.

I can't tell if he feels her coldness or not, and he isn't reacting because he's too busy eating.

When the phone rings, Ma smiles at the caller ID and goes into the basement to answer it. It must be her friend with a lead to another murder item. One thing is for sure—Ma will never be without her hobby. Someone is always going to be murdered.

I stare at Enzo's jaw as he chews. After eating all his carrots and half of his meat and potatoes, he wipes his mouth on a paper napkin and finally says, "Why do you look like that?"

"I took a part-time job at Jolly Time Agency where Emma worked. The dead clown."

He stops mid chew.

I smile. All I need is his attention. "I was thinking. If you give me the details on her murder, I can help you figure out who killed her."

Emma leans forward and practically drools in his lap.

He raises a brow. "I can't tell you about a case. Besides, it's not my case. I don't know much."

"Maybe, but you can find out something. You must have friends in the department. And maybe I, or Emma, can help you make detective faster."

She purrs. "Yay, dicks."

I chuckle and shake my head when he gives me a questioning look. "She likes detectives."

He glances to his left. "She's here?"

"Yep. And while she doesn't remember how she died, I've already spoken to a few people who knew her." I tell him what I've learned about Wesley and a possible memory of her last being at his house.

Enzo sighs around a mouthful, swallows, and glances over his shoulder. "Fine, but this is between you and me. Don't involve them," he whispers.

He's talking about the family. "What? You don't trust them?"

He frowns. "Of course, but this is my career. Only us. Pinky swear, or I'm not giving up anything."

I place my elbow on the table and stretch out my pinky like I did so many times growing up. Being the youngest, it was the only way to learn the gossip. "I swear."

He clears his throat and leans over his plate. "The preliminary toxicology report came back. It shows Rohypnol in her system."

Emma and I gasp in unison.

"That's a date rape drug," Emma says.
"And the reason you don't remember anything," I add.
She nods.
Enzo goes back to his meat.
"This isn't a spur of the moment, heat-of-passion killing," I say. "It's premeditated murder."

CHAPTER ELEVEN

———

I'm off on Tuesdays, so I spend the next morning Googling the three wives. There's a website and Facebook page for The Jam Shoppe—Stacey Anne Ingles' store. Oh my God, jam. Is it the free sample Emma ate from this store? I search faster, but there's nothing personal about Stacey Anne or her husband. The Jam Shoppe displays their jars, each with a red gingham bow. Why would Emma order a sample from one of the wives? Is it possible she didn't know it was Stacey Anne's shop? I need to show this to Emma ASAP, but she and Billy aren't here now.

I find a LinkedIn link for Naomi Anderson, but without an account, I can't see it, and I doubt there's anything incriminating on a professional site. There are no photos of her or her husband either. Fawn Stewart, however, is another story. She's on Facebook, Twitter, Instagram, Pinterest, and YouTube, where she posts makeup tutorials. I should email the link to Danielle. I spend way too long stalking Fawn and her eight hundred seventy-four friends.

When I've wasted all morning in front of the computer, I decide to stalk her in person and jot down the address of the salon. But before I log off, I do a Google search of Billy. Since I don't know his last name, I enter his first name, spring break, and alcohol poisoning. Why didn't I ask for his full name? This would be so much easier.

I find an article about a college student dying at a party. Is this it?

On March twentieth, police officers responded to a call about loud music coming from a house at 55 St. James Place. When they arrived, they found a party thrown by Holy Mount College students.

The house is in town, but the school is three towns away. It's a private Catholic college with a good reputation. Ma wanted us to go there. Pop wasn't so adamant. I'd like to think it was because he believed we had a right to choose our own religious beliefs, if any, but I'm sure it was really about the money. Sending the two of us to private colleges would've put them in debt for years.

Enzo ended up at Farmingdale University, a state school where he lived on campus for four years. Although it felt like much less since he was home weekly for Ma's cooking and laundry services. I lived at home, going to Nassau Community College for two years, and then transferred to Adelphi, which is a private school but a short commute. Since I only went there for two years, Ma and Pop were able to manage the cost.

I get back to the article.

There was drinking and drugs at the party, and several occupants were either high or over the legal limit of alcohol. The house owner, Andre Collins, is being held for questioning since many of the guests were under the legal drinking age. A couple of the partygoers were taken to South Shore Beach Hospital for further observation. William Wyatt—that must be Billy—*was discovered unconscious. He was pronounced dead from alcohol poisoning at the hospital.*

I sigh and rub my face, grateful I didn't put on makeup earlier. Poor Billy. That's not a cool way to go. What is he sticking around for though? Probably his family. I need to find the time to connect with him, learn his inner demons, and eradicate them. He needs to move on. And I need one fewer ghost in my life. Not to be too insensitive and all.

* * *

I drive over to Fawn Stewart's work, Randall Lawrence Salon & Spa, on Park Place in the East End. Emma comes along for the ride. Maybe she can help. You never know when you may need the dead's assistance.

I'm about to get out of my car when Fawn walks out of the brick building. I recognize her instantly due to the thousand selfies scattered across her social media pages.

She gets into a little red Corvette and pulls out of the parking space. So I do the only thing a deli worker-slash-part-time clown can do. I metaphorically flip my original-*Charlie's-Angels*-feathered hair and follow her.

Several blocks away she pulls into a spot in front of an office building and sits there.

"What is she doing?" I ask after double-parking several cars back. I'm blocking in a beige sedan. If the owner comes out before Fawn moves on, I'm screwed. I'll have to circle the block and risk losing her.

"Her husband, Kurt, works here," Emma says.

"She must be waiting for him. It's a bit late for lunch though. What's he do?"

"Something in insurance. He's not a talker."

I don't comment.

Three men and two women in navy and black suits exit the building and walk around the corner to the parking lot.

"That's her husband," Emma says with a sigh. "The one holding the briefcase. He's gorgeous and so great in bed. He does this thing where he holds my legs over…"

I stick my fingers in my ears. "Lalalala. I don't want to know."

She smirks, and I assume it's safe to stop acting like a child.

I lower my arms. "Never give me the details."

She keeps her eyes straight ahead, but her smirk turns into a smile, so I believe we're cool.

Kurt Anderson is blonde, pale, and even with the suit looks like he belongs in a Calvin Klein underwear ad. Definitely not Plaid Guy.

"How'd you meet him?" I ask, suddenly wishing I owned binoculars and one of those devices that pick up sound from far off.

"When I first moved to town I got here a day early, and my landlord had a family emergency. He wasn't here to give me the key, so I took a room over at the Beachcomb—the hotel down on Broadway. Kurt was there for a business meeting, but afterward he hung around, and we met by the pool. I never learned why he didn't leave right after his meeting. I guess fate wanted us together."

She makes it sound like they had a romantic relationship and not an affair with no chance of a happy ending.

Several cars pull out of the parking lot, and Fawn follows the black SUV. And I follow Fawn. What kind of wife doesn't get out of her car to greet her husband but follows him when he leaves his office? The kind that's been cheated on more than once.

They pull onto South Shore Beach Road and head down toward the water. When he turns on Pacific Avenue, a street full of two-story, private homes, my gut tells me Fawn is either livid or in tears.

"Obviously you're not the only one he's cheated with," I say.

Emma scoffs. "It's great that you think my wanton feminine ways can attract all men, but a man who cheats is a man who's going to cheat. If he's loyal there's nothing another woman can do to change that. So maybe save the judgment for the one in the committed relationship."

Whoa, where did that come from?

I turn and stare into her eyes. She's right though. Emma hasn't broken any vows, and she's only responsible for her own actions, not anyone else's. She didn't make promises to Izzie or any of these women. Whether or not she knew Paulie was married, he's the one who cheated.

I nod and turn back to our stakeout. "Sorry."

Then I shudder. If Izzie knew I apologized to the clown, she'd disown me.

* * *

After Fawn returns to the salon without confronting her husband or his car, Emma disappears, saying something about a toga-wearing man in her apartment building, and I head over to Wesley's. I have just enough time before my shift at the deli to snoop around. I'm hoping since he's a teacher that no one else, like a housekeeper, is home. And when I pull into his empty driveway, I'm thrilled I get my wish. Although what I can find searching the outside perimeter is beyond me. I just don't think I'll get another tour soon. Eventually he and Danielle will get suspicious.

Just the same, I get out of my car and head toward the back of the property where there's that breathtaking view of the Atlantic and no peering neighbor eyes. On a quick glance, though, it doesn't look like many people are home. There are no visible cars parked outside any of the houses.

Wesley's yard is small considering how much he must've paid for this place. You'd think each house would come with a lot of land, but that's not Long Island. At least not this area. You'd have to drive farther out into Suffolk County to find more space. Here, or at least in the West End, it's more like the City where you and your neighbor can lean out your windows and carry on a conversation as if you're standing side by side. You don't buy or rent a home in South Shore Beach because you want to raise chickens or don't like people. This town's draw is the boardwalk and the beach.

I head back toward the garage and notice two sets of tire tracks on a strip of grassless dirt above the gravel driveway. One set is thinner than the other. Clearly a car and some type of truck or SUV. I pull out my phone and snap photos of them. Not sure if it'll do any good, but that's what they do on those TV crime shows.

I'm about to turn and head to my car when something glints against my sunglasses, blinding me for a second. I look up and catch movement. From the house next door, a dark-haired young man directs his phone at me. He's leaning over the railing of a balcony, and he has no shame about leering. Then again, I'm the one trespassing.

"Hey," I shout up. "Did you just take my picture?"

"Maybe."

"That's illegal."

He laughs. "No it's not. You're thinking of video, and that's only illegal if there's audio."

Is that even true, or is he BSing me? And who is this kid? "How old are you?"

"Sixteen. How old are you?"

"Ninety-five."

He whistles. "Wow, you look fine for being ancient."

I can't help but smile. "So do you film your neighbors often?"

"Only the hot ones."

He thinks I'm hot? Well… No, Gianna, don't be flattered. He's a child and shouldn't be encouraged.

Then it hits me. "Any chance you saw a hot redhead here Saturday night? It would've been late."

He looks off for a second and walks into his house.

What the heck? Way to end a conversation.

I consider going over and knocking on their door, but the kid's probably full of crap anyway. I turn back toward the driveway and start walking to my car.

A screen door slams, and footsteps hurry toward me. "Hey."

I glance over my shoulder. He looks much younger close up. A face full of freckles, light brown eyes, and a small scar above his right eyebrow.

"You a cop?" he asks.

"Nope."

"Good. I hate cops. They're so nosy."

I almost laugh. He just snapped a photo of a stranger. Isn't that the same thing?

"I saw the redhead."

He has my attention now. "Saturday night?"

He nods. "She's around here a lot. Not as much as that other lady but still a lot."

He must be talking about Danielle. "What time did she get here? How long did she stay?"

He shrugs.

"But you said you saw her."

"I saw her leave, not arrive. And she wasn't alone."

I'm at full attention now. "Did someone leave with her? Wesley? The guy who lives here."

"Don't know the dudes name, but he carried her out. And it wasn't the house owner."

Another man. Plaid guy?

"Did you recognize him? Was he wearing a plaid shirt and a Yankees' cap?"

"I was too busy watching the chick to be checking out his wardrobe. She has a nice rack."

Guess he hasn't figured out she's the body on the beach. "You didn't get his plates by any chance?"

He smiles.

I nearly squeal. "You did?"

He raises his phone and shakes it. "Better. I got pics of him and his car."

"Let me see." I reach for his phone.

He snatches it back and slips it into his pocket. "My rates are high."

I scoff. "Seriously? You're going to extort me?"

He wiggles his eyebrows. "A guy's gotta eat."

I scoff a second time, louder, and hold out my arms. "You live in the lap of luxury. I doubt you're having to resort to Spam and bologna."

He wrinkles his nose. "Won't touch the stuff."

One thing we have in common—on the Spam. I have been known to eat a bologna sandwich. It's really good on rye with mayo.

Before I know what he's doing he grabs my phone. "Hey."

When he hands it back, he's listed himself as contact No Spam. Cute. "When you get two grand, give me a call. Cash only." He takes off, back to his house.

Two grand. "Are you crazy? How do I know you even have pictures? You probably captured something from three weeks ago."

He ignores me and keeps walking to his door.

I should call the cops on his butt. But then they'll get the info, and I'll still be clueless. What if it's Paulie? I doubt it, but what if? And if I'm being honest, I simply don't want to hand over real evidence to Kevin. I'd rather the killer go free. Almost.

"Hey, why aren't you in school?" I shout after him. "Maybe I should call the truant officers."

He glances back and wiggles his phone. "That won't get you the info either."

Little creep. There's just no way. Even if I had that kind of money sitting around, I wouldn't give it to this thief. He probably doesn't even have any pictures. No. I'll find another way to get the information.

CHAPTER TWELVE

I figure one more stop is in order before I find food. My stomach is growling so loudly I'm surprised other motorists don't shriek and crash their cars, fearing Godzilla is close enough to attack. I chuckle at my goofiness and drive to The Jam Shoppe.

According to their adorable website with scrumptious pictures of jam on scones, crackers, and flaky rolls, it was established four years ago by Stacey Anne Ingles. It also says how she grows her own organic fruit, and every jar is made with special care, natural ingredients, and love. Gag me!

The "About" page shows her picture. She's a blond woman with big green eyes, and she's holding a jar of jam. No other personal pictures are available though. With no pictures anywhere of Stacey Anne's husband, I wonder if he's Plaid Guy.

I'm not sure what to think about Emma being at Wesley's. Her story resonates with No Spam's, but they're both unreliable. Then again, Wesley's a stranger. He could be a serial killer for all I know. Until I get definitive answers, I'm keeping all possibilities open.

As I pull up to the store with the red awning, a tiny blond woman exits and locks the door. That's Stacey Anne. I follow her to a small house over on Indiana Avenue, and that's when Emma pops back in.

She laughs as we watch Stacey Anne walk into her house.

"What's so funny?" I ask.

"You. Have you never watched a PI show on TV? 'Cause you suck at this."

"Hey," I say in a way to sound wounded, but really I can care less if my sleuthing skills are mocked. She's right. I haven't a clue and am copying my limited knowledge of crime shows. I need to spend the evening with *Law & Order* or *CSI*. Hey, *Castle* has Nathan Fillion. That's an instant rise on the hotness thermometer.

"You can't watch someone into confessing. You need answers. You need to approach them," Emma says.

"So somehow I need to get close enough to a jam maker, an estate attorney, and a hairstylist. The first and last may not be too hard. But I'll need help."

She bows her head. "I am at your disposal. It's not like I have anywhere else to be."

"Thanks, but I need the corporeal variety."

I shift the car into drive and go to my apartment. When I climb the back stairs, contemplating going into the deli and grabbing some eggplant parm rather than cook, I spot Alice seated on the top step.

My heartbeat jumps into my throat, and I rush up. "What are you doing here? Are you okay? Where's your mother?"

Her eyes grow bigger and bigger the more I speak. "Chill, Aunt Gianna, everything's fine."

I narrow my gaze and stare at her hard. "You're sure?"

She shrugs. "No one's dead, if that's what you mean. I wanted to see your place."

She's lying, but as long as she's not bleeding I can take a little time to yank the truth from her. I push my key into the lock. "Okay. Come in."

As I push open the door, I pray Billy isn't here. I'd like a quiet hour or so with my niece.

But there he is seated on the couch watching TV.

"Oh look at that." I take the remote and turn the set off. "I must've left it on. Silly me."

"Hey, I was watching that," Billy says with a whine.

I glare and whisper, "Scram."

Alice doesn't seem to notice. She drops her backpack on the floor and walks around looking at things, but I don't have much displayed yet.

Billy huffs and disappears. I have no idea where Emma wandered off to, but it doesn't matter right now. I don't want Alice getting suspicious if I start nodding or whispering at the thin air. When she was first born, Izzie made me pinky swear I wouldn't let Alice find out about my ability until Izzie says it's time, and that won't be before high school. That's another year at the earliest.

As far as I'm concerned, we can keep it from her until she's thirty. I'm not in a rush to try to explain and possibly lose my cool-aunt status. What if she's freaked out? What if being around me becomes scary for her? Nope. Waiting is great!

I stand in the middle of the room watching Alice. "How'd you get here?"

"I took the bus."

Smart. The public bus runs twenty-four hours a day.

"How's school?"

She shrugs. "Some of it sucks."

"Yeah, it did for me, too."

She glances at me with a smile. "At least you don't tell me it'll get better."

I smile. "Ah, that's Pop…um…Nonno's favorite line. He used to say that when I was in school, too. Don't hold it against him. He means well. And just so you know, it does get better. College is a lot easier on the social level."

She smiles. It makes her chubby cheeks and round eyes look even more cherubic.

"Does your mom know you're here?" I ask.

"I told her I was stopping at a friend's before going home."

It's nice to be considered a friend.

She peeks in the bedroom and circles back around and plops onto the couch. "Can I get something to drink?"

"Sure. I have water, milk…" I open the fridge, forgetting what Ma bought. "And apple juice." What am I five? I seriously need to make a pit stop at a liquor store. I am, however, grateful she added lavender scented Plug-Ins to the bath, bed, and main rooms. She must've noticed the salami stench because I forgot to mention it.

"I'll have juice."

I notice the cold cuts, the fruits and vegetables, and a couple of slices of cheesecake. "Are you hungry?" I grab a glass, and when I don't hear a response, I glance back.

She's shaking her head.

I hand her the juice and sit beside her. "You know anything you tell me remains here, right?"

With her head bowed she asks, "Anything?"

I take a deep breath and think about it. "You can talk about anything with me. The only things I'll have to tell your mother are if you're doing drugs…"

She wrinkles her nose.

Good.

"If you're pregnant."

She busts out laughing, and her face colors. "I'm only thirteen."

Great, now I've embarrassed her, but it's nice to know she's isn't sexually active.

"Or if you're doing something else harmful."

She still won't look at me. "Like what?"

"Cutting, suicidal attempts, binging and purging, starving yourself. Things that can kill you."

She nods, sips her juice, and places the glass on the coffee table. "What about bitching?"

I hold back a chuckle. As sure as I am my niece curses, this is my first time hearing it. "That's completely confidential."

She takes a mammoth-sized breath and slowly exhales. "Okay, so I'm going crazy at Nonna and Nonno's. Mom is always up my butt about my schoolwork and my friends, and she never lets me have fun anymore. Ever since she and Paulie started fighting, she's been so hard on me."

How much does she know? "Do you know what they're fighting about?"

"Mom accused him of other women."

Darn, she overheard them.

As a child, when Ma and Pop would argue, they'd either whisper in their bedroom at night when they thought us kids were asleep, or sometimes they'd go into the garage and scream at one another. One night, I woke up, heard the yelling, and got scared. Izzie was already awake at our window, listening. I sat beside her, and she put an arm around my shoulders and told me it would be okay. And she was right. The next morning, Ma was singing while Pop made breakfast.

Our parents only did the yelling bit once in a while, and they always stayed together. I think the fact that they made it a point not to argue in front of us solidified them somehow. Like, as long as they agreed to that rule and were doing something together, they could get through anything.

Alice sighs. "Mom accuses him all the time, even though he swears he's not doing it. Sometimes she screams so loud at night, it wakes me up and scares me."

Come on, Izzie. I don't have any real experience as a mom, but doesn't my sister realize she's hurting the person who matters most to her?

"And I know about the woman at the beach. I know she and Paulie were…together," Alice says.

I try to hide my surprise. "What makes you think that?"

She scoffs. "Come on, Aunt Gianna. First, I'm not stupid. I could tell something was wrong on Sunday, especially when the cops showed up. And second, I overheard Mom and Nonna arguing about whether or not Mom should take Paulie back."

Crap.

"Did your mom say if she would?"

Alice shrugs. "Not that I heard. So, are they getting divorced? Are Mom and I living with Nonna and Nonno for good now?"

I can't figure out what Alice wants. Paulie's only been in her life for six years, officially her stepfather for three, so while she may not think of him as Dad, she may. "I honestly don't know yet. I don't think your mom does either. They're going through something very difficult right now, and it'll take some time to heal. Do you want them to stay together?"

"I guess so. Paulie's cool, and I want to go back to my house. I want my room, my friends, and my freedom."

I smile. "Yeah, that's gotta suck. Do you want me to mention it to your mom?"

She thinks for a minute and shrugs. Gotta love the indecisive emotions of a teenager.

"Okay, how about I wait, and you let me know."

She nods.

"Any time you want to talk you just have to text me. Morning, noon, or night, okay?"

She smiles wide. "Cool."

We talk about the latest celebrity gossip for the next hour. She's totally pro-Lorde and anti-Bieber, which means I think she's cool, too. Then we get into the car and head to Ma's.

Izzie's is the only car in the driveway when we arrive. Good. I'd like to talk to her without our parents listening. Izzie and Alice may be staying with them, but their life with Paulie is their own business.

I go inside and wink at Alice. She heads to the kitchen, and I find Izzie up in our old room putting away laundry. "That looks like a lot of clothes. You've decided to stay here indefinitely?"

She glances at me before shutting the bottom dresser drawer. "I don't know. What do you want, Judas?"

I take a deep breath and prepare myself for Hurricane Isabella. "Your help."

She scoffs. "As if."

"It's important. There are other women whose husbands slept with Emma, too." Not that Emma and Paulie had sex. Wait. Why am I defending their actions?

She laughs. "That doesn't surprise me."

"They were very angry. Maybe one of them killed her. If we can prove it, you won't have that hanging over you."

"What do you mean 'we'? I'm not helping this clown cross over. She can stick around and rot." She grabs the basket of clothes and pushes past me.

I follow her into Enzo's old room, the one Alice is staying in now. Light blue walls and a navy rug. No wonder ballerina Alice doesn't love it here. "This isn't about helping Emma. It's about helping you and my niece."

Didn't I already explain this the other day?

She ignores me while putting away Alice's T-shirts, jeans, socks, and underwear, and she moves into the hall to put towels into the linen closet. When the basket is finally empty, she turns to me with a sigh.

"Fine. What do you want?"

"One of the women is a hairstylist, and someone I know needs a trim." I blatantly stare at her uneven ends.

She runs her fingers through the back of her hair. "I could use a professional. But how does that help find out if she's a murderer?"

"You'll ask questions. Make her open up. You're good at that. And isn't a hair salon a bed of gossip anyway. It was on *Steel Magnolias*."

That makes her laugh. And just like that, I have my sister back.

"I can do that. Give me her name and number, and I'll make the appointment."

"Great."

She frowns. "But how will this help the police? Are they going to believe what I tell them?"

This I already worked out. "They will if you're wearing a microphone."

She smiles. "Cool."

Just like her daughter.

CHAPTER THIRTEEN

When I get back to my apartment, Julian's black truck is parked in the lot. For a split second, I stare at his tires and wonder if he's the one who took Emma from Wesley's, but that doesn't make sense. He's been in town less than a week. Why kidnap an unconscious woman and then…what, kill her?

I'm still laughing at my absurdity when I step from my car. I don't acknowledge him and walk through the back door, which doesn't have a lock, and up the stairs to my door.

He follows right behind like a hungry puppy.

"What are you doing here?" I ask as I let myself into my apartment.

"We haven't had a chance to talk." He closes the door behind him. "Really talk."

I toss my bag on the floor by the couch and kick off my shoes. Then I walk through my bedroom to the bathroom and hold up a hand. "You're not following me in here."

I slam the door and go about my business. When I'm done, he's seated on the sofa flipping channels on the remote. He'll be greatly disappointed that I don't have the gajillion stations he's accustomed to. "Say what you need to so you can leave."

As I stand there and wait for him to speak, I realize my anger, my disgust at seeing him, isn't there. All I see is the way I used to curl up beside him while he watched those boring documentaries and the way his skin glistens when he steps from the shower. And I hear Ma's words. That we had a misunderstanding because I haven't told him my secret.

"You okay?" he asks. "You have this weird look on your face."

"Yeah. Fine, but I don't think you came here to discuss my face."

He smirks. "It's a beautiful face."

My insides become jittery, and I look away. No, Gianna, there won't be any mushy feelings. He's still the semi enemy.

I turn to the kitchenette and decide to keep busy. Yep, need to keep my thoughts off the past. And his abs. After I add water and grounds to Mr. Coffee, I stare at the wrapped package of sliced chicken breast in my fridge. My stomach grumbles. I should have stayed at Ma's for taco night. I consider being rude, making food, and not offering him any, but unfortunately, it's not in me. Not with him anyway.

"Hungry?"

Julian gets up and sits at a stool at the breakfast bar directly across from me. "What do you have?"

I pull out lettuce, tomato, mayo, and bacon, then grab a small frying pan and get to work on the pig. "How about a chicken club?"

"You make the best sandwiches."

Yep, on my gravestone.

We don't speak while I cook. He seems to be content watching me flip bacon, and I have nothing to say. He shouldn't even be here, and we definitely shouldn't be sharing a meal. But I can't work up the courage to tell him to go either. Ma's words about how he moved here for me swim in my head, drowning reason and logic.

I grab the bread off the counter and slide six slices into the toaster oven. "I was surprised you weren't at the police station."

"I had to work."

I nod. "Right." That was another thing wrong with us. He worked all the time and never discussed it. I wanted to understand. The cases were privileged information, and he could lose his job if he shared, but I still felt left out.

After blotting the bacon on a paper towel, I assemble the sandwiches. One great thing about living on top of a deli is all the free, sliced cold cuts I want. It's also the first thing I'll be sick of by the end of the month.

"What smells so great?" asks Emma. She steps into the kitchen through the wall, bypassing the sink.

I try not to flinch at her arrival.

Then a screech sounds from my bedroom doorway, and I nearly slice my finger off while cutting the sandwiches in two. I glance over and see an astonished Billy. I give a quick frown, as if to ask *what the hell is wrong with you?*

He points to the sandwiches. "I'll never be able to eat bacon again. That's worse than death."

Emma laughs and slides up to Julian.

I bite my bottom lip and smile.

"What's going on?" Julian asks.

I set his plate in front of him. "What do you mean?"

"Something just happened. I can tell. You changed." He looks over his shoulder.

Billy puffs out his chest. Emma blows in Julian's ear. And I realize I've stopped calling her Cupcake and him D.N.

"Hey," I shout. Emma may be dead, and Julian and I may be apart, but he's off limits. I glare at her.

She holds up her hands in surrender and backs off. Nice to know she's capable of that.

When I look to Julian, his brow is furrowed. "What?" he asks.

"Um, nothing. Just 'hey, it's done.' Now, *manga*."

I don't bother sitting beside him, so I hop up on the counter beside the stove and pull my feet in beneath me.

We each take a huge bite and sigh in unison. It will be a very accurate epitaph.

Halfway through, I'm in need of a drink but too lazy to hop down. I nod my head toward the fridge. "Why not pay for your dinner and grab me a beverage."

One corner of his mouth lifts. "Yes, Ma'am." He finds two glasses in a top cabinet and pours water from the Brita pitcher, knowing darn well I'm not a fan of apple juice. Too bad Ma doesn't remember that.

I take my glass from him, and our fingers brush together. His touch is warm and inviting. I clank the glass against my front teeth, in my attempt to no longer touch him, and slosh water on my chin. Fate's way of a cold shower? Not funny.

He returns to his seat, but when he's facing me again, I notice the smirk on his smug face. He knows our chemistry is something I could never walk away from. The day I left his apartment, I had to do it while he was at work, just in case he tried to talk me out of it. I probably would've melted into a puddle around his expensive shoes. I wouldn't have left Connecticut. Izzie would've had to deal with Emma on her own. Or maybe she wouldn't even know. Would Emma have died if I hadn't returned home?

This is crazy thinking. I'm not responsible for Emma's death, and neither is my family. It's the Plaid Guy. I know it. He killed her and would have even if I moved to Tahiti, took up surfing, and dated a guy named Hiro.

Julian finishes his sandwich and keeps staring at me. Eating while being watched is no fun. And there's no sense in stringing this out. It's only torturing me, so I say, "Spit it out. What do you want to say?"

"I want to talk about us, about why we broke up."

Swallowing the last chunk of sandwich is difficult. I jump down, place my plate in the sink, and walk into the living room. "You know why. We're not compatible."

He swivels in his seat. "Bull. We fought. Every couple does. That doesn't mean we can't make it work."

"He wants to try," Emma squeals.

"He must really love you," Billy says.

I scoff and place a hand on my hip. "And that's why you're here? To make us work?"

He stands and is in front of me in one giant step. This apartment is too small. He brushes a curl from off my cheek and lets his fingers linger. "Exactly."

Darn. I didn't think Ma was right.

I shake my head, even though all I can think about is pressing myself against his tall, firm leanness. "It didn't work."

He smiles, slowly and deliberately. "We try harder."

Yes, harder. That's exactly what I want.

I stare at his lips and remember how they feel pressed against mine. How his tongue usually tastes like fruit—lemons, limes, oranges, cherries. He always has Lifesavers or candy drops in his pocket. Sifting through them before laundry was like Halloween each week.

A noise sounds beside me. Emma is fanning herself with her hand, and I'm brought back to reality. I'll need to remember to do something nice for that woman.

I take a step back, drawing my line in the sand. "Too much has been said. You didn't want to see me anymore. You specifically said you needed space." That's the universal phrase for *it's over*.

"Aww, give him a chance," Billy says.

"I meant right then. I needed time to process, to think, to calm down. I didn't mean forever." Julian moves closer. If we keep this up, he's going to have me up against the windows in several more inches.

I poke him in the chest with my index finger. The tingle and Band-Aid are gone. "Well, you should've been clearer."

He runs his fingers through his thick hair. "There was so much going on. Grandma had just died, and you were acting weird, and then the letter. I wasn't thinking clearly."

I pray he doesn't want answers to my weirdness now. I can't tell him the truth and run the risk of him… Wait. What? Leaving? I've already done that, so what's the worst that happens? He already thinks I'm insane.

"But we can talk it all through now and move past it."

"You're not a talker," I remind him.

He stares into my eyes. "But you are."

A lump forms in my throat as my chest swells. Has he always been this charming?

"Aww, he's so sweet," Emma coos. "Tell him the truth. Tell him about us."

Billy jumps up and down.

I turn my head slightly so I can't see him in my peripheral. He's making me more anxious, plus he looks so darn cute, I don't want to start laughing.

"I didn't mean to accuse you of lying about the letter. I'm sorry," Julian says.

"Now you have to tell him," Billy says.

Julian knew his grandmother hadn't written him a letter before she died. He'd accused me of writing it. And he'd been right. He was in so much pain from her death, and he was wrapped up in some big case at work. I couldn't bear to see him like that, so I wrote down all the things Delia told me before she moved into the light. I guess I hadn't been convincing enough in making him believe she wrote it before her death and stuck it into her favorite book. Unfortunately, it was the book he said he'd flipped through daily since she'd died, and he'd never seen a letter before.

So this is the moment. I either tell him the truth and risk him walking away for good, or continue to lie and have him stay away for good. What a choice. Despite the fighting, breaking up, and calling him every name I can think of, including some made-up ones, I know what I want. I made the wrong choice when I walked out on us without trying. I've been trying to tell myself I hate him, but that's far from the truth. Seeing him at Lindy's then Ma's, having him call the lawyer for us, and even him showing up today wanting to talk has all made me realize I still love him. And even if he chooses to never see me again, at least I'll know I've done all I could.

How's that for facing my issues and not running away?

Okay. Here it goes. "Don't be sorry. Well, maybe for some of the things you said, but you were right."

His eyes widen and darken. The worse is that he hates me. I can handle that. Right?

"What?" His tone is soft, like he can't believe what I just said.

No, I can't handle it. Nope. Nada. I am a coward, and my feet are itching to take flight. But it's too late now. If I lie my way out of this, I'll definitely lose him forever.

"I wrote it, but they were her words." I hold my breath and wait for him to process it all.

He opens his mouth, but no words come out. He does this three times before I wonder if he's having a stroke.

I take in a lungful of air 'cause dying right now isn't going to help anyone, especially if I need to call 9-1-1. "Say something."

"I haven't a clue what you're talking about," he says.

I softly sigh. I guess expecting him to jump to the conclusion that I see dead people is a bit ridiculous. "I can see, hear, and communicate with the dead, and sometimes I help them move on."

His eyebrows raise, and a corner of his mouth lifts. "You talk to the dead? Come on, be serious."

I stare at him, waiting, hoping, not sure of what else to say. I know he believes in souls and that people can linger after dying. He said he felt his grandmother still around a few times. So that's half the battle. But how do I prove I can communicate with the afterlife? Maybe I can remember something his grandmother told me, but I've already shared it all with him. It's not like she's here now and can tell me the name of his imaginary friend or favorite toy.

When I don't start laughing, he frowns. "You are serious."

Emma and Billy dance a jig from the TV to the breakfast bar and back again.

Julian steps away, walks in a circle while rubbing his jaw. "Oh my God. That kind of explains all those times I caught you talking to yourself. It seemed like in depth conversations."

I bob my head from side to side. "A few of those times I was just talking to myself."

He stares into my eyes. "And Grandma came to you after she died?"

"No, she came to you."

His eyes widen again. Pretty soon they're going to fall out of his head.

"I was just able to see her, and you weren't."

He sits on the couch and lowers his head toward his knees.

There goes that pain again. When will I learn to keep my mouth shut?

I sit beside him and place a hand on his back. "She loved you dearly, and she wanted to make sure you knew that. She wouldn't leave until I promised to write the letter."

He looks up and sniffles. "But it was a week between her passing and my getting the letter. She was around that whole time?"

I nod.

It takes him a moment to compose himself. "Why didn't you tell me she was there?" There's a clipped edge to his tone.

"Are you mad at me?" I ask, pulling back.

"Yes. No. I don't know." He gets to his feet. "If I'd known, I could've had that last week with her. You know how much I loved you. You saw how hard I was grieving, and you kept it all a secret?"

I didn't think it was possible to feel worst, but as wrong as I now see my choice was, I can't help but feel defensive. Everything looks different in hindsight. I did what I thought was best.

"I'm sorry." It's all I can say. I never thought of how this would affect him when he found out the truth. I never expected him to find out.

"So why didn't you say anything?" he snaps.

Great. I have to admit how selfish I am too. I explain what happened with Hilary and Micky. Yes, it was a thousand years ago, and no, I don't still harbor feelings for Micky, but the pain, the betrayal, the fear of not being believed, of being abandoned, is still very real and vivid.

"I would've believed you," he says, which makes me feel like dog poo.

"How was I supposed to know that?"

"You should've trusted me. We were living together."

I think about this for a second and then shake my head. "You make it sound so simple, but you don't know what it's like to live with this." My voice cracks.

He takes a big breath and returns to his seat beside me. "You said to help *them* move on. So there have been others?"

"Since that time I died. That's when it all began."

Something in his gaze shifts, and why I'm like this is making sense to him now. "Of course. And since you've been home? Seen any ghosts?"

He laughs, perhaps expecting me to say no. When I don't immediately, he becomes serious. "You have?"

I point to the set of Irish dancers. "There are two right there."

They both stop and wave.

"They're waving hi."

Julian frowns and tentatively waves back.

I try not to laugh, but it's so darn cute, so I do.

"Who are they?"

"One is Billy."

He bows for Julian.

I smile. "A young, college student who died of alcohol poisoning. I haven't had much time to find out more about him yet. Been too busy with my other guest, Emma."

She curtsies.

"She's the one that was..." A thousand crude words enter my mind, and had this been Sunday I would've used one of them. But somehow, in the past few days, I don't hate her anymore. Of course, I will not admit this to my sister. On the growth and maturity meter, though, I am soaring along.

"She's the one caught with Paulie that night."

He jumps to his feet. "The one murdered?"

"That's the one," she and I say in unison.

Julian looks astonished again. He's going to need a stiff drink after he leaves here. Maybe even some therapy. "Why haven't you told the police who killed her? Was it your sister?"

I actually laugh. "No, of course not. She wouldn't do that. Emma doesn't remember who killed her. She'd been roofied."

"How do you know that?"

I curl up my top lip. "Can't say."

It takes a second, but he seems to work it out. How else would I get the info but from my cop brother? "Okay, so since we're doing full dis..."

My cell plays "Before He Cheats" from my bag, cutting off his words. I smile wryly at my choice of ringtones and pull it out. "Hey Izzie, what's up?"

"It's not Izzie," says Ma.

Did I change the wrong ringtone? I pull the phone from my ear and look at the number. Nope. That's Izzie's number. "Ma? Why are you using Izzie's phone?"

Ma lets out a dramatic sigh. "She's been arrested."

CHAPTER FOURTEEN

Julian insists on taking his car to the station, which I have no problem with since my hands are trembling, and I'm likely to drive myself into a tree. I may see a lot of ghosts, but murder and cops and the legal system are not my forte.

In the eloquent words of Evie, from *The Mummy*, British accent and all:

I am a sandwich-maker.

When we arrive, I find Ma in the same narrow hall outside the interrogation rooms I waited in my last time here. It still smells stale, like old cigarettes and coffee, but smoking in public buildings hasn't been allowed in years. It probably permeated into the walls and the furniture.

Instead of sitting in one of the uncomfortable chairs, Ma's pacing, digging a trench in the linoleum with her sneakers. She gives each of us a kiss and hug. "The attorney, your boss, is with her," she says to Julian.

I glance at his rugged profile, and I'm glad he's by my side.

He goes in search of coffee, water, a sedative, while I sit with Ma. "Where's Pop?"

Izzie's cell is in Ma's hand. "He's making some calls. He knows the editor at the *Herald*. He's hoping this won't make the local paper."

Nice try, but how likely is it they won't print a juicy story about an angry wife killing her husband's clown? That's like asking a nun not to pray.

Ma rolls her eyes. "He's wasting his time. This is food for those vultures. But you know how your father gets when he's made up his mind."

Actually, she's talking about herself. Pop's the laid-back one. He doesn't get involved unless he has to.

"Where's Alice?"

"She went to a movie with a friend after dinner. That's why I have Izzie's phone. I called the friend's mother and asked if Alice could spend the night."

That's a great idea.

I wrap an arm around Ma and lean my head on her shoulder. "It's going to be fine." Although, I'm not sure I believe that.

Julian returns with three, tiny cups of coffee and sits on the other side of Ma.

"Thank you for being here and helping Gianna through this," she says to him.

"Of course. Do you know what they arrested her on?"

Ma sniffles and pulls a tissue out of her jacket pocket, but she doesn't use it. She's a rock, and I've rarely seen her cry. "Um, the detective said they found Izzie's blood on the bat, and one of the deceased's bloody hairs on Izzie's dress."

I softly gasp. "That's impossible. Izzie wasn't near Emma."

Fire flashes in Ma's eyes. "Of course she didn't do it."

"What about the blood on the bat?" Julian asks.

I think to the tiny cut on Izzie's hand. "It's from the glass and plastic shards from Paulie's truck. Izzie never stepped foot near Emma."

Ma nods. Julian reaches behind her and squeezes my arm.

"Where's Enzo?" I ask. Maybe he knows more.

Ma takes a deep breath. "He ran off. I don't know. He said he'd be back."

I replay Ma's words in my head. The detective said... "Which one?" I ask.

Ma frowns. "What?"

"Which detective told you about the evidence?"

"It was Kevin."

Of course! Suddenly everything doesn't seem so gloomy. Yes, getting arrested sucks, but I wouldn't be surprised if on closer examination this evidence turns out to be fabricated.

Julian must be following my train of thought because he says, "He can't lie about finding the hair."

"That doesn't mean it wasn't planted." I expect him or Ma to argue with me, and when they don't, I realize it's not as farfetched as I fear.

I hand my cup to Julian. "I'm going to go find Enzo. Will you stay with her?"

"Of course."

When Ma doesn't protest, I hurry off and head to the other side of the building.

I find Enzo talking with another officer in the hall. I don't want to interrupt in case it's something important, but so is this. I pull out my phone and text him. Thanks to an ever slow cell service, I wait what feels like an eternity before he looks up. I nod for him to join me, and I take a few steps back.

He's by my side in two shakes of a lamb's tail. What I want to know is, who thought up that phrase? Some farmer who got his jollies watching lambs shake their tails? And then what? He told his wife, and she told the women at her knitting circle, and before they knew it, it was being said across the country?

"Did something else happen?" Enzo asks.

"You mean other than our sister being arrested for a murder she didn't commit? What are you doing here and not by Ma's side. When I got there, she was all alone."

"Pop was with her when I left."

"He's off calling his friend at the *Herald,* and Ma's trying to hold it together alone." When I'm frustrated, I may exaggerate a tad. Ma's never been known to cower at tragedy. It pumps her up and makes her stronger. And with us three, she's lived through her share and more.

"What's up with this evidence crap?" I ask. "Kevin's a filthy liar, and there's no way they actually found anything but sand and lint on Izzie's clothes."

Enzo grabs my upper arm and pulls me after him. We're moving so fast I barely have time to see the little stick man on the door he pushes me through. But sure enough, there's no mistaking the urinals and pine air freshener.

He kicks in the two stall doors before he says, "You can't blurt that out in the hall. Look, I know Kevin's a jackass."

"And he deserves to be demoted and to have hot wax poured on his 'nads," I add.

Enzo winces. "Ouch. But just because we think this doesn't mean we can publicly slander his reputation."

"Enzo, I hear you, but whenever I see him I remember him accusing me of Craig's death. I have no doubt that he's trying to frame Izzie because of his insane vendetta against me."

He rubs his eyes. "If that's true, you can't prove it by accusing him of it."

I blow a raspberry. "Fine. Have you learned anything else about Emma's death? Have they even searched for Plaid Guy?"

He looks over his shoulder and says so low I almost can't hear him, "I don't know what a Plaid Guy is, but the last items in her stomach were beer, saltine crackers, and some type of peach and blueberry jam."

That jam again.

"What? Does that mean something?" he asks, apparently noticing a change in my expression.

I fill him in. Just as I'm done and waiting for his explosive reaction, 'cause it should be explosive, especially the part about mixing peaches and blueberries, shudder, there's a sound at the door.

Enzo takes off as if his shoes are on fire and rushes into a stall.

My instincts aren't nearly as fast, so when an older, uniformed officer walks in, I'm standing in the middle of the room, staring at him. And smiling. Can't forget the smile. It makes some people uneasy. Especially when I look like I ate a canary.

"It's mint," are the words that tumble out of my mouth after my brain frantically tries to come up with a reason I'm a statue in the men's room.

The officer frowns, as he should 'cause I sound and must look like a lunatic. "Excuse me?"

I point to the walls. "The paint is the color mint. Just like out in the hall. I wanted to check to make sure of the continuity. And now I have. Bye."

I sprint out before he arrests me for telling a lie. The color is actually seafoam.

* * *

I don't get to see Izzie tonight, none of us do, but Mr. Hamilton reassures us she'll make bail in the morning. He says we all need to go home and relax. Ha! He doesn't know us very well. In two houses and one apartment, there will be much pacing, much worrying, and plenty of caffeine to punctuate it all.

Julian is called in to his job to work a new case, and I'm sad to see him go.

I flop onto my couch, channel surfing beside Billy. "I hate investigator's hours." I wanted to finish my conversation with Julian. I still don't know how he feels. It's a good sign that he accompanied me to the police station, but for all I know the work excuse is a ruse. He could be so angry with me that he's at his job quitting, hoping to put a state back between us. Or he's slinging back some beers telling the bartender how he used to date a crazy chick.

Bartender.

I grab my phone, search for Lindy's on Google, and dial the bar.

"Why do you look like you just won the lottery?" Billy asks.

I glance at him as someone at the other end picks up. I should seriously start playing the lottery. Maybe I'll be a Mega-Million winner.

"Lindy's," says a sultry female voice.

"Hi, I was at your bar Saturday night, and I forgot to leave the bartender a tip. I paid for my drinks and was going to tip him before I left, but I ran into an ex, and you know how that goes. We got to arguing about how he works all the time and never made time for me, and before I knew it, I ran out, and the poor bartender didn't make any money off me."

"Okay." She sounds less than enthused. A man cheers in the background, and glasses clink together.

Billy shakes his head, probably wondering what the heck I'm up to now. When he passes over, at least he'll get to tell the other souls that his last days weren't boring.

"Can you tell me his name?" I cross my fingers.

"Um, it's Andy."

I smile. "Great. Is Andy working tonight?"

"Nope. Not until Saturday."

"Thanks. Any chance you can give me his…"

The line clicks. She hung up.

"Number," I say to no one.

Billy quirks his brows. "Trying to make your man jealous?"

"Hardly. I want to know what the bartender saw the night Emma died." More specifically, if he saw Plaid Guy. If I'm not the only one then he can tell the cops, too. They'll believe a stranger more than a suspect's sister, right?

"Are you staying in tonight?" Billy asks.

I turn sideways, lean my back against the armrest, and pull my knees to my chest. "What are *you* doing tonight?"

He points to the television. "What I do every night. What choice do I have?"

"You can move on."

He looks offended. "Why would I want to do that? This place is nice." He pats the sofa cushion. "Comfy."

This old thing? The other side has a dip, so when you sit, you sink down. Now I know he's lying.

"Other than the creature comforts and how wonderful they are, which you can't even enjoy, why are you sticking around?"

He shrugs. "Beats me. Just don't wanna go."

Which means there's a reason. It's usually they're afraid of missing family or just afraid.

"Where's your family? Any reason you stay here and not there?"

"They live in town. It's boring there. Here I have you and Emma." He stares into my eyes. "You guys can see me."

And there he's all alone, and hanging with sad, grieving people isn't any fun, even if you love them.

"Is there anything you want to say to them? Something you didn't get a chance to before you passed."

His head is bent down, and he's looking at the floor. "You'd do that?"

I jump to my feet, eager to help. I also don't want to sit here and think about poor Izzie in a holding cell all night. "That's my job. Come on. Let's go visit them."

He smiles and floats beside me. "That job sucks since you don't get paid."

"Volunteering is good for the soul. It's like chicken soup."

* * *

Ten minutes later, I pull up to a small, one-story house in the West End. I have to park several houses farther up because parking on these narrow, cramped streets is like fitting an elephant into a shoe box. I chuckle. Sometimes I make the corniest analogies.

When we're standing in front of his door, he hesitates. "How are you going to do this?"

"I don't know, but I'll figure it out." If he makes me nervous, I may turn around and go home.

I knock and glance at the time on my phone. It's early enough in the night to be almost rude. Ma and Pop always taught us never to visit or call someone too late or too early and never to visit people unannounced. I've tried to live by their rules. Except the one about throwing salt over my shoulder if I spill some. I'm not superstitious, and that one is just plain silly. Why waste perfectly good salt?

A woman in her forties opens the door. "Yes? Can I help you?"

"Mom," Billy whispers.

"Hi. My name is Gianna, and I was friends with Billy."

Sadness creeps onto her face. "Oh."

"I don't mean to bother you. I wanted to stop by and tell you how sorry I am for your loss."

She presses her lips together and looks past me, as if she can see her son. She takes a step back and opens the door wider. "Please. Come in."

I step into the living room and immediately start to sweat. Gosh, it's stuffy in here. I glance at the two windows and see they're both shut.

"Have a seat. Would you like something to drink?"

I'd like a fan. "No, thank you."

The room is dim. There are no lights on, only the TV, and it's turned down so low I can barely hear a sound. She and Pop would hate hanging out together. I glance at Billy, wishing he could read my mind, because I don't really know what to say.

I sit on the dark green sofa. It's definitely more comfortable than mine.

His mother sits in an armchair close to the TV. "How did you know Billy?"

"Through Holy Mount." I hold my breath and hope this is the Wyatt residence and I found the right article. It's a safe guess. I mean how many college students died of alcohol poisoning over Spring break?

When she nods, I freely breathe. Thank goodness I know how to Google.

Bill sits on the other end of the sofa, right by his mom.

"How long have you been there?"

"Um, this is my second year."

Hopefully I can pull off nineteen reasonably easily. She doesn't seem to notice the tiny, and I do mean teensy, lines between my brows. Ma says I frown too much. Can I help it if other people have a way of irking me? Plus, being around the dead all the time doesn't help much.

"Billy and I had a class together."

"Oh, which one?" she asks.

Darn. Why did I say that? I will him to speak up with my mind, but he's staring at her like he hasn't seen her in years. My heart goes out to him, but he needs to tell me what he wants her to know. I'm going to melt if I stay in here much longer.

"Um, English." That's a safe bet, right? Everyone has to take that.

She nods.

"I'm sorry I didn't come by sooner. I was just so sad, and I didn't want to crowd you and your family." I bite my lip, hoping there's more family and she's not the only one. Not so much because of getting caught in a lie, but I don't know if I can deal if she lives here all alone. There has to be nothing worse than grieving by yourself.

"Thank you."

When Billy doesn't come out of his catatonia, I get fed up. "Um, would you mind if I had a glass of water?"

"Of course." She gets up and walks out of the room.

I take a throw pillow and toss it at Billy. It goes right through him and luckily stays on the couch. "Hey, you," I whisper. "I'm dying here. No pun intended. You want to help out? I'm not here for me."

He rolls his shoulders, as if he has a kink in them. I'm pretty sure ghosts don't experience muscle cramps. "Sorry. The last time I was here, she was sobbing to my aunt. This is the first time I've seen her looking normal since before I died."

I nod in sympathy, but we have to get down to business. "What do you want me to tell her?" I whisper.

His mother reenters before I get any answers. She hands me a glass of tap water with no ice. Yum.

I smile, pretend to take a sip, and set it on the end table beside me.

"Tell her that I love her and Dad and that I was always grateful for everything they did and gave me. Even if I didn't always show it."

"Um, Billy always told me how much he loved you guys." I repeat the rest, too.

His mother sucks in a breath, and I wait for an outburst of tears, but she holds in it.

"And tell her that eating blueberry pancakes every Sunday morning is my favorite memory."

I tell her and feel awful at her pain. Maybe I should leave the ghost hunting alone and concentrate on sandwiches.

Her shoulders shake, and she starts to cry. I get up, swipe a tissue out of a box on a side table, and hand it to her. I glance at Billy, and he's gone. Vanished. Probably unable to handle the tears. I get it, but it's not like I know the woman.

After she calms down, she says, "Thank you, dear. This hasn't been an easy time, with the arrangements, the funerals. Mr. Wyatt and I appreciate your stopping by. He's not home now, but I will tell him every word."

I smile. "Please give Mr. Wyatt my condolences too." I figure this is a good moment to hightail it out of here, but I realize what she just said. "Funerals? There was more than one?"

She sniffled and dabs her nose. "Yes, you must've heard."

I shake my head, not caring I'm blowing my cover. "I, uh, I couldn't handle it, so I quit and haven't gone back to school yet."

She grabs my hand. "Oh, I'm so sorry. The night of the party, Billy wasn't the only one who drank too much. Another classmate. Um, Stephanie Murdock also died. Not that night. She slipped into a coma and passed away a couple of days later in the hospital."

Crap. Billy doesn't know this. Were they close? Should I ask his mom and really look clueless? Would she even know? Do I tell him?

I get up, say good-bye, and nearly run out of the sauna. Outside, I wipe the perspiration from my forehead and open all my windows when I get into the car.

Billy appears in the passenger seat.

I decide to hold on to this information for the moment. "Why is your parents' house so hot?"

He smirks. "Mom's from Florida. She's always cold."

Makes sense.

"Okay, do you feel like moving on?" I ask.

He shuts his eyes and concentrates. After a moment, he looks at me. "Not yet."

Darn. What now?

"Um, were you close to a Stephanie Murdock?"

He frowns. "Where'd you hear that name?"

I shrug. "Your mom mentioned her."

Billy shakes his head and stares out the windshield. "Nope."

CHAPTER FIFTEEN

Wednesday morning, I'm woken by another creepy dream of Freezer Dude. After peeing and brushing my teeth, I call Ma to find out about Izzie. Pop is going to the courthouse while Ma opens the deli like usual. I leave a message with Enzo to get back to me when he knows more, and I start to call Julian but decide he needs to make the next move.

I need to prove Kevin is a rat bastard. Since I don't have a degree in forensic science or a crystal ball, my best choice is figuring out who really killed Emma. And who Plaid Guy is, 'cause I'm betting they're one and the same.

So after dressing and cramming a banana into my mouth, I grab my portable mug of coffee and drive to Stacey Anne's house to discuss the finer things about jam making. I park in front and make a quick decision to knock on the side rather than front door. Something about the two potted plants and a carelessly tossed pair of garden gloves by the side steps tells me this is the informal entrance. I'm hoping to come across as easy, casual, and friendly.

When I asked Emma about the jam last night, after Billy and I got home, she said she wasn't sure of the company name, but it had a red and white gingham ribbon tied around the neck of the tiny jar. And she didn't put two and two together that the jam came from Stacey Anne's shop because the jar had no label on it, and there was no return address on the box it all came in. That would've been her first clue that there was something wrong with it.

I knock again on Stacey Anne's door, but when I don't hear movement inside I wonder if anyone's home. Her light blue car is parked out front. Maybe she's still sleeping?

"Can I help you?"

I'm startled by the soft, high-pitched voice behind me. I spin around to see the woman who's even more petite close up and looks to be about twelve. She's dressed in denim capris, a yellow blouse, a full red apron, and dingy, white, slip-on sneakers. She reminds me of a softer version of the clowns.

"Hi, I'm looking for Stacey Anne Ingles. I'm Gianna from Mancini Deli over on Park Place." Gosh, I hope she doesn't follow the news closely. Izzie's arrest is probably everywhere local.

The girl-woman holds a basket of strawberries and pruning shears. "Oh yes, I've been there. Great food."

"Thanks." Ma and Pop will be so proud.

"How can I help you?" She steps toward the door. Right up near me, she definitely looks more like early thirties. There are fine lines in the corners of her eyes, laugh lines. She's happy. Or she spends so much time outside she has squint lines.

"I tasted some of your jam, and I am looking into possibly selling it in the deli or adding it to one of our dishes." And what exactly would that be, Gianna? Pastrami on rye with extra strawberry jam?

Her brows shoot up, and a smile covers her face. "I'm honored, but I have my own storefront."

"It can't hurt to sell more though, right?"

She opens the door. "Come inside, and we'll talk."

Yes! Now I have to figure out how to steer the conversation where I want it to go. This is so much harder than I thought it'd be.

I follow her into the kitchen, where she sets the basket of fruit by the sink and motions for me to have a seat at the round table by the window. The decor is a cheery yellow with lemon, lime, and orange slices on the curtains and the wallpaper border. Her cabinets have glass doors, and her dinner plates are a mixture of yellow, green, and orange to match.

I'd have to wear sunglasses to hang in here for long.

I sit and look out the window. Her backyard is magnificent—a garden of fruits of various colors. It's gorgeous. Ma and Pop would love it. They used to have a huge vegetable garden, but the upkeep with the deli was too much. Now, they only grow tomatoes and basil, which they use in practically everything.

"Would you like some tea?" She sets the kettle on the stove.

I think ruefully of the half cup of delicious coffee I still have in my car. "Thank you."

As the water boils, she busies herself with taking out dishes, and I busy myself by looking around the room. It's a normal looking kitchen. Canisters, a baker's shelf with a deep fryer, electric grill, waffle maker, salad spinner, and a box of something. I lean forward and peek inside. Red and white gingham ribbons.

Bingo!

The last thing I check out is a small, built-in desk where a photo of her and a man sits. They're smiling into the camera, cheek to cheek. That has to be Andrew, her husband. And he's definitely not Plaid Guy. Not unless he lost about a hundred pounds since that photo was taken.

She places a tray on the table and sets a lemon-colored, ceramic mug, lime saucer, and a spoon in front of me. "I grow my own tea, too, and this is a special blend, ginger chamomile. I hope you enjoy it."

"You grow tea, too. Wow." I hope I'm not poisoned.

"I just started doing it. I haven't added it to my inventory yet." She hurries back to the stove, gets the kettle, and pours water into our cups. Once she returns it to the stove, she grabs a small jar of jam and a plate of crackers and sets them in the middle of the table.

I stare at the jar of peach and blueberry jam. "That's an interesting combination."

She giggles. "My husband thought the same until he tried it. Go on. See for yourself."

I smile because we've now entered the personal zone. Bringing up her husband clearly means it's an open topic, and I can do the same, right? I smear some of the weird, purplish concoction onto a cracker and ask, "How long have you been married?"

"Only a year."

And he's already cheated on you? Oh, you poor thing. "You're newlyweds."

She's staring at the cracker in my hand, obviously waiting for my approval. So I bite into it and hope it's not so awful that I visibly cringe.

It's not overly sweet. Blueberry is definitely the more prominent taste, with a hint of peach. "Wow, that's great." I'm a bit too enthusiastic, but surprisingly, it's actually good.

She beams but doesn't reply to my comment, so I bring it up again.

"Your husband must be so proud of your business."

"Yes, he is."

"What's it like being married?" Oh that's lame. But how exactly am I supposed to bring up Emma?

She shrugs, still smiling, but sadness passes her eyes. "It's great. Why do you ask?"

"My boyfriend, well, it's getting serious, and I've been thinking about marriage a lot lately. Any tips?"

She stares out the window. "Don't rush into it."

"Is that what you did?" I try to make it sound light and giddy, but she turns her gaze on me, and it's dark and scary.

Exactly what is the jam lady capable of?

* * *

When I get to the deli, it's mobbed. Not only is there a line inside, but there are people gathered out front. I doubt our new caprese pasta salad is driving the town to visit in droves, so it must be Izzie's arrest. Pop is there. Ma must've called him in early. It doesn't look like she's leaving any time soon either.

I grab an apron in back and am tying it when Pop comes in for a sleeve of plastic cups.

"I haven't seen it this busy since we opened again after Hurricane Sandy," he says.

"How's Izzie? What happened?" I ask.

Pop looks weary. His eyes are sad, his skin paler than normal. He needs a vacation. "The judge set bail at a hundred thousand dollars."

"Oh my God," I shriek. "Is she still in jail?"

He shakes his head. "No, I went to a bail bondsman. We only have to pay ten percent."

"So you have ten grand just lying around?" I know my parents aren't piss poor. They own their house, and this building. They must be doing all right because they put two kids through college and still manage to lease their cars. Every five years, they trade them in for something new. Plus, they're generous on birthdays and Christmas. But I don't know what they have, or had, socked away for a rainy day. I hope this ten G wasn't all of it. Pop doesn't talk about money though, so it's no surprise when he doesn't answer me.

"We also had to put up collateral." He grabs an extra sleeve of cups.

"What kind of collateral?"

He looks me straight in the eye. "The deli."

Whoa. Wait. Does that include my apartment? Of course it does, Gianna. It's attached to the deli. Don't be so selfish. "What does this mean?"

He pats my shoulder. "Nothing. Izzie will go to court, and everything will be fine." He heads up front.

Or I'll find the real killer, and this nightmare will end even sooner.

I take over for Pop by the salads and finish scooping a pound of antipasto. When I hand it off to Pop to ring up, the next person in line steps up.

"Gianna, dear, how is your sister?" Mrs. Pearson, old, gray, and as thin as a twig, grabs my wrist and jerks me toward her over the counter. Due to my lack of height, my sleeve grazes across a splatter of oil and vinegar. There goes that shirt.

"She's fine. What can I get you?"

Not happy with my answer, she gives me a look of disdain and curls her lip up at the items under the glass dome. "I'm not sure."

I snatch my arm back, forcing her to let go, not interested in standing here waiting for her to make up her mind when it's obvious she's only here to find out gossip.

"Who's next?" I shout, not caring when another glare comes my way.

Luckily, the next person orders a pound of potato salad and a half a pound of tortellini and doesn't want to gab. By the time I get through the inside and outside line, Mrs. Pearson still hasn't ordered anything. She ends up on the other side of the counter where Pop is slicing ham. He goes in the back to get another side of pig, and Ma pops her head out front to let me know she's finally heading home and will call me later.

"Oh, Rosa, dear," says Mrs. Pearson. "How is Isabella? She didn't kill that poor girl, did she?"

"She's fine." Ma ducks back into the kitchen, and I almost laugh at the old woman's expression. Almost 'cause I'm also fuming at the audacity of her. Doesn't she realize she's talking about Ma's daughter? And for her to act so casual about it, not to even express sorrow or concern.

"Everyone is so rude," Mrs. Pearson says under her breath.

"So is asking questions that are clearly none of your business while pretending to order something," I say. Loud.

The young man ordering the ham smiles to himself.

Mrs. Pearson cringes and storms out.

Pop comes back in with the ham and catches the tail end of the old biddy's departure. Literally. "Did she get anything?"

Just a lashing. "Nope." I wink at the young guy.

The bell above the door rings, and I turn with a smile. I immediately drop it when Kevin and a trio of cops walk in. Great. Sometimes I wish my folks owned a funeral parlor. Then if Kevin came in, maybe it would be on a gurney.

He steps up to me, stares straight into my eyes, not even glancing at the rows of salads encased between us, and smirks. "Let me see, what do I want for lunch today?"

I fake a smile so big, my cheeks start to hurt. "How about a demotion with a side of planting evidence?"

His face tenses, and my grin goes from saccharine to sugar cane. I lean closer, pretending I'm about to whisper, but still speaking with my outside voice. "If it wasn't true, you wouldn't look so guilty right now."

One of the other cops stares at Kevin's profile. The other two walk over to where Pop is restocking the Provolone.

Kevin narrows his eyes. "You think you're clever." He's definitely using his inside voice. We're so far inside, I can barely hear him. Which means he doesn't want his colleagues or Pop to hear him either. No witnesses?

"No, just right." I refuse to let him rattle me. I'd like it to be the other way around.

"No one will believe your lies. In fact, when I get done with you, no one will believe when you say the sky is blue."

I roll my eyes. "What are you yakking about?"

The right corner of his mouth lifts. "Do you really think anyone will care what the girl who talks to ghosts says?"

Involuntarily, I widen my eyes. He knows? But how? Then it hits me. Hilary. That witch!

My expression makes Kevin smile. Darn. I really need to develop a poker face.

"That's right," he says. "I know your crazy little secret."

This time I lower my voice. "I don't care what you know. We can each deny it and say the other is lying. But the difference between our secrets is that you can't prove whether I see ghosts or not. I will, however, prove that you tampered with evidence."

He stiffens and glances around to see who's listening. His buddies are giving Pop sandwich orders.

I go in for the kill. "And then what will happen? Mancini deli may get more business so everyone can see the crazy girl who fills plastic cups with potato salad, while you're drooling in your beer somewhere wondering what happened to your career."

I don't give him the satisfaction of replying. I turn and join Pop in creating a ham and Swiss on rye with extra mayo and an eggplant panini with roasted red peppers and spinach.

When the three orders are done, the cops step outside and wait for Kevin. He still hasn't ordered anything, and I doubt he will. It's clear he wants the last word but won't speak in front of an audience. The big baby!

Since I want him gone, I ask Pop to give us a minute.

Pop eyes Kevin, not sure if he wants to leave us alone. He never asked me about the assault I mentioned on Sunday. He probably asked Ma or maybe even Enzo. The phone rings, and Pop reluctantly goes in back to answer it.

I put my hands on my hips and face the jerk. "What?"

He obviously has nothing planned because he stands there like a doofus. "I'd watch my back if I was you."

"That's really hard to do without a mirror," I shout as he walks out.

* * *

I go to Ma's after work, still smelling like oil and vinegar from Mrs. Pearson yanking at me over the counter. When I get there, I find Izzie in the kitchen wearing Ma's apron.

"What are you doing?" I ask. I expected to find her curled in the fetal position in bed, an empty bottle of Pinot Noir beside her. Not standing at the sink, filling a pot with water.

"Making spaghetti. You hungry?" She gives me a smile.

The basement door is ajar, and when Izzie turns the water off, I can hear Ma humming "It's a Doggone Life".

There are so many things wrong with this picture that I don't know where to begin worrying.

First, what happened to Wing Wednesday? Second, why is my sister acting like all is right in her world? And thirdly, why isn't Enzo here with a fork and a bib?

Maybe I'm sleeping, and I don't know it.

Izzie glances back at me. "Well, are you?"

"No," I say in a daze. "Are you alright? You seem kinda chipper."

She shakes her head. "I realized that I can cry and whine or I can fight back."

This sounds promising. "Oh yeah? How?"

She smooths the side of her head, to the elastic band of her stubbly ponytail. "How do you think? My mug shot was horrendous, Gi. My appointment with that hairdresser, Fawn, is Friday. I can't go to court looking like the bride of Frankenstein."

I don't know what to say. I don't *have* anything to say. She's stunned me, and that's not easy to do.

"Okay." It's all I got. "I'll pick you up?"

She turns on the stove. "Yes, that's great. Be here at eight. I made it for before work, but that was before the arrest. I won't be going back to the deli for a while."

I step forward, ready to hold her up as she crumbles, but she sees my movement from the corner of her eye and whips around.

"Don't," she says. "No hugs or sad voices. This will be fine. It has to be. And I won't break down. I have a daughter and a…" She abruptly stops.

"Okay, it's cool. You know where I am if you need something."

She picks up the wooden spoon as if ready to stir…I don't know…the water, and she points it at me. "Just make that clown talk."

I smile. "I will." I'll do more than that.

CHAPTER SIXTEEN

The next day, I head down to work early to help Ma and to cover Izzie's shift. We're packed all morning and afternoon, and when Pop comes in, he mutters something about closing for a few days—until the celebrity of knowing a murder suspect dies down. As much as I need the money, I won't mind a breather either. I need to kick this sleuthing into high gear. So far I have a bunch of theories, but none of them are concrete.

All night, I replayed Izzie in Ma's kitchen, boiling water and acting as if her world wasn't in pieces. Being the oldest, she's always put on a brave face, especially in front of our parents, but when she and I are alone, she usually lets it all out. Maybe she's afraid if she starts, she won't be able to stop.

After my shift, I go upstairs, take a quick shower to get the meat stench off my skin, and dig into my jewelry box. Most of it is costume stuff. I love my accessories. Bangle bracelets, which may or may not still be in style, all kinds of earrings from studs to dangly ones, and rings and necklaces that show my quirky style. There are only a few real pieces. One being the diamond pendant my cousin gave me when she got married. She almost didn't walk down the aisle because of an anonymous note, but luckily, true love prevailed.

I was her maid of honor, and while the rest of the bridal party got diamond chips, I received a one-carat, square pendant looped onto a silver chain. I don't wear it often, and it doesn't mean a lot. It reminds me of Julian. We met the day before Claudia's wedding.

It's the only item I have to pawn to pay my little extortionist, No Spam. There isn't anyone I can ask to borrow the money from, especially not after Ma and Pop just coughed up ten grand. Of course, I could tell Enzo and get the cops involved.

I've considered this. It would be easiest and wouldn't strain my wallet, but I don't want to risk Enzo's future promotion by doing something unethical. He'd be required to get the detectives involved immediately, and I don't want Kevin getting his hands on the picture. If there isn't a picture and No Spam is lying, it would make Enzo look like a fool. No, until I know more, I want to handle this on my own.

And if I'm being fully honest, I may have fantasized once or twice about finding the goods to not only clear Izzie's name but to bring down Kevin too.

I head over to the only pawnshop in town, and Emma and Billy decide to go along for the ride.

"So what do you guys know about a ghost trying to pull a human over to the other side? Anything?"

They both look confused. Great. Nothing. How do I find out what Freezer Dude wants and how to stop him?

The pawnshop owner only offers me four hundred for the necklace, not even a quarter of what I need, but it'll have to do. After I leave the store, I debate texting the teen. I could use this money for groceries and bills, or give Ma and Pop a little extra for rent next month. They shouldn't be taking care of me. I'm an adult. At least in age. But what if this boy can get Izzie off?

I stare at the cash then shove it into my purse. First, I'll see how it goes with Fawn tomorrow.

* * *

When I leave the pawnshop, I head over to the agency. I haven't ordered any of the costume items I'll need yet. I don't want to spend money on something I'll probably only use a couple more times. Those outfits are expensive. My next gig, according to a message from Danielle, is tomorrow. I'm hoping I can borrow the clothes I wore to the Conroy party and figure now's a good time to ask.

When I get there though, Danielle isn't at her desk. I go through the side door and hear someone taking a deep breath and then a sniffle.

I head toward the sounds and come to an ajar door. I softly knock while wedging it open further with my foot. "Hello?"

It glides open, revealing an office as colorful as the lobby, and Timothy is seated behind a large, white desk. He widens his eyes and swivels away from me so I can't see him wiping them. "Gianna, what are you doing here?"

"I'm sorry. I didn't mean to startle you. I was looking for Danielle."

"She went home early." He turns back around. "Can I help you with something?"

"My outfit won't be in by tomorrow, and I'm wondering if I can borrow what I wore last time?" I sit in a chair across from him. I don't wait to be asked, mostly because I don't think he'll invite me in.

"Yeah, that's fine. It's not like you can run to Walmart and pick up a costume." He laughs, but it sounds strained.

"Right." I lean forward. "How are you doing?"

He looks at me, probably a bit startled I'm asking.

Billy is either still in the car or went back home, but Emma kneels beside Timothy, her brow creased. She looks as upset as he does.

Before he can answer or kick me out, I say, "Were you and Emma close?"

She hasn't mentioned if their relationship was a one-time thing or ongoing, so maybe his tears are about something else.

When he nods, she sharply inhales. "We screwed around some," she says, "but it was just fun."

Obviously, it was more than that for him.

"I loved her," he says.

Emma gasps. "I had no idea."

I watch them for a few minutes. Her by his side, him not aware she's there. I'm filled with a sudden urge to see Julian and to throw myself into his arms.

* * *

Julian's apartment is on the corner of Monroe Boulevard and Broadway. It's a two-story building with an open terrace in the center. I find apartment 2B in the back and knock on the door. The hallway smells like curry, which is coming from the apartment next door.

When he opens it, I take one step over the threshold and throw myself at him. I wrap my arms around his neck and push my mouth against his. He immediately pulls me closer, his hands firm on my hips. And for several dizzying seconds we pretend the last four months never happened.

I can't believe I almost let him go. I don't expect us to pick up as hot and heavy as we were. He needs time to get used to my talents, and I like having my own place. Even if I'm not actually alone.

As my nether regions start to tingle, he pulls away.

It takes me and my sore lips to figure out what the heck just went wrong. Why is my mouth cold and not puckered?

"What?" I ask. "You don't believe me?"

He takes my elbow and guides me inside, shutting the door behind us. "About your ability? No, I believe you."

"So you don't like my kisses anymore?" I give out a light laugh, as if I'm joking. But I'm suddenly very serious. He may end up with a shoe upside his head if he's not careful how he answers.

One corner of his mouth lifts. "That'll never be a problem."

I smile in relief. These are expensive shoes.

"Then what?"

While he hesitates and my uneasiness returns, I check out the room. It's windowless with a desk and a couple of file cabinets. His work area. To the left is a doorway leading to a kitchenette and probably a living room. The bathroom is straight ahead, and an arch before it is probably the bedroom. Not shabby for one person. It's definitely bigger than my place. And appears to be ghost free.

He leads me into the room with the kitchenette. The far wall is covered with a couple of bookcases and a plasma TV. A brown leather sofa and armchair, as well as a couple of tables and lamps, fill the rest of the room. The TV is new, but I remember cold Connecticut nights cuddled together on that sofa. Plus several vigorous horizontal mambo sessions. Leather on a bare bottom isn't always luxurious though. Especially on a humid summer day.

He motions for me to take a seat, but I can't. Partly because of the memories and partly because my stomach is in knots not knowing what he's going to say. Maybe he doesn't want to get back together. Maybe he's decided I'm not worth the heartache.

"I want to talk," he says.

My heart sinks. Or maybe he really moved to New York for his job after all. He always put it before us anyway.

I wag a finger in his face, trying to sound playful and not like I might burst into tears. "You know, we should take things slowly. There's no sense in rushing into anything. You have your place here, and I live over there." I point in the opposite direction. "We can see each other once in a while and…"

He grabs my hips and jerks me forward. "Once in a while will not be enough."

A smile breaks out onto my face as his mouth crushes mine.

* * *

I open my eyes to sunlight and blink several times. The night's memories of Julian carrying me to his bed spring to mind, and I roll onto his side of the mattress to find I'm alone.

"Hey," I say. "Where are you?" I sit up and stare at the empty room. A room I hadn't paid attention to last night. It's very minimal. There's a large mattress and box spring on a metal frame and a small dresser. That's it. Where's his old bedroom furniture? The longer I think about it the more I remember it wasn't holding up well. He must've ditched it.

Water sounds. Then the faucet goes off, and a door opens. Julian, dressed in gray trousers and a light blue button-down steps into the room. He smiles at me, and my insides turn to mush.

"I really wish I didn't have to see a client."

I realize the sheet has dropped to my waist, and I'm buck naked. I rise to my knees and am thankful I don't manage to tumble off the mattress. "Are you sure you have to leave right now? What's fifteen more minutes?"

He laughs and turns to the tie on his dresser. "What I want to do to you will take longer than fifteen minutes."

Goody. I was exaggerating my abilities of reaching another touchdown after the two games we played into the wee hours of the morning.

"But it'll have to be later. Tonight? Maybe dinner first?"

I plop back down on my butt and try to remember what day it is. "Uh, no can do. I have a birthday party tonight."

He frowns. "A catering thing?"

That's right. He doesn't know I'm slumming it as a clown part-time. "No, but it's a long story, and you don't have the time."

I grab my tee off the floor and wiggle into it. I reach for my phone as he smacks my butt. It's seven-oh-five. Shoot, Izzie. I grab my clothes and rush into the bathroom.

"Where's the fire?" he asks.

I pee as fast as possible, not fully emptying my bladder, and dress as if there is a fire. I wash my hands and fly out the door. "I've got to meet Izzie. I'll call you later."

Then I'm gone, into my car, and racing to my apartment. I have enough time for a quick shower before meeting my sister.

When I get inside, a very pissed off Billy greets me. "Where have you been all night?"

Emma is pacing the floor in front of my couch. When she sees me, relief floods her face.

"What's going on? Why are you guys in a tizzy?" I drop my purse onto the floor and head to the bathroom, stripping along the way. It's not like Billy hasn't seen me naked before. It's hard to know when a ghost will walk in on you undressing.

"You didn't call," Emma says. "We were worried."

I laugh. How would I call them? "I'm fine. You sound like my parents."

"You were gone all night, and the last I knew, you were looking into my death."

The emotion in her tone makes my step falter. I stop and look back. "I'm fine. I spent the night with Julian."

Her mouth drops, and her eyes twinkle. "Oh do tell all. And I mean every explicit detail."

I smile and head to the shower. "I don't have time. Izzie and I are meeting Fawn. Now it's time to find out who murdered you."

She pops up in my shower, and I yelp.

"Why are you doing this? After what I did with Paulie, why are you helping me?"

It amazes me how she's directly under the spray and doesn't get wet. "Um, I was never one for showering with other women. You think you could step out?"

Her eyes widen, and she glances down at my boobs. "Oh yeah, sure."

Suddenly, she's gone, and I step under the hot water.

"So?" she asks from the other side of the curtain.

"I don't know. I guess I feel like this is my calling. It's what I'm meant to do."

"Oh." She sounds disappointed, like I was supposed to give some long speech about how I'm doing this because I care about her. Truth is, I do, in my own way, but this is more about my sister and niece. I don't want to hurt her feelings more though, so I change the subject.

"Where's Billy?" I ask.

"He saw a cute girl outside and wanted to check her out."

Figures. I rinse the shampoo from my hair, add conditioner, and lather up. I have a really good feeling about meeting Fawn. Izzie and I may find out who really killed Emma.

* * *

Fawn drapes a bib over Izzie's sundress and smiles at me through the mirror. Luckily, the place isn't busy this early, and she's allowing me to sit in the unoccupied chair beside them.

We didn't have enough time to stop and buy a hidden microphone. It would've taken us even longer to learn about them, too. Not only was I running behind due to my tryst with Julian, but Izzie's having a sluggish morning, as well. We decided to use what we have. In my lap is my cell phone. I have my camera app open, set to video, so I only have to press the large green circle when I want to record. Between Stacey Anne's jam that was in Emma's stomach and may or may not, but probably may, have contained a powerful drug, and Plaid Guy, I doubt we'll catch anything incriminating here. But Izzie had the appointment, and she really needs that trim, so what the heck. Recording this can't hurt.

"I'm so grateful you were able to get me in so fast," Izzie says.

She had the foresight to make the appointment in her maiden name, and luckily the news hasn't released her photo yet. Pop's friend helped us out there. But that's just local. Izzie's name and photo have been mentioned and shown on the national channels. Hopefully, Fawn hasn't seen it and won't recognize her.

The mirror in front of me has two small pictures of children taped to the edge of it. They must be another stylist's kids. I look around Fawn's mirror and all along her section, but I don't see any pictures—none at all, not of Fawn, a man, nothing. From her Facebook photos, I already know her husband isn't Plaid Guy, but photos can be so telling. I guess a lack of them is, too.

"You're lucky. We had a cancelation." Fawn grimaces at the uneven ends of Izzie's hair. "Did you do this yourself?"

"Yeah. I know it looks crazy. I was experiencing extreme hatred for my husband."

"And you took it out on your poor hair." Fawn grabs a spray bottle of water and spritzes the back of Izzie's head.

"Stupid, huh?"

Fawn shakes her head. "No. You'd be surprised how often I see it. But it's usually when a wife has decided to leave the marriage. She wants to look different, and the hair's the easiest place to start."

Izzie and I exchange looks in the mirror. Part of it is for show. In the car we rehearsed what we'll say and how much information we'll give Fawn. We want to be ready for anything. But Izzie also doesn't want to blab her business all over town. She's embarrassed that her husband can't keep it in his pants. And now she has to face down the humiliation of an arrest. I'm certain most people have at least heard about it by now. This town is only so big.

"My husband is a cheating louse," Izzie says.

Fawn, with scissors and comb in hand, stops mid snip. "Oh, I'm sorry. Men can be such jerks."

"Tell me about it." I roll my eyes. I cough dramatically and press the button, hoping I'm the only one who heard the beep.

Izzie bites her bottom lip. She must've heard it, too. Since Fawn doesn't look over, I assume we're good.

"I don't understand why they can't keep it zipped. Is it that hard?" I ask.

Fawn giggles. "Right."

"Sounds like you know," I say with a grin.

Fawn doesn't respond or look up right away. It's almost as if she didn't hear me, but then she glances my way, and her expression is anything but friendly. Too bad I'm not holding the phone up to record her face. She returns her attention to Izzie's hair and trims.

Izzie raises her brows at me through the mirror, as if to say, *now what*?

And I'm not sure. Emma's right. I suck at this.

"There are some women who seek out married men. They latch onto them and won't give up until the guy gives in." Fawn's tone is heavy and full of anger.

"Not all guys give in," I say.

Fawn and Izzie stare at me as if I'm crazy. I know we're here to get the truth, but Fawn's husband is a probably a serial cheater. It's possible whoever he visited in that house has something to do with his work, but Fawn's certainly concerned enough to follow him. She can blame his actions on Emma or other women all she wants, but the truth is some men are simply unfaithful.

"Sorry. Never mind." I press my lips together and shut up. I even scoot back in my seat to give the illusion that I'm no longer a part of the conversation.

Izzie clears her throat. "My pig of a husband swore up and down he wasn't cheating, but I knew. He was coming home later than usual. He was always tired, rarely wanted to have sex, and as soon as he'd come in the door, he'd take a shower."

I glance down at the phone. I only have a three-minute window before it turns itself off. I decide to end it and start a second video. I start another coughing fit. By the time we leave, I'm going to be hoarse.

Fawn shakes her head. I fear she heard the beeping that time, but she keeps cutting. "A friend of mine's husband is a habitual cheater. He ends it with one and starts with another. He, however, was harder to catch. He never comes home late from work. He's been leaving the office early, meeting his bimbo, and then going back to work."

She's definitely talking about herself. Ah-ha! I knew it.

Oh, oops, that's not something to be happy about.

Izzie tries to shake her head, but Fawn is holding a side section of hair. "What did she do?"

Fawn gazes at her through the mirror. "Do?"

"Yeah? Did she leave him? Get even? Run the girl over with her car?" I ask.

Izzie and I laugh, but there's no mistaking the look of surprise on Fawn's face.

Oh crap! Was she the one who almost ran Emma down?

CHAPTER SEVENTEEN

Izzie and I head to my car and sit there—each of us staring out the windshield. Of the three wives Emma mentioned, one may have drugged her jam, and the other allegedly almost used her car to mow her down. What about the third one? Is Naomi Anderson innocent, or did she push her down the mall escalator? And what kind of coincidence is it that all three of these women did something to harm their husband's mistress?

"What do you think?" Izzie asks.

I turn and look at her hair. Fawn took off just enough to make it even, and she blew it out to create soft waves around Izzie's face. "First, I think your hair is gorgeous."

She flips down the visor and stares at herself in the mirror. "It is, right?"

I smile. I'm glad she's not crying in a fetal position on her bed. "And second, I think she's the one who tried to run Emma over."

"How will we find out? Enzo should help."

I don't say anything. I'll never break a pinky swear. "There's still one more wife I want to speak with." One more husband I need to find a picture of. Surely there's one of Naomi and hers on her desk at work.

"So, what are you waiting for? Let's go." Izzie fastens her seatbelt.

"Naomi Anderson won't see me without an appointment, and the closest one I could get was in two weeks." She must be in high demand.

Izzie frowns. "What does she do?"

"She's an estate lawyer, and I made the wrong choice in saying I needed to speak to her rather than it was an estate emergency." Another novice mistake. I don't know if that would've helped or not.

"Let's go anyway. Maybe we can sneak in. But first I need to stop at the house. These shoes are killing me."

I glance down at her zebra print pumps. She's complaining about her heels? "What's wrong with them?" I ask and put the car into drive.

She pushes the heel of one off and displays a raw scrape on the back of her ankle.

"Yikes."

We stop at Ma's long enough for Izzie to throw on red pumps with a slightly scratched heel and for Pop to grill her to make sure she's okay. Then we pick up coffee from Dunkin' Donuts, and I drive over the bridge and head to Front Street in Hempstead.

I pull up to a three-story building and have to park across the street, several businesses down. My stomach's in knots, like I'm about to get caught for doing something wrong. And while I don't mind doing mildly wrong things—it's often fun, exciting, and gives my complexion an extra sheen—I really dislike getting caught.

The reception area is small. Izzie checks out the shiny plate of names screwed into the wall, and I head over to the receptionist. She's thin, curvy, and has long, pointy nails like daggers. I intend to stay on her good side.

"Can I help you?" she asks in an acidic tone.

Someone woke up on the cranky side of the bed this morning. "Yes, I'm here to see Naomi Anderson."

She taps her keyboard. "What's your name?"

Yes, what is it? I already made the appointment under my name, and Izzie's is too high profile now. So what did that leave?

"Um, Hilary Burton." As the words tumble from my mouth, I want to bathe my tongue in bleach.

"I'm sorry, but I don't have you listed for today. Are you sure your appointment isn't for next week?"

"No, I'm certain. I made it a month ago."

She trails her index nail down her screen and shakes her head. "Nope. Sorry."

"I know it was made. Perhaps it was deleted."

She gives me a look of disgust.

"If I can just see her for five minutes."

Before I'm done speaking, she's shaking her head. "Ms. Anderson sees clients by appointment only."

"I do have an appointment. You just can't find it." I probably shouldn't be antagonizing the Wicked Witch of the West.

She points a dagger to the ceiling. "That is incorrect. I am beyond efficient."

I start to insist, but forcing it is only going to make her meaner when I come back in a couple of weeks for the real appointment. And her being right doesn't make me too confident on insisting anyway. I stomp back to Izzie. "What a witch. All she needs is a pointy, black hat."

Izzie stands tall and stares at the woman. "Okay, I'll distract her, and you barge through," she whispers. "Naomi Anderson is in room one-seventeen. It must be close by."

I nod and crack my neck, ready for my mission

She walks over to Cruella. I can't hear what Izzie is saying, and the woman seems to be having a hard time, too. So Izzie leans down, obstructing her view of me.

I hightail it across the tile, grateful I'm wearing my boots with the rubber soles, and down a hall of office doors. The last one says, 117. Naomi Anderson.

I take a deep breath and push open the door. Three women turn and gasp.

It takes my brain a full second to process, but when it's done, I can't help but smile as if I won a jackpot. In a way, I have. I was totally right about this not being a coincidence. I just didn't realize they knew one another.

Seated behind her desk is a striking brunette who I assume is Naomi. Seated in front of the mahogany monstrosity is Fawn and Stacey Anne.

I love being right.

* * *

That evening, as I yank, tug, and pull on my clown getup, I realize my day hasn't been as productive as I'd hoped. Yes, catching the three women together is very telling, but what precisely does it tell? It doesn't prove anything. They know one another and what? I assume they're in cahoots with the car, escalator, and jam, but why the jam? From what I know so far, none of the women were at Lindy's or Mitch's Tavern, so what did roofieing her accomplish? And I'm no closer to finding out who killed Emma.

After almost getting trampled as Fawn and Stacey Anne ran out, throwing eye daggers at me the entire time, Naomi threatened to call security if I didn't leave. So no answers. Not that I expected them to spill, but…okay…maybe I was expecting it a teensy bit. Is it too much to ask that criminals be compliant and confess?

When I'm done dressing, I head out and find Danielle dressed in a blue and multicolored polka dot dress with tights, a curly pink wig, and ballerina flats.

She smiles at me. "Are you ready? You can either follow me there, or we can take my car."

This is a perfect moment to dig up dirt and try to salvage this day, so I chose the latter.

Danielle obviously doesn't come from money. We get into her old and battered Nissan, and she drives over the bridge through Island Park.

"So how long have you been a clown?" I ask.

"Three years. When I was a kid, my family went to the circus a lot. I loved the clowns. As I got older and everyone else grew wary of them, I still loved them."

She and Wesley have the same interest and reasoning. I laugh. "Some people definitely have a phobia. I blame it on Stephen King. Are you close to your family?"

She stops at a red light. "They're not around anymore."

"Oh, I'm sorry." That has to stink. If I didn't have Izzie, Enzo, Ma, and Pop, I'd be beside myself. Lost.

"Thanks. What about you? Why'd you decide to become a clown?"

"A friend recommended it. It sounded like fun." At least these lies are easy to remember.

She smiles. She doesn't do it too often. She should. It's pretty. "And are you close to your family?"

"Very. If it wasn't for them, I wouldn't be here." I grin at my cleverness. Sometimes, it really takes very little to amuse me. I guess that's better than the alternative.

"Since you don't have family, does this mean you'll have a small wedding?" I need to steer and control this conversation somehow.

"Not at all. Wesley has four sisters. Three of them are married with children. It'll be a big wedding. I'm meeting his sisters and mother tomorrow to go dress shopping for the engagement party. His family is very conservative, and everything is done a particular way. It's all so new to me, and I hope I don't fudge it up."

"I'm sure you'll do fine." I went with Izzie and my cousin when they went dress shopping. Both times were the same—a bit frustrating but not the worst experience in my life. I wouldn't necessarily volunteer to do it again though.

We pull up to Best Western and park.

"This is where the party is?" I ask, while following Danielle inside and to the elevator.

She presses for floor two. "Yep. You'll see."

I'm not so sure I'm ready for this. It feels weird. And I'm super nervous. What kind of parents hold a birthday party in a hotel?

When we step off and walk to room two-oh-three, soft music thumps through the door. Danielle knocks. It opens and a young redheaded man with a can of Budweiser in one hand and a wad of singles in the other stands there. His face drops upon seeing us.

We obviously have the wrong room.

"It's a couple of clowns," he screams.

Another man, short, broad, with thick dark hair, comes up, pats his buddy on the shoulder, and smiles to us. "Welcome. You're right on time."

They step back so we can enter, and I grab Danielle's wrist. "What's going on?"

She giggles low and throaty. "Some guys find clowns sexy. We're hired to be the pre-entertainment. Don't worry. We won't have to strip."

Well, thank my psychedelic costume for that.

When I walk inside, I'm startled by the room full of raunchy men. One sits in a chair front and center. His ankles are secured to the chair legs with duct tape, and his arms are tied loosely behind his back.

Oh my God, it's a bachelor party!

The poor guy's eyes widen, and his face colors so badly I fear he'll have a heart attack. "Are you kidding me?"

The short guy who welcomed us shouts, "You wanted to be entertained."

All the men cheer. One rubs the top of the bachelor's head.

Someone pushes me forward. I stumble and right myself by his feet. I glance to Danielle, who starts swaying her hips. The skirt of her dress bounces around.

Too bad Emma isn't here this time. I could really use an instructor. And a Valium.

I copy Danielle and try to think of any movies I've seen with exotic dancers. None immediately come to mind, so I fake it, rotating my hips and listening to the music.

One guy slips a dollar into my pocket. I laugh and let loose. The bachelor still looks horrified, but after a bit he's laughing and howling like his friends.

Another few minutes and Danielle and I have the room hooting and hollering. At one point, I bump and grind with Danielle and wonder if I've mortified her, remembering what Emma said about Danielle and Wesley waiting for marriage. She doesn't seem revolted by my dirty dancing, especially when she joins in and we're rubbing our butts together. Maybe Wesley is the only religious one, the only one who wants to abstain.

There's a knock at the door, and when it opens, a busty woman dressed as a sailor walks in. Our time has come to an end. I'll never admit it, but I'm kinda bummed.

One of the men cuts the bachelor free. He rises, punches his friend in the arm, and gives Danielle and me a hug.

"You were a great sport," I shout into his ear. "Have fun."

When Danielle and I walk out, the sailor is using the same moves we did, but she's shimmying out of her top.

* * *

Back at the agency, I change, scrub off the makeup, get into my car, and check my phone. I have a missed text from Enzo. He wants me to call him. I'll do better than that. I turn the key in the ignition and head over to his house.

I park, stop, and listen to the silence. I inch up his walkway and creep to the side of his house. It's never not a time for a scare. I peer into the living room window. It's empty, but the window won't budge. Next I hit the spare room. Same problem. I check Enzo's room next, but it's locked, too. Doesn't the man believe in fresh air?

Maybe I'll get lucky, and the back door will be unlocked.

I reach the corner, turn, and walk straight into my brother. I yelp.

He grins.

I slap his arm. "What the heck are you doing standing here?"

"Waiting for you. I saw you pull up. I know how you think. You can't scare me. Never gonna happen."

I growl, more at his smugness than at not scaring him. I'll get him one day. He can't expect me forever. "I got your text. What's up?" I can't help sounding testy.

"Let's go in."

I follow him into the living room and plop onto his sofa. "What new information do you have?"

"What makes you think I have any?" He pulls two bottles of beer from his fridge and tosses one at me. "Can't a brother invite his kid sister over for some alcohol and conversation?"

"No."

"Smartass." He grabs a notepad on the coffee table and sits beside me. "I may have peeked at their case file."

Oooh, this will be good. I twist the cap off my beer and take a swig. "I guess there's no way to prove Kevin is a lying rat bastard?"

"No, but he and Sanchez did question those women you mentioned. Um, Naomi Anderson, Fawn Stewart, and Stacey Anne Ingles."

I set my beer on the table and lean closer. This is better than I thought. "And?"

"There's not much more than you already know. Stacey Anne was home all night with her husband. Naomi was out to dinner with clients, and Fawn was home alone."

There goes her husband being home from work on time. "Fawn looked very upset when Izzie made a comment about running over the woman who cheats with a husband. And Emma was almost gunned down."

"Yeah, they know about the near hit-and-run. It was made by a rental, rented by Naomi."

"What?" I scream and jump up almost knocking over my beer. "Why isn't she in jail?"

"Because she didn't kill her. She has an alibi, and the hair on Izzie's top belongs to Emma."

"You mean the hair Kevin planted." I'm furious, but I also feel sick. This is all my fault. If I'd learned to keep my mouth shut and my knees down, Kevin wouldn't be so furious, and Izzie wouldn't have been arrested.

I rub my forehead. "There's one guy I can't quite put my finger on. It's Wesley Vaughn. He works at the high school as a teacher and as a clown for the Jolly Time agency. His family is loaded, and he and Emma were close."

"Did they sleep together, too?" He scribbles this on his pad.

"No, from what I can tell they were only friends, but I'd swear he lied about Emma being at his house that night. And where there's one lie, there are usually more."

"I'll look into him."

Friends or not, maybe Emma and Wesley fought, and he bashed her skull in. How would he have gotten his hands on the bat though? Was he at the bar, too? And what about that morning? Who picked her up? There are too many unanswered questions.

This is when I should tell Enzo about No Spam. I won't have to fork over that cash.

"Did Sanchez and Rat Bastard Kevin look into the Plaid Guy I saw at both bars? Or did they talk to a bartender named Andy?" I planned on being at Lindy's tomorrow night for his next shift.

Enzo checks his pad. "I didn't write anything down, so they must not have."

Of course. Once they had that hair, nothing else mattered. I don't want No Spam's picture ending up in Kevin's hands. I realize I may be foolish to think I could be a better investigator than him.

Investigator!

Why don't I ask Julian to help? He can find who killed Emma. Of course. Why didn't I think of this before? Can he help get the photo from No Spam? That's silly, Gianna. How could he? He's a PI not a cop. He has no authority, and he's not going to steal it from the kid.

One thing is for sure. I need concrete answers. No more pansy-assed questions. And the only way I know of to get what I want is to pay my little extortionist.

* * *

The next morning, I awaken after another disturbing and odd Freezer Dude dream. I check my phone. I had texted No Spam last night after leaving Enzo's, but he never got back to me. I send another text and go pee. I'm finishing tinkling when I hear the chime on my phone.

Meet me at diner on PP and Jeff now.

I assume that's Park Place and Jefferson Avenue. I dress in a knee-length navy blue skirt, a cute white sweater that falls off the shoulder, and navy suede flats in record speed and dash out to my car.

This is it. I can feel it. I'm going to get answers, and I will take the picture to Sanchez. Not Kevin. Sanchez will have to reopen the case. One hair doesn't mean anything. Well, one hair and fingerprints on the murder weapon, but who's counting?

When I pull in, No Spam's already seated and eating.

I slide along the booth seat across from him. "Were you already here when I texted?"

He nods while stuffing French fries into his mouth. "Yep."

The waitress comes over. I order coffee, too nervous to enjoy food.

"So, are you going to tell me about that night?"

His brows go up. "You got the money?"

I pull an envelope out of my purse and place it on the table, drug dealer style. I slide it over to him.

He licks the ketchup off his fingers and peeks into it. He slides it back. "That's not even half."

I slide it back but don't take my hand off. "Yeah, well this is all you're gonna get. If you don't accept it and give me the photos, I'll call my brother, the cop, and have him deal with you."

His eyes widen, but he still tries to act nonchalant.

"I'm sure he'd be happy to sit your butt in an interrogation room all day. Maybe get a search warrant for your house. Inform your parents."

He holds up a hand. "Okay. Fine. I get it."

I remove my hand, and he takes the envelope and sticks it into his backpack.

The waitress arrives with my coffee.

When she walks off, I ask, "So? Where is it?" If he even thinks of leaving here without giving me the goods, I will tackle his scrawny butt to this sticky floor.

He picks up his phone, swipes, and after twenty seconds or so, he lays his phone back on the table. He returns to his food as if I'm not here.

"Well?"

My phone vibrates.

He smirks.

I snatch it out of my purse. It's a text from the little creep. He sent me the photo. But as I tap the message, I realize it's not a photo. It's a video. Even better.

I press play, and I'm staring at the moon, then a panoramic view of the beach. A door slams in the background. Hushed voices and shuffling feet.

Wow, his phone can pick up sound great. I need to get one of those.

The camera turns, and now I'm staring at Wesley's driveway. A man is carrying something over his shoulder. It's Emma wrapped in a sheet. I can make out part of her face, and a lock of red hair spills out from between the sheet. The person walks to the back of his truck and sets her down.

The camera shifts back to the doorway. Wesley's standing in it. There's blood on his hands and shirt. He seems to be crying.

So he did kill her. And then he called someone to get rid of the body.

The camera shifts again. The truck is pulling out of the driveway. Once it reaches the street, it stops for a second, and the driver turns his head to look at Wesley.

That's when I get a clear view.

That's when my world turns upside down.

That's when I start to hurl.

Phone still clutched in my hand, I jump up and run outside. I barely make it onto the pavement before bile comes up. When my stomach is emptier, I'm too embarrassed to let anyone know I upchucked. And I'm too pissed to care.

I jump into my car and start it. It doesn't matter that my hands are shaking, and I may end up in a wreck. I have to confront the man in the video. I have to know why Julian helped cover up a murder.

CHAPTER EIGHTEEN

I don't remember the drive to Carter, Hamilton & Levine, only pulling up to the front of the three-story building. I barely take note of the foyer, brushing past a man in a suit and taking the elevator to the third floor. I push through the double glass doors and stand in the middle of the carpeted floor, staring at all the offices but not actually focusing on them.

That's when I realize it's quiet, not the bustling atmosphere of a lawyer's office, or at least not what I expect of one. The receptionist's desk is empty. Everything is made of glass—the office doors, even the walls, so I can see inside each one. Several are dark, and a couple have lights on. It's Saturday. Of course it's not super busy.

I dial Julian's cell phone, holding it away from my ear so I can hear if it rings from one of the offices. But it goes straight to voicemail, which means the phone is off and he's on a case. It's the only time he turns it off. Am I even sure of that, though?

How well do I know Julian? Yeah, I lived with him for almost a year, but every time he walked out of that apartment, I didn't know where he really went or what he actually did. Does he even work for Carter, Hamilton & Levine? Yes, because how else would he have called Mr. Hamilton to help Izzie and me? But other than that he had a grandmother, I know nothing else I've seen with my own eyes. He had a couple of friends but no family. At least, not any he invited over.

He told me his parents died when he was a boy and he moved in with his grandmother. But I have no corroboration. No one to tell me whether or not he's lying. Well, obviously he's a liar. He sat on my couch while I told him Emma is sticking around. He didn't admit the truth. He did, however, seem eager to know if Emma identified her killer. Maybe he's afraid of getting caught?

Ugh! I squeeze my head. This is such crap. Julian didn't kill Emma. It's obvious from that video he was just helping Wesley out. But why?

One of the offices ahead is lit up, and the door is ajar. I step closer. It's Mr. Hamilton's. He's here. Maybe he can give me some answers. It's empty, so I step in and wait. There are mounds of paperwork on one side of his desk, and a law journal is open by his chair. Several folders litter the floor, and a half-eaten sandwich and a small bag of chips sit by his phone.

I turn to take a seat in one of the chairs facing his desk and notice the framed photos on the wall. Various gentlemen in suits posing for cameras. I'm not sure why they catch my attention until I get to the last one. It's Mr. Hamilton standing outside a construction site. His smile is big—the infectious kind that makes you want to smile back. I'm not smiling though, because beside him is Wesley's father. He looks like he did in the photo in Wesley's house, an older version of his son.

"Gianna, did we have an appointment?"

My pulse jumps. I turn to see Mr. Hamilton standing in his doorway. I glance back at the photo, my head spinning. "No."

He walks in and steps behind his desk. "Is something wrong with Isabella? Is Detective Burton harassing you?"

His tone is gentle and full of concern, and that makes me smile. At least on the inside. "No, I'm sorry to bother you. I'm looking for Julian, and I saw your door open."

He sits in his high-back, leather chair. "Julian's on an investigation. I'm not sure when he'll be back. Would you like me to leave him a message? Although, he'll probably check in with you before me."

"What makes you say that?"

He smirks. "It's obvious he's smitten with you."

My chest tightens. "Oh, yes. Thank you." But I don't leave. I stand there, staring at the photo. It's not unheard of that Mr. Hamilton knows Mr. Vaughn. He could be his attorney. But it sure feels like a huge coincidence. Or a slap in the face. Wesley's family lives in Connecticut, so why would he have an attorney on Long Island?

"Is there something else?" Mr. Hamilton asks.

I point to the photo. "That's Mr. Vaughn, right?"

Mr. Hamilton stands and walks beside me. "Yes. That was taken several years ago, right before they broke ground to put in a strip mall."

"Is that on the island?" I ask.

"Yes, in Hempstead. Why? Are you interested in strip malls?"

"I just recognized Mr. Vaughn. I know his son, Wesley."

Mr. Hamilton turns and stares at me. The skin between his brows puckers. "You do? What a small world."

Tell me about it. "It's weird to me because Mr. Vaughn lives in Connecticut, so why does he have a Long Island attorney?"

Mr. Hamilton turns his body straight to me. "Mr. Vaughn is a friend."

"Oh." I didn't think of that. Now I feel foolish. "If you see Julian before I do, can you please tell him I'm looking for him?"

"Of course. Have a good day."

"You too." I walk to the elevators, and when I get inside of one, I look back. Mr. Hamilton is standing in the middle of the reception area watching me leave.

* * *

I pace my living room from breakfast bar to windows, going over what I know and what I saw. But it doesn't tell me anything. I'm no clearer now than this morning when I got that darn video. What am I supposed to do? Should I call the cops? Tell Izzie? I've left Julian four messages since leaving Hamilton's office.

I pivot and glance up, taken aback by the strange expressions on Emma's and Billy's faces. They're both seated on the sofa, close enough that they're whispering to one another. They're unnaturally quiet and still.

"What?" I snap and resume pacing.

"We're a bit concerned about you." Emma says.

"You're acting a little crazy. Crazier than you normally do," Billy says.

His comment barely registers. When the heck is Julian going to call me back?

"She won't even take my bait," Billy says to Emma. "Maybe she really has gone crazy."

Emma shushes him and hovers in front of me.

I have to stop short or step through her, and while that won't hurt either of us, it freaks me out.

"You don't seem well. Can we help?" Emma asks.

I shake my head and walk around her. There's nothing they can do. But then I remember this is about her, and I stop short again. "Are you sure you've never seen Julian before, while you were alive?"

She nods emphatically. "I'm positive. There's no way I'd forget someone so yummy."

"Are you sure?" I ask again, just in case.

"She's sure," says Billy.

I scoff. "How would you know? You two are BFFs now?"

They look to one another and share an expression I don't understand. "What's going on?"

Emma says, "We've discovered that we can read each other's minds."

I laugh. That's absurd. And yet here I am talking to ghosts. "What?"

When they don't smile or laugh, letting me know it's a joke, I let my jaw hang. "Seriously? You're both telepathic?"

Billy chuckles. "We're not psychic."

"Well, not before we died," Emma says.

Billy nods. "But as ghosts, we know what the other is thinking."

I slump onto the couch. As the ghost whisperer, shouldn't I have learned this way before now? "Why haven't previous ghosts told me?"

Emma shrugs. "They probably don't know. We didn't until a bit ago. With all your pacing, I could suddenly hear what Billy was thinking."

I stare at him. "That I've gone crazy?"

His timid nod calms down my mind long enough to take a deep, cleansing breath. "Too bad you can't read the thoughts of the living."

Emma giggles. "That would be awesome. Then I could know how a guy really feels about me right away."

I lower my head to my hand. This is so not about flirting. But then it hits me, and I look up. "Wait a minute. If you can read the minds of other ghosts, you can help me find out some answers. Like why the freezer is so important. And who that scary Freezer Dude is."

It may not be the most pressing issue right now, but it can be a problem solved.

Billy jumps up. "Let's go."

* * *

Pop decided to close the deli today, to take the entire weekend away from the chaos that the place has become since Izzie's arrest. Living above it though, Pop has given me a spare key in case of an emergency. I don't think sneaking in and talking to dead freezer people constitutes an emergency, but Pop doesn't have to know that.

I shut the back door and join Billy and Emma in front of the freezer. They both look from me to the door.

Billy bugs his eyes out. "Dude, you have to open it. We can't."

"Oh right." I grab the handle and yank it.

A blast of cold hits my sleeveless arms, and I jerk back, immediately thinking of Freezer Dude and those wretched dreams. It isn't until this moment that I realize how scared I am of him.

Billy and Emma pretend they don't see my reaction. I grab a stool under a work table and stick it in front of the door, just in case it shuts. They walk past me into the freezer. My steps aren't nearly as quick as theirs.

I'm halfway in and ask, "So why do you think the dead pass through here? Do you feel some kind of pull?"

They shake their heads, one after the other, like we're playing a game of Simon Says. Then Emma says, "It's not the freezer. It's what's under it."

"What do you mean?"

"I think if the freezer was gone, the pull would still be here. Like it's a part of the land."

I never looked into the land. "Like the movie *Poltergeist*?"

Billy rubs his hands together. "You think the deli was built on graves?"

"I doubt it's that Hollywood, but maybe something on a smaller scale? Like maybe it's the building." I make a mental note to find out what was here before the deli.

Billy walks to the far end and places his hand on the back wall. It goes through, and I expect to see him sucked into oblivion, but he's still standing there. He pulls his hand back out. "I don't see a weird guy."

Great. So now I look crazy for sure.

I walk over and stand beside Billy. I squeeze one eye shut and tentatively place my hand on the wall. The cold makes me flinch, but nothing else happens. I'm not sucked into a hell dimension. Freezer Dude doesn't poke his head through. No maniacal laughter.

Is it possible I imagined the last time? Some residual terror from my dreams and the time I died? I bet a shrink would say it has to do with my moving back home or something to do with mommy issues. According to them, everyone has some.

I look at the tip of my index finger. It's fine. No more tingling since that day. Had I imagined it?

* * *

When I get back upstairs, Izzie calls. She needs to get out of the house. I can't sit around and wait for Julian to call me, so I pick her up and drive to Lindy's. I need to speak with Andy anyway.

I open the door, and music blasts at us. The tables and bar are full. There are even people on the dance floor.

"Whoa, what happened?" Izzie shouts.

My thoughts exactly.

We have to wait for two college-aged, giggly girls to get up and go to the bathroom, which is almost immediately, and we snatch up the same stools we sat on last week. I pray we don't have another fatal night.

Reading my thoughts, Izzie shouts, "No matter who walks through that door or what we see leaving, we don't get involved."

I smile. "Deal."

Andy pours two beers on tap for a couple on the other side of the bar and walks over. "Hey, ladies. Good to see you again. What can I get for you?"

He remembers us. That's a good sign. Maybe he'll remember Plaid Guy and Emma, too.

"A club soda with lime for me and a glass of Merlot for her." I'm definitely playing designated driver tonight.

"No," Izzie shouts. "I'll have the same as her."

She must need a break from all the alcohol. I say to Andy, "Also, I'd like to ask you some questions about last Saturday."

A woman in a skintight, royal blue dress leans over the bar, displaying her melons. She waves a twenty-dollar bill. "Excuse me."

"I'll get you the drinks, but I can't chat this minute. I'll swing by when I get a second, okay?"

And I'll make sure of that. I smile. "Sure thing."

When he places our drinks on the bar, he winks at Izzie. Does he recognize her from the news?

"Hey, why are you so busy? Last week, it was dead in here," she says, handing him a ten.

After making change and laying it on the bar, he holds up a finger to tell the woman he'll be right there. "Since all that murder business at Mitch's Tavern, some people say they're scared to go there." He shrugs. "Their loss is our gain."

He sprints over to the woman, and Izzie and I clank our glasses.

"They should give you free drinks," I say, making her laugh. Hearing it helps me relax.

From the moment I hung up after she called, to changing into a black skirt and an off-the-shoulder pink top, to picking her up and driving here, I went back and forth between telling her about Julian or not. She's my sister, and everything I've done this past week is because I love her. But, whether I like it or not, I love him, too, and I'd like to hear what he has to say before throwing him under the bus.

I guess I just answered my own dilemma.

"Ma told me about Kevin and Hilary," Izzie says. "How do you feel about that?"

Ugh, of all conversations, I'd rather talk about insect repellant or how I spent my childhood believing Pluto is a planet, and now it's not anymore.

"I *feel* Hilary's a fool to be attracted to pond scum." Ah, that made me feel better.

Izzie smirks. "How do you feel about Hilary?"

"Didn't I just answer that?"

"No, I asked about the two of them. I want to know your feelings about just her. She was your best friend for many years, and she screwed you over. I know you're past it, but this must have brought up all kinds of emotions."

I glance at her sideways. "What? Are you a shrink now?"

She sighs. "I think I've been living with Ma too long. She never stops with the questions, and sometimes, when she's nagging, she gets kinda shrill. That woman can peel paint off a wall with her voice alone."

I snort then chuckle. "Especially when she and Pop are arguing over the most mundane thing. But part of the reason we love her is because she always has our backs."

Izzie giggles. "Yes, and you're avoiding the question."

I roll my eyes. "I have mixed feelings about Hilary. Part of me pities her. Kevin just happens to propose marriage, and they rush to do it that same day, the very day, I move back home? I don't want to think everything's about me, but that screams it's about me."

Izzie smiles and nods. There's a teensy-weensy chance I'm reading Kevin's actions wrong, but if my sister agrees, I'm more sure that I'm not.

"And another part of me hopes she's miserable. She told him my secret."

Izzie coughs on her club soda. "What?"

"Oh, I didn't tell you? Yeah, that day he came to the deli, he referenced my seeing…them. The only one who could've told him was Hilary. Or Micky, but he's not in town anymore, and I never confirmed it with him, so he probably thinks she lied."

Izzie shakes her head. "I can't believe her."

I check out Andy. He's on the other end of the bar pouring shots. Someone's popular tonight.

Izzie sets her empty glass closer to Andy's side of the bar, wanting a refill.

"Why aren't you drinking tonight?" I ask. Not to say my sister's a lush, but if she's going to drink, I'd think it would be while her marriage is falling apart.

She purses her lips and glances at me. I know that look. She has a secret. I'm about to press her on it when she says, "I'm pregnant."

I'm not quite sure I hear her right, or maybe that's just the shock making my ears ring. "What?"

She nods. "I found out the morning before I was arrested. I've been late, but I assumed it was the stress."

I can't tell if she's happy or not. "Oh my God. Wha—what are you going to do?"

She sighs and plays with her napkin. "I'm having it. I don't know what this means for Paulie and me, though. I still want to wring his neck. But we've been trying for a year now, and it's just like fate to give us what we want when I'm not sure if I want to be with him anymore."

Not sure means she's considering it. At least she's open to all possibilities and not running away like I do…did. Of course, I should've run farther so Julian couldn't reach me.

"Does Paulie know?" I ask, trying to keep my focus on my sister. She needs me. Her problems are more important than mine.

"No. No one does, so don't say anything."

I press my lips together, zip and lock them with my fingers, and throw away the key. "Do you want him back? Can you forgive him?"

"I don't know. He says it was just that one time, that all my nagging and accusing was for nothing because he wasn't cheating. Until the night I caught him, and they didn't have intercourse, as if that makes it better."

I'm sure on some level it does, though. "You guys have spoken?" I ask.

"He emailed me."

I want to laugh at that, but I also want to remain respectful of her feelings. Paulie's not much of a computer person.

"Hey, ladies, what's up?" Andy stands before us out of breath.

What exactly was he doing down there? I'm also impressed he remembered us.

"Last Saturday, as we were arriving, there was a guy dressed in a plaid shirt and a Yankees' cap who was leaving. Do you remember him?"

He takes Izzie's glass and refills it. "Yeah, it was so slow I remember everyone from that night. He ran out after that clown did." He gives Izzie a hard stare. He must recognize her but doesn't say so. Good man.

"Do you know who he is, or did he pay by credit card?" Izzie asks.

Andy shakes his head. "Nah, sorry. I've never seen him before."

The lady in blue shouts for him. Gosh, she's getting annoying.

He's about to run off when I say, "Hey, did the cops ask you about him?"

He shakes his head again. "Nah, they didn't talk to me at all." Then he hurries off.

I narrow my gaze and look to my sister. "They didn't even investigate her entire night. Once they found that hair, they didn't care about the truth anymore."

CHAPTER NINETEEN

After we finish our drinks we leave, and I drop Izzie off at the house. I'm still buzzing with this new information when I unlock my apartment door and flip the switch for the living room lamps. I'm about to shut the door when I hear a thundering sound growing closer. Suddenly the door jerks farther open, I stagger back against the wall, and Kevin makes his way inside.

Crap!

"Get out," I shout, but Kevin ignores me and staggers into the living room.

His footing is uneven, and I bet if I make him take a breathalyzer, he'll fail miserably. Great, exactly what I need, a drunk cop who hates me.

Panic flashes inside me. I know I shouldn't feel as invincible as I do. He is taller than me, leaner, and has more muscles. And he's licensed to carry a gun. My hate for him, however, makes me cocky. I want to take this jackass down so badly I can taste it. It's spicy with a hint of cardamom.

"What do you want?" I snap.

He whirls around and almost topples onto my coffee table. He points a finger in my face. "You are a bitch."

"Flattery will get you nowhere." I can't resist smart-mouthing to him. Not only does he make it easy, but it's also loads of fun.

He grabs my forearms and squeezes tightly. Then he backs us into the wall by the TV.

My head hits it pretty hard, and I grit my teeth to stop myself from crying out. Maybe I've pushed too far this time though.

He doesn't let go but instead digs his fingers into my flesh tighter and deeper.

Tears gather in the corners of my eyes, and I'm not sure how long I can last before the pain makes me give him the emotional response he's dying for.

He presses his body against mine, and his booze-infested breath is enough to make me pass out. Unfortunately, I stay wide-awake.

"You're a filthy liar," he says. "You can't see ghosts. You said that to get attention. Admit it."

Billy and Emma appear at my side.

"Okay, I admit it," I say. "Now, you admit you placed that hair on my sister's clothes."

He smirks, and I know that's as good of a confession I'm going to get. Too bad my roommates can't testify in court.

"He's hurting her," Emma shrieks. "We have to do something."

Billy disappears, and suddenly the lights start flickering on and off.

Kevin glances to the lamps.

Emma steps right next to him and slides her arm into Kevin's stomach. She looks at me with her glorious eat-crap grin.

Kevin's grip on me loosens, and he starts to turn green. "What's going on?"

"What's wrong with you?" I ask, pretending I know nothing. "If you puke on me, I'm suing."

Emma giggles and withdraws her arm. "That's fun."

The lights stop flickering, and Billy reappears, but only long enough to jump into the television. The set turns itself on.

Kevin flinches and looks to me as if I'm going to give him moral support. "What are you doing?"

What, now I'm telekinetic too? I frown and think back to the drama class I took in college. I don't think the lessons on diction and costume will help, but I'm betting acting natural and improvisation will come in handy now. "What are you talking about? I'm standing here, being harassed by your ugliness."

He finally lets me go and takes one step back, staring at the TV.

I decide this is too good to miss and stay in my spot. "What's wrong with you?" I ask because I want to prove I really am a bitch.

Emma giggles.

Billy makes the channels jump from one to another. Snippets of the news, a late night talk show, a commercial about TP and another about Cheerios filters through the room. But I pretend I don't hear a sound.

Kevin points to it. "Something's wrong with your television."

"Why?"

He stares at me. "You don't see this?"

"See what? You need a doctor. Like a shrink."

He gets back up in my face. Oh great. Joke about his mental health, and he gets testy.

The TV turns static, and my first thought is Carol Anne from the *Poltergeist*. It causes Kevin to blink and forget what he's going to say.

"Get out," whispers Billy from inside the TV. I don't know how he's doing it, but he makes Emma laugh, and Kevin's eyes bug out.

I draw blood from biting my bottom lip. Darn, I wish I could get this on film. I'd sell tickets and make a killing.

Emma's laughing so hard, she clutches her belly and floats back. She falls into one of the stools, and it rocks back and forth, finally crashing onto its side on the floor.

Whoa. She and I stare at one another in surprise. I thought they could only manipulate electronics.

"What was that?" Kevin whispers, not sure if he should be looking at the moving furniture or the possessed television.

"What was what?" I whisper back.

"Get out!" Billy shouts so loud even I flinch.

Kevin doesn't notice though. He gives out a girlish scream, flies out my front door, and something thuds before I hear the downstairs door slam against the wall. He probably missed a step at the speed he's traveling.

Billy pops out of the TV with a big smile on his face. "How'd I do?"

I finally laugh. "You're my hero. You both are. Emma, how'd you make the stool move?"

She shrugs, still sitting on the floor. "I have no idea, but I feel drained now. It used a lot more energy than I expected."

* * *

When someone pounds on my door, I bolt up and look around the room. What's going on? I'm disoriented for a sec. My arms throb, and Rachel Weisz and Brendan Fraser are kissing. Oh darn, I dozed off on the sofa while watching *The Mummy*.

The knocking continues. My roommates aren't here. Oh crap. What if it's Kevin again?

I toss the blanket off my legs and walk to the door. There's no light on the other side, so looking through the peephole gives me nothing but blackness.

Another knock. "Gianna, it's me."

Julian.

I twist the lock and unfasten the chain. I'm going to talk to Pop tomorrow about getting a lock on the downstairs door. I open this one and glare. "Where the heck have you been?"

I walk into the kitchen, parched from sleeping, and let him enter behind me.

"I've been on a case all day. I only got your messages just now. What's going on?"

When I turn with a glass of water, his eyes bulge, and he grabs my elbow. He's staring at the bruises on each of my arms. They're obviously fingerprints. "What happened to you?"

"It's nothing."

"Bull. Someone did this to you, and I want to know who."

I experience a moment of delight. He wants to protect me, and I would pop popcorn for a Julian-slash-Kevin fight. But I don't believe in violence. Verbal sparring is fine, but skin on skin ain't my thing, so I won't initiate it.

"So you can kill him?" I ask.

He blinks then frowns. "What?"

I pull out of his grip and walk around him to the sofa. I grab my phone out of my bag and scroll to the video. When it pops up, I press play and shove the phone in his face. "This."

He stares at it for two seconds then tries to take the phone from my hand, but I'm expecting that, so I'm faster than him.

"Nope. You aren't going to delete it. It's my proof that you killed Emma. How could you let Izzie take the fall?"

He runs his fingers through his hair. "Do you really think I murdered that woman?"

I sigh. "No, but you're obviously involved somehow. Did Wesley kill her, and you helped him out? Maybe you two are friends. His dad lives in Connecticut, your home state. Maybe he's the real reason you took this new job and moved to Long Island."

"You don't understand," he says.

I sit on the couch, a bit dizzy from the entire night. "You're right. I don't. I don't understand how you can let Izzie take the fall for something you know she didn't do."

He doesn't respond, but his face tells me I'm right about that at least.

I suck in a breath. I don't want to be right. I want him to tell me I'm mistaken, or I'm seeing things, the video has been doctored, or he has a twin brother—anything else. Anger, hurt, betrayal swirl inside me until it's one big muddled emotion that makes me want to scream, cry, and punch something, or someone, at the same time.

He sits beside me. "I won't let that happen."

I breathe for a few seconds, needing to calm myself. "What do you mean? It already has."

"I mean I won't let her go to jail. If I have to quit my job to save her, I will."

I'm surprised again. He'd do that for me? Wait, what? "Your job? What the hell does your work have to do with this?"

He rubs his eyes and lets out a loud breath. "I'm not supposed to say."

Not supposed to? Did he really just utter those stupid words?

The ugly comes out in me. I twist my body so I'm sitting sideways, facing him, and tuck my feet beneath my legs. "Oh, but you will. See, this is about my family, whom you know means the world to me. And I already told you my secret. The one that has cost me so much in the past. The one I was ready to lose you over to keep hidden."

His brow creases.

"And I gave you sex. That means you are going to spill. Now."

He runs his hands through his hair and looks like he may barf. Please don't do it on the couch. "This can't go anywhere. No one can know. Not your sister or your parents, or, especially, your brother."

What does Enzo have to do with this?

"And my boss cannot know I told you."

My stomach sinks. This is more serious than I thought. I nod. "I won't tell a soul." Well, a soul may learn if they're listening, but I won't be doing the squealing.

"I'm more than a simple investigator. I'm a fixer."

"What's that?"

"I fix problems for Hamilton's clients."

Okay, that doesn't sound too bad. "What kind of problems?"

"Anything that may tarnish their reputations or get them into trouble with the law."

Fear slithers down my spine. "Anything?"

He nods. "Most anything. I haven't killed anyone."

Why do I get the distinct impression that he wants to add *yet* to that sentence? "And this is what happened with Emma? How?"

"All I know is that Mr. Vaughn, Wesley's father, is Mr. Hamilton's client. He called my boss to help his son with a situation. Hamilton called me. When I got to Wesley's, Emma was dead."

I knew it. "Wesley killed her."

"I don't think so. He was distraught, almost inconsolable. He said he went to sleep, woke up to use the bathroom, and he found Emma, in the spare room, beaten to death."

"With the baseball bat?"

"It was on the floor near the bed."

"And he didn't do it? You believe that?"

"Yes. His back door was slightly open. It looks like someone broke in and killed her."

I stand up and start pacing. "Doesn't he have an alarm system?"

"He forgot to set it."

I give him a look that says, *I don't believe that.*

"Emma came by drunk, or so he thought she was drunk. She was crying about how screwed up her life was. They talked for a bit, and he told her she could crash in the spare room. I guess that was common for them. He went to bed and didn't think about the alarm."

"That sounds too convenient."

"I thought so, too, but I watched him carefully the next few nights. He drank too much and cried himself to sleep, often forgetting the alarm."

"So you put her body and the bat on the beach? You ruined the crime scene."

He gets up and takes my hands in his. "It's what I do. Mr. Vaughn is running for governor of Connecticut. A murder tied to his son could make him lose the election."

I stare at him with disbelief. "And letting a woman's killer go free because the cops don't know all the details is okay? Letting my sister get arrested and causing stress and anguish in her life, as well as her daughter's and family's, are okay? And let's not forget the ten grand my folks had to fork over. You can't really believe that."

"I told you I won't let her go to prison. I've been trying to figure out who really did it on the side. If I can't, I'll do something to get her free."

"Do something? You mean, you'll fabricate some lie? You won't tell the truth?"

"I can't."

Is he serious? I pull myself out of his grip. "Of course you can."

"This is my job. This is my career. Not only will they sue me for breach of confidentiality, but I'll never get another job like this again."

"This is wrong. Can't you see that?" I'm astonished I even have to say this.

"It's gray."

"What?"

"You believe the world is black and white, right and wrong, but it's more than that. There's a whole swirl of gray smack dab in the middle that you never look at."

So this is now about me?

"You've been helping this ghost find out who killed her. From the information you know, you've probably been talking about it with your brother, which means he's getting help from a ghost, too. That's all gray."

I turn my back on him. I don't want to hear him justify his actions. Covering up a murder is wrong. That's all.

"You need to leave."

CHAPTER TWENTY

"How are you doing?" I ask Alice as I sit on the edge of her bed. I just arrived for Sunday dinner, and the house is unusually quiet. Pop's reading the newspaper—TV off. Ma's in the basement singing "Hopelessly Devoted to You," while the water for pasta simmers on the stove, not quite at a boil. Sunday definitely signifies a new week in her repertoire. If she comes upstairs singing "Greased Lightnin'," God help us. And Izzie is in the bathroom. From the sounds of it morning sickness has arrived.

Which leaves Alice.

She pulls the ear buds out of her ears and clicks off her iPod. "Everything sucks," she whispers with a glance to her doorway. "The kids at school keep saying I'm going to be an orphan."

I take a deep breath and only come up with three ways to strangle a bunch of eighth graders in the time it takes me to exhale. "Kids suck. First of all, your mom's not going to jail, and you'd never be an orphan. You got me."

She frowns and grins at the same time. Not an easy feat "I can live with you?"

"Duh. Although if you did, I'd probably have to go from cool aunt to strict mom-like-person."

"That's fine," she says way too enthusiastically.

"You know, the real bit of reassurance in this conversation is that your mom isn't going to jail. I promise." And I mean that. If it means turning in Julian, I will. There's no way the district attorney will agree to try this case if he learns the police screwed up the evidence.

I push a lock of light brown hair behind her ear. "What else are the idiot kids saying?"

"That Mom did it because Paulie had a whore."

I don't know how to answer that. "And what do you think?"

"Mom wouldn't kill anyone. She can barely punish me."

I laugh, and soon Alice joins me. I get up and kiss her forehead. "Don't worry. I'm not. It's all going to work out. And when you come down for dinner, leave your phone up here."

She looks horrified for a second but then smiles and nods.

I go down as Enzo's walking in the front door.

"What's wrong?" he asks, eyes wide.

"What do you mean?" I take a quick peek outside to see if Julian is around. No black truck.

"It's so quiet in here," Enzo says.

I snort. "Pop's reading. So whatcha got?"

"Who says I have anything?"

"The way you're still here talking to me and not in the kitchen attacking the meatballs."

He smirks. "I ran the background checks on your co-clowns."

I look him over for papers or a folder.

He reads my mind and pulls out several folded sheets from his inside jacket pocket. He unfolds them, and the top sheet has a photo of Wesley's driver's license.

We stay huddled by the front door so Pop doesn't see us from the kitchen.

"Wesley's clean. He's never even had a speeding ticket. Timothy has a couple of DUIs from over five years ago. He started Jolly Time after a stint in rehab."

I guess becoming a clown is one way to stay sober.

Enzo flips to a page with Danielle's license picture. "I had trouble finding information on Danielle. There's no trace of her before the age of twenty-two when she first got her license and moved here."

The hairs on the back of my neck salute. "That's weird."

"Yeah, it's unusual. But from what I found on the family, they lived on a farm in West Virginia, and were like the Amish—no electricity, grew their own food. Maybe she was off the grid until she moved here."

That sounds like another world compared to my life.

"I did, however, discover a twin brother. He was caught for shoplifting at the age of eighteen, so I was able to pull up his mug shot. He did a bit of probation and hasn't reappeared since."

The pages are stuck together, and he's having an issue prying them apart.

"Danielle said her family is dead."

"I didn't find any death certificates for anyone. But it wouldn't surprise me." He finally manages to separate the pages. "Here, this is Daniel Lewis."

I suck in a breath and stare down at Plaid Guy.

* * *

I manage to choke down Ma's fabulous cooking and stay long enough for coffee before I can't sit still anymore and need to find answers. I don't think taking Enzo's discovery to Sanchez will do any good at this point. They didn't check into Plaid Guy when I told them about him. Will my word that Daniel Lewis is Plaid Guy really change things? And may I point out that naming your twins Daniel and Danielle is just cruel? Anyway, I don't believe Sanchez takes me seriously.

But Enzo disagrees. We may all believe Kevin set Izzie up, but Sanchez and the rest of the department are the "good guys," according to my brother. He can't be a cop and not fill them in. So while he takes his info to Sanchez, and Sanchez alone, I call Danielle in pretense of getting my next gig.

"I don't have anything on the books," she says.

"Who is that?" Wesley asks in the background.

She tells him and protests as he grabs the phone from her.

"Hey, Gianna. Timothy, Danielle, and I are headed to the beach for a little memorial for Emma. Would you like to join us?"

"I'm on my way," I say and get instructions as to exactly where and then hang up. This won't give me one-on-one time with Danielle, but it's better than nothing. I'm not sure if I should tell Emma or not, but I decide to at the last second.

She looks like she might start crying, if she still could, and marches out my door. "Let's go."

On the ride over, I ask, "Did you know Danielle has a twin brother?"

She shakes her head. "Despite how close Wesley and I were, I don't know anything about her family."

Why doesn't Danielle talk about them? Why did she tell me they're dead if they're not? Then again, I think she just said they're gone. I assumed she meant dead. Regardless of what she said or didn't say, why does she want to hide her family?

We all meet on the beach a block from where her body was found. Timothy is already there on a blanket with a wooden picnic basket.

I sit beside him, and we smile at one another. I doubt he knew I was coming, but he doesn't act like my being here is bizarre. Emma sits on the other side of him and stares out at the water. Wesley and Danielle arrive a few minutes later.

I'm not certain, but it feels like Danielle is giving me the cold shoulder and doesn't want me here. That makes sense if she knows her brother is involved with Emma's death. Have they all yet connected the dots and know I'm Izzie's sister?

Timothy pulls a couple bottles of apple cider from his basket and opens the first one. He tells Wesley to grab the glasses and Danielle to take out the food.

She pulls out red pepper hummus, crackers, a block of cheddar cheese, a knife, strawberries, and several packs of Hostess Cupcakes.

Emma and Timothy smirk. "Those were her favorites," he says.

There are only three glasses, but Timothy hands me one and holds the bottle near his chest. He clears his throat and says, "To Emma. You always lived life to the fullest. You loved parties and laughter and snuggling by fires."

Wesley smiles, his eyes moist. Danielle squeezes his hand in comfort. She's a good fiancée. But she's a terrible person if her brother killed Wesley's friend and she keeps it a secret from him. Why would Daniel kill Emma though?

"Emma, you will be sorely missed and never forgotten," Wesley continues. "I love you."

Emma whimpers. She can't actually cry anymore, but if she were alive, I bet she'd be sobbing.

A lump the size of a walnut sticks in my throat, and swallowing doesn't make it go away.

Wesley raises his glass. "You were a great friend, Emma. I'll miss you more than you know. And..." He gazes off into the distance, but little does he realize he's staring right at her, or through her. "You deserved so much more than you gave yourself credit for."

Danielle squirms on the blanket and says, "Emma, I wish we could've been closer. I'm sorry you'll miss the wedding."

Emma rolls her eyes and laughs. "Leave it to Danielle to make it about her."

They all put their glasses or, in Timothy's case, the bottle to their lips.

"Wait," I say.

They stop and look at me.

"Sorry, I'd like to say something."

Timothy smiles and nods his approval.

"I didn't know you well," I say. "In fact, the first night I met you, I didn't like you." I smirk at the memory of her in Paulie's car. In comparison to where she and I are now, it feels like that clown was a completely different person.

"But as I got to know you through others," I add quickly so the three living people around me don't think I'm crazy, "I'm sorry I didn't get more time with you. I will miss you." When you move on.

She smiles at me. "Thank you."

We raise our glasses, Timothy says, "To Emma," and we drink.

We spend another hour on the blanket, eating and drinking, and laughing at Emma stories. I don't get a chance to talk to Danielle alone, and I'm okay with that. There's always tomorrow. Tonight is Emma's night.

* * *

When we get back to my apartment Billy is standing at the windows, looking down at something outside.

Emma rushes over to him. "They had a memorial for me. It was awesome. You should've come. Everyone said wonderful things about me. It was really sweet, and I didn't realize how much I meant to Timothy."

She turns to me. "It's a shame I didn't spend more time with him before I died."

I don't know what to say. I'm better at smartass comebacks than heartfelt sentiment. I smile and nod.

She looks back to Billy. "Got nothing to say?"

He doesn't reply so she waves a hand in front of his face.

"Ghostal plane to Billy. What's so important?" She follows his gaze. "Oh."

"What is it?" I ask, hurrying over to them.

On the sidewalk across the street is a girl. She's standing in front of the used clothing store and just staring ahead. Other than passing cars, there's no one else around.

"Who is that?" I ask.

"Maybe Billy's soul mate?" Emma asks.

He still doesn't respond. If that's true, he must have it bad. It's hard to make her out from up here, but it looks like she's petite with dark brown hair and is wearing a really cute jean jacket.

"So you know her, or this is one of those from afar loves?" I ask.

Still no response.

As we watch, the girl turns and heads toward the street. She walks right through a parked car. Whoa! She's a ghost?

"Stephanie," Billy whispers and disappears.

Stephanie? His mother mentioned that name.

Suddenly Billy appears outside on the sidewalk by the girl.

I take off and run down, hoping they're both still there by the time I make it around to the front and across the street. Too bad I can't fly.

A car honks as I dart out in front of it. I'm not that close—don't know why the driver is so angsty. Although, I guess a woman running into the street after dark, without stopping or looking or giving any kind of warning, is honk-worthy.

When I reach the other side, Billy is standing in front of the girl. They've stepped back onto the sidewalk closer to the store and are staring at one another. I feel like I've walked into the middle of a conversation and missed a lot. But the longer they stare, the more I realize they're dumbfounded and I haven't missed a thing. Good, 'cause I hate being late for a party.

"I can't believe I found you," the girl says. On closer examination she's adorable—freckles, pixie nose, small bow-shaped lips, and black-rimmed glasses. She looks like one of those American Girl dolls.

"Found me? You've been searching?" Billy says with much sighing. "I didn't even know you were dead."

"Is this Stephanie?" I ask. "Your mom mentioned Stephanie Murdock slipped into a coma and died a few days after you did."

The girl nods.

Billy's eyes widen, and he stares at me. "Why didn't you tell me?"

"I started to, but you said you weren't close." In hindsight I should've told him then regardless.

Billy hangs his head.

Stephanie smiles. "We were starting to be. Or so I thought."

Billy looks up into her eyes, eagerness in his. "Yeah, me too. I—I was gonna ask you to go to the movies with me."

She smiles. "I would've loved that."

Emma's across from me. The four of us form a square. Of course, to the passing cars it looks like I'm standing on the sidewalk mesmerized by the brickwork on the used clothing store.

"You said you were looking for me?" Billy asks.

She pushes the glasses up on her face and nods. "After I died I went home. No one was there. They were planning my funeral. I thought I'd disappear right away or at least after they buried me, and I wanted to say bye to you, so I went to your house. I learned you died a couple of days before me."

Billy grins. "You know where I live?"

She bats her lashes. "Remember the time Randy gave you a ride home during the thunderstorm? I was in the backseat."

He nods. "That was a crazy night."

"Why haven't you passed on?" I ask Stephanie.

She looks me up and down as if she's just realizing I'm standing here. "You're alive, and you can see me...us?" She glances at Emma too.

"Yep. I'm special."

"She's awesome," Billy says. "I've been crashing at her place." He points to the apartment above the deli.

Aww, I'm awesome. Nice to know I'll have a favorable reputation with the other side once he moves on.

"Isn't that the place where you cross over?" she whispers to Billy.

"Yeah, but it's cool. You don't get sucked in. It's totally by choice."

"Why are you here in this spot now, tonight? And why haven't you crossed yet?" I ask again.

She answers, but she's not looking at me, only at Billy. "When I learned you were dead, I wasn't sure if you passed yet or not. Something kept pushing me on, telling me to keep looking. I've been passing by the deli every night just in case you hadn't crossed. I almost gave up and moved on yesterday."

They beam at one another, all cheesy and cute and very high school. Emma places her hands on her chest and makes an "aw" sound. I'll admit it's a touching moment.

As if Emma and I are invisible, Billy and Stephanie hover to one another. I figure they'll just get really close. It's not like they're solid and can touch each other. But the closer they get, the brighter they become. It must be their souls.

Swirls of shining white light shimmer off and around them, like a thousand lightning bugs all at once. It's so mesmerizing I can't look away. I feel like I'm watching a sci-fi movie.

Billy slides his hand along her cheek, and starbursts feather from their contact.

She leans into him, causing fireworks to dance above their heads.

The more they touch and explore one another, the brighter it becomes. I can barely see their outlines anymore. I take a step back. Emma does the same.

When they pull apart, they return to normal, and I feel like a voyeur. Boy, I could use a cigarette, even though I don't smoke. That was powerful.

"I can move on now," Stephanie says.

Billy smiles. "Me too."

Oh my God, this is it?

They float across the street, over to the deli.

No, wait, I'm not ready for this. I run ahead of them and realize my keys are upstairs. Shoot. I'll never make it up and back before they're gone.

I get in front of Billy. "Stop!"

The passenger in a passing car stares at me long after they pass.

Billy looks at me. "What?"

"I'm so glad you're ready to move on. I'm glad you're at peace, but you can't leave without saying good-bye." My voice cracks.

Gosh, I didn't realize I'd feel this way. Billy's just a kid, a ghost. I've never gotten emotional over ghosts before. I haven't spent time with many before either.

"Dude, I'm not leaving without saying *adios*."

I smile, relieved. "Will you wait long enough for me to get the key and see you off?"

"Of course."

I run upstairs with a lump in my throat. I won't break down. I won't cry and make this harder.

Once I'm in the deli, I lock the door behind me—something I'll be doing a lot from now on—and find my three friendly ghosts by the freezer.

"I'll miss you," I say to Billy. "The first day I saw you I wanted you gone, and now—I just want you happy."

He winks at me then Emma. "Thank you for seeing me and letting me stick around as long as I wanted."

I didn't have much choice in that, but I smile.

He turns to Emma. "You're awesome, too. Find out who killed you, and make sure this one doesn't get into too much trouble." He nods toward me.

Emma giggles. "I'll keep my eye on her. Maybe I'll see you again when it's my turn."

Billy grins. "Hope so." He takes Stephanie's hand. "Ready?"

She nods.

I open the freezer door and watch them walk to the far end.

Billy turns back and waves at us.

I wait for a magical, intensified moment, but there isn't one. They walk through the back wall and disappear.

I look to Emma. "That's it?"

"Wow, that's uneventful," she agrees.

I shut the door. "You're next, but I promise to make it more exciting."

"Are you gonna hire trumpets?"

I head outside and lock up behind me. "No. I'm thinking of hiring a clown."

She laughs as we make our way upstairs. Once inside, we both walk to the sofa and plop down. Well, I plop. She sorta just lands.

I grab the remote, draw my knees up to my chest, and lean my head back against the cushions. "What do you want to watch?" I click the TV on.

She shrugs. "I don't know."

I start flipping channels, and we spend the rest of the night doing exactly that, a la Billy style.

CHAPTER TWENTY-ONE

The next morning, I head over to Danielle's place. According to her driver's license, she lives in a one-bedroom apartment on Baltic Avenue, over by the train tracks. It's a small building with only four apartments, two on the first floor and two on the second. Danielle's is on the bottom right.

There are no spaces in front of the building, so I have to park a block away. On the walk to her apartment, I notice the area is pretty quiet. There are few cars driving around, and either people are already at work, or a lot of the residences are empty. Honestly, I'm not very fond of this area. If South Shore Beach has a seedy, run-down section, this is it.

I grip my keys in my hand, positioning the apartment key between my thumb and index finger, ready to use it as a weapon if necessary. Of course, it's just nine a.m., and how many muggers are waiting for a curvy brunette to walk by?

When I reach Danielle's apartment, I climb two steps to her creaky front porch and knock. Her car is parked in a narrow, pebbly strip beside the building, so I know she's home. But she doesn't respond, so I take a step to my right and peer in the window. The shades are up, but the sun bounces against the glass pane, creating a prism. I have to look down rather than straight ahead in order to see into the room.

It's a small living room. There's a sheet thrown over the couch, an old box TV on a stand with wheels, and a couple of folding end tables. She definitely hasn't spent a lot of money on her place. There's a card table with a couple of chairs in a room to the right, probably the kitchen. A hallway to the left must be the bedroom and bathroom area. Great. But where is she?

I'm about to knock again when someone walks from the kitchen toward the bedroom. I tap on the window, ready to wave, but when she turns to me, it doesn't quite look like Danielle.

Oh my God, is it Daniel?

Suddenly freaked out that I may be face-to-face with a killer, I turn around and run back to my car. When I get behind the wheel, my hands are trembling. What is wrong with me? I should've waited for him to open the door, to demand answers from his sister. She's there somewhere. But he's a murderer. At least I think he is, and I'm assuming he's been hiding out, not wanting to be seen. Otherwise, why would Danielle pretend she has no family?

I press on the gas and get the heck out of there. I'll call Enzo and tell him everything as soon as I park. He's the professional. He'll know what to do. I'm pretty sure *stay out of it* will be among his advice.

I pull into the lot behind the deli, park beside Ma's car, and dial my brother. It goes straight to voicemail. I leave a message and am about to get out of my car when my cell rings. I don't recognize the number and answer it.

"Hello?"

"Gianna, this is Danielle. Were you just at my place?"

Crap. She saw me run away like a baby! Does she know her twin is a murderer? "Um, yeah. I thought we'd hang or something. Maybe get lunch?"

At nine in the morning, Gianna? Think. Stop rambling.

"Oh, that'll be fun, but why did you leave?" She sounds sincere, like she doesn't know I saw her criminal brother.

"Um, I had to do something. I'm sorry. I probably should've called first anyway, in case you have company."

She laughs. "Like who? Wesley's at school. I don't have a lot of friends. I'm on my way to look at more dresses, and Wesley's sisters are all working. Do you want to join me?"

That's a good idea. We'll be in public, and I can try to squeeze some answers out of her.

"Sure. Do you want me to meet you somewhere?"

"You can, but I'm driving past the deli now. I can pick you up."

I hear the sound of tires on gravel and look into my rearview mirror. Danielle pulls in behind me. My stomach tightens. That was fast. She must've left her place seconds after I did. My internal radar goes off. What does she actually want? I doubt it's dress shopping or not just that.

"Maybe this is a bad time," she says through the phone. "I saw you near my place while I was leaving and thought you could help. We could do lunch after. We don't really know one another, yet we work sometimes closely together."

I think of the bachelor party. Can I trust her though? It's possible she doesn't know her brother killed Emma, if he did. And it's possible Danielle never felt jealous over Wesley and Emma's closeness. But what if that's not the case? Even if she doesn't know the truth about her twin, how many women would not feel insecure in the other matter?

"I'm sorry," she says. "You're busy. We can do lunch or something another time." Her car starts reversing.

"No, wait," I shout into the phone while watching my opportunity back out. "I'll be there in a second." I hang up. Despite my reservations an opportunity to find solid evidence can't be passed. I push aside any suspicions. I'm usually suspicious anyway.

I get into her car and immediately feel awkward. She must think I'm crazy to run from her place like that. "I'm sorry about earlier. I'm really not insane."

She grins. "I don't think that." She looks flawless in a light gray pantsuit. Her hair is pulled back into a bun with several wavy tendrils framing her face.

My phone rings again. It's Julian. I skip the call, toss the phone into my purse, and fasten my seatbelt.

"Someone you don't want to talk to?" Danielle asks as she backs out and pulls onto Park Place.

"Yeah. My ex."

"Relationships are hard."

"Yes, but you're lucky. Wesley seems awesome and completely in love with you."

She smiles and color dots her cheeks. "I am lucky." She drives several blocks and pulls into a gas station. "I need to fuel up."

"Sure." I don't know what I was so nervous about. Regardless of who Daniel is, Danielle is nice, and when this is all over, maybe we can be friends. If she doesn't hate me for turning in her brother.

She grabs her purse from the floor behind my seat and sets it on her lap. She rummages through, and after a moment or two, her movements become frantic. She leans over, looking behind my seat, and goes through her purse again.

"Problem?" I ask.

"I can't find my wallet." She gets out, goes around to open the back door, and searches everywhere. When she's done, she gets back behind the wheel and sighs. "I must've left it at home."

"I'd offer to pay for gas but..." I am beyond strapped.

"Oh no. It's not a big deal. I'll swing back and get it. It's not like I can buy a dress on my good looks alone." She giggles.

She turns around and drives to her apartment. When she pulls into her parking space, trepidation fills me. She opens her door, keys still in the ignition. "I'll be right out."

I nod and bite my lip.

She squints at me. "Are you okay? You can come in if you want, but I'll only be a second."

Is she trying to keep me out? Maybe going in and confronting her brother is best. No, that's stupid, Gianna. Provoking Kevin is one thing. Confronting a murderer is suicide.

"Look, when I came by earlier, I saw a guy in your place." I watch her reaction intently.

She looks to her apartment then back to me. "It's not what you think. I'm not cheating on Wesley."

I smile. "I don't think that. I believe he's your brother."

She frowns and looks down at her lap. "You do? How do you know about him?"

I'm not sure how much I should tell her. If I directly accuse Daniel of Emma's murder, she's likely to push me away, and I still don't have any proof. Sanchez may be reasonable or fair or whatever, but that planted hair is still incriminating. And even if Enzo is charming, I doubt he can be that convincing. It's going to take more than just my word to get Sanchez to dig deeper.

I need evidence. I need to get inside that apartment and look for something tangible.

"I don't," I lie. "He, um, looks a lot like you. I assumed." I can't let her know Enzo's been feeding me info. I won't let anything jeopardize his job. It's bad enough Julian knows.

She lets out a long breath. "You're right. I have a brother. I kept him a secret because he hasn't been a part of my life for many years. I have reasons to keep it that way, too."

Like his criminal ways. "But he's here now."

She nods, staring out the windshield. "He came back, needing a place to stay for a few days, but he's gone now. Left right before I called you."

Darn, does that mean he took any evidence with him? "Why did he leave?" I ask.

She shrugs. "I'm not even sure why he came back. He doesn't talk much, and he definitely doesn't share. Daniel's always been quiet, reserved, depressed."

I lay a hand on her arm. "I'm sorry, Danielle. I didn't mean to pry."

She smiles. "It's fine. But I want to go shopping, so let me run inside real quick."

Maybe I can still salvage this. "Do you mind if I use your bathroom?"

"No. Come in."

We enter her apartment, and it smells like apple pie. Yum. It reminds me that I only had a banana for breakfast. "Do you bake?" I ask.

She points to a red candle in a glass jar on a rickety bookshelf. "I can barely boil water."

We laugh, and she points to the left. "The bathroom is right through there. I think I left my wallet in the kitchen."

We split up, but instead of going into the bathroom, I peek in the bedroom first. I don't really have to pee. I'm just hoping I'll see something quickly. I know I won't. I need more time than what it takes to grab a wallet off the counter, but I'm not sure I'll get another chance inside any time soon.

I turn on the bathroom light, shut the door from the outside, and tiptoe into her bedroom. There's a full-size, hastily made bed, a couple of tables, and a small dresser. The room is neat, although Ma would have a fit if the sheets didn't have hospital corners. There are a few things out—alarm clock, bottle of perfume, makeup bag, a small jewelry case, and a box of tissues—but none will prove Izzie's innocence.

I head to the closet first. One, if Daniel left anything behind, it's probably in there, and two, from this spot, Danielle can't see me unless she steps all the way into her room.

Her closet is tidy—each article of clothing is perfectly spaced from the next one and looks pressed and hung evenly on the hanger. She cares about her brightly colored wardrobe. I wish I felt the same about my own. If I owned designer garb, I might. I'm not sure these are brand names, but they sure look like it. She owns a lot of maxi skirts too. With her height, she can pull it off.

I push aside several of them, checking out her shoe collection, hoping to find some manly remains, something that belonged to her brother. She doesn't have that many pairs, which surprises me, but some women don't love shoes. I notice something shiny wedged into the back, right corner of the closet floor. I bend over, move a pair of black strappy sandals, and grab the item. I roll my eyes. It's an empty, silver gum wrapper. Wow, that's incriminating.

I stand straight and hear a soft whoosh. As I turn to see what it is, pain explodes from the back of my head, and then darkness…

CHAPTER TWENTY-TWO

I open my eyes and stare at beige fuzz. My head pounds, and something is stuffed in my nostrils and on my mouth. I blow at it and realize I'm face down on carpet. I roll onto my side with a heavy groan. I try to sit up, but the shoes and clothes in the closet sway. What the hell happened?

"Crap. You're awake."

I try to decipher the voice, but it sounds warped, and I think of Charlie Brown. And dogs. And spindly Christmas trees. And turkey. Gosh I'm starved, but I'm riding on a wave of nausea, so I doubt I can eat even if that was an option.

I roll onto my back and squint at the daylight pouring into the room. It seems to be the same brightness coming in from the same direction as before. Maybe I haven't lost much time. "Wh—what's going on?"

Someone kicks my foot. "You're a meddling nosy body—that's what's going on."

I burrow my chin in my chest and stare at the person ahead, but it's hard to make out because he or she is moving so fast. Back and forth, back and forth. Pacing.

"You couldn't just leave it all alone. Why do you care anyway? Because of your sister. It's not my fault she was blamed. I had nothing to do with that." The person stops and stares at me.

Danielle? Why? She's helping her brother. Ugh, why didn't I listen to my radar? Since when am I so trusting?

She walks to her dresser and jerks open a drawer. "I should've known it wouldn't work. Everything I want goes to crap eventually. I don't understand why I can't keep something good."

What is she mumbling about? I need to get out of here, but I can barely see straight. And what do I do if I make it to the door? Walk home? She'll find me limping along the street in a nanosecond.

She sheds her jacket with her back to me. This is the time to try something, but the only weapons within my grasp are shoes. Even if I grab one, there isn't enough space between us for her not to know what I'm up to. And what will I accomplish with a shoe? Stomp Danielle into submission? I have to try though. I can't die here without fighting back.

I roll to my side again and reach into the closet. The closest shoes are a pair of brown, cowboy boots and the black, strappy sandals. There's a small heel on them, but unless I gain direct access to an eye or her jugular, I doubt they'll do any good. I grab them anyway.

A drawer slams shut and another opens. "All my hard work all these years. I can't let it fall apart. I have to at least try and hold onto what's mine."

She must not notice my movements, so I take it one step farther and struggle into a sitting position, my back pressed against the open closet door. It creaks, and she turns around. One second she's at the dresser, and the next she's crouched down in my face.

"Where do you think you're going?" Her breath smells like spearmint.

"My head hurts," I whisper, hoping I sound more pathetic and weak than I feel.

"Aww, you poor baby. That wouldn't have been necessary if you'd left me alone." She points to the bed. Propped up against the side of it is a shovel.

She hit me with a shovel? I'm surprised I'm not dead.

"I was never good at baseball," she says. "Got laughed at in school for not having a lot of upper body strength. You're lucky I only hit you once so far. Unlike Emma. I had to make sure she was gone for good."

I expect a crazy, toothy grin, but she actually looks upset.

She killed Emma? "Why?" I ask, continuing to use my inside voice.

She rolls her eyes. "Why do you think?" She stands straight and reaches into the closet and up to the top shelf.

That's when I notice what she's wearing. Jeans and a plaid shirt. *The* plaid shirt. So she's dressing like her brother to what…kill me and dump my body somewhere? Did she go to the bars that night, dressed as her brother, already knowing she was going to kill Emma? She's blaming poor Daniel for all of this? I blamed the wrong ass twin?

I consider kicking her, but really, what will that do?

"You said 'so far.' You plan on killing me too? Why, and why haven't you done it yet?"

"You're full of questions, huh?" She bends back down. This time her hair is pulled back off her face, and she's wearing the Yankees' cap.

I suck in a breath. I didn't see their resemblance until now. Granted, I didn't get a close look of Plaid Guy that night. The cap hid most of his face, but they're the same height and have the same build. But nothing clicked when I first met Danielle. I feel so stupid.

"If I kill you with the shovel now, there are too many variables. I can't kill you in the same manner I killed Emma. No one will believe your sister murdered you, and I can't have the police reopen the case, so you must die another way. Maybe you can drown in the ocean."

While I process her words, she stares at my eyes, mouth, and hair. It's quite distracting. I almost tell her to take a picture; it'll last longer. But I catch myself.

"You saw me that night. When you walked into Jolly saying you're a clown I should've known you'd be trouble. I wanted to believe it was all a coincidence, but they don't really exist, huh?"

"Why are you blaming this on your brother, Daniel? What's he done to you?" I ask.

She smiles. "I'll admit that's a good assumption. False but good. Maybe I could've pulled it off for a while, but I would've had to tell Wesley I've been lying about my family. That they're living their pathetic, phobic existence pretending they don't have a child. But Wesley doesn't like lies."

What is she talking about? "How does he feel about murder?"

She ignores me and goes back to the dresser. "And then I'd have to be Daniel again, be a boy, and that's not possible. I suffered too long as him."

As him? She's pretended to be her brother before? Maybe it's a twin thing, like when they trade places. I've heard of that, but don't the twins need to be identical to pull it off?

Something niggles in my brain.

Danielle doesn't have a birth certificate. She didn't appear until age twenty-two. Is that because she didn't exist until then? Is Danielle Daniel?

"Daniel?" I ask softly.

Her head turns and drops, and she glances at me from the corner of her eye.

"You don't have a brother," I shout.

She places her hands on her hips but doesn't look at me. "Pin a rose on your nose."

Oh my God, I can't believe it. Danielle is transgendered. That wouldn't be shocking if she hadn't been lying about it. "Why not tell the truth? And why kill Emma?"

She doesn't answer me.

If I can keep her talking, maybe I can find a way out of this before she kills me. "No one will believe my death is an accident or suicide or whatever your plan is. I called my brother, the cop. He knows I'm here."

She stares at me through the mirror hanging above the dresser. "That's a lie. I was with you the whole time."

"Look at my phone." I'm hoping she's not a clock watcher so I can pretend my before call to him was actually made after.

She rummages through my purse and finds the phone while I curl my legs toward me, trying to get closer to standing. If she would turn away for a few moments, I might be able to get to my feet.

"Shit," she whispers before tossing the phone onto her bed. She begins pacing again.

Suddenly beautiful, wonderful Emma appears. "Oh my," she says after taking it all in.

I'm so relieved, I lean my head back against the door and start giggling. I'm still not a giggler, but it's all I'm capable of at the moment.

"What's so funny?" Danielle asks.

Emma squats by my side. "Are you okay?"

"Not really," I say still laughing. "She killed you. And she's about to kill me."

Emma gasps.

Danielle stops pacing. "Why are you talking gibberish?"

Maybe if she thinks I'm delirious, she'll pay me less attention.

"How can I help?" Emma asks, but I don't have any answers for her.

She hovers over to Danielle and gets right in her face. "Why? Were you afraid Wesley and I were too close?"

I look into Danielle's eyes and say, "Emma's here. She wants to know why you killed her."

Danielle smiles and then frowns. "You're losing it."

"No, really. She wants to know."

Danielle rolls her eyes. "Fine. You won't be around much longer anyway. It was because she learned my secret."

Emma turns to me and shakes her head. "What secret?"

Danielle jerks open a drawer, looking for something. "Where are those sleeping pills?"

Oh crap. She's planning on drugging me. I won't be able to fight back then. I repeat Emma's question.

Danielle sighs. "She saw the truth at our last party."

Emma's frown is deep. She looks as confused as I feel. "Our last party? I saw the pills in her purse. I can't be dead because of pills." Now she looks sick to her stomach.

"Emma walked in on you in the bathroom and saw birth control pills in your purse. But they were hormones, right? They were in a BC package, so she assumed. Surely that's not worth someone's death."

"She saw more than that," Danielle snaps. "Wait, how do you know what happened?"

I ignore the question. "What else did she see?" I ask.

"She and Wesley were very good friends, and I couldn't have her blab. He's such a good person. I don't know what he saw in her. She had no morals."

And killing someone makes you a good person? But I don't say that in case Danielle grabs her favorite shovel again and decides to finish me off after all.

"It was dumb luck she was drugged and couldn't see where she was going. When you and your sister found her with your brother-in-law, it was perfect. I couldn't have planned it better. I saw you toss the bat in his truck, and he didn't drive off right away. Taking that bat was easy."

Well that explains that, but I'm still not sure about the secret.

"What else did Emma see in the bathroom?"

"How do you know that?" Danielle shouts.

"She just told me. She's standing right in front of you."

Danielle flinches but remains in her spot. Then she chuckles, but it sounds wavy, as if she's not quite sure whether she shouldn't actually believe me. "You are crazy."

Emma fumes and disappears. Wait, where is she going?

"Besides, it had nothing to do with pills, although, if they're found... No, they won't be."

Suddenly, noise sounds from the other room. Voices. It's the television. Emma pulled a Billy.

Danielle frowns.

I smile. "Told you she's here."

Confused, scared, compelled, whatever her reason, Danielle walks out of the bedroom to investigate.

I scramble to my feet as quickly as possible, using the door and wall for support. The room sways, but I manage to stay upright. I wobble to the bed and hear a whirring sound, like a blender. If I make it out of here alive, I owe Emma big time.

I grab my cell from the bed and dial 9-1-1. I only have a second and not enough time to explain what's happening to a dispatcher. So upon answering I whisper the street address and "She's going to kill me", and then I slip the phone into my pocket. I seize the shovel, make it into the hall, and hear Danielle returning. The bathroom door is open, the light off. I step into the darkness and raise the shovel. It's heavy, so I rest the handle against my shoulder.

Danielle turns the corner, stops, and looks back to the living room.

I hold my breath, praying she doesn't see me.

Emma hovers beside her. "I want to kill her for taking my life. I don't even know what her stupid secret is."

It definitely sucks to die for reasons you don't understand.

Danielle takes a step into the bedroom, her back toward me, and I step out of the shadows. She twirls around as I raise the shovel. A mask of horror slips over her face, and as I'm about to have it become intimately involved with the back of the shovel, she pushes into me.

I slam into the wall, and tiny white stars decorate my vision for a second. I want to nurse the pain throbbing in my left shoulder and at the base of my skull, but I know I need to move fast. I push back, using all of my weight, but she's taller and stronger. I'm somehow still holding the shovel, and it's wedged between us.

She grabs its handle and tries to wrench it free from my grip, but there's no way I'm letting go. We struggle, each of us hanging onto the handle with all our might. We spin and dance down the hall into the living room. She's so much taller than I that there are moments when my feet don't even touch the floor. It would be cool if I wasn't fighting for my life.

"Oh my God, what else can I do?" Emma screeches.

I have no idea where she is. The spinning through the room is making me dizzy. I take a step back and hit up against something solid. It's the television set. Danielle throws her weight on me. The wheels on the stand roll slightly, and I shift my feet quickly so I don't end up flat on my back. But the TV stand hits the wall, and the corner of the set digs into my back.

Danielle pushes me harder and harder into it, until I'm bent over it backwards. I have no place to go. Somehow I need to loosen her grip on me.

"Should I jump back into the TV?" Emma asks.

I turn to focus on her, and Danielle uses my movement to turn the shovel so the handle is pressed against my throat. She's going to strangle me with it.

Emma screams, "No!"

A flash to my night in my apartment with Kevin comes to mind. He's the last person I want to think of, but then another thought flashes, and I'm suddenly very grateful. Why hadn't I thought of it before?

I take one hand off the shovel handle and place it on her shoulder. Then with all my strength and the extreme desire to live, I bring up my leg and knee her in the balls.

Pain puckers her brows together, and her grip on the shovel loosens.

"Yay!" Emma shouts.

I push into her with my body. She staggers back a couple of steps and holds onto her junk. I take a swift step to the side, to get away from being blocked in, and realize I'm still holding the shovel. I lift it and smack it across the side of her head.

She crumbles onto the floor. Her eyes are shut.

God, I hope I didn't kill her.

Emma's jumping up and down cheering.

I don't feel nearly as celebratory. I fall onto the sheet-covered couch and hear the blessed sound of sirens.

CHAPTER TWENTY-THREE

Shadows dance before my closed lids. I open my eyes and spot Julian standing above me. What the fettuccini? I didn't even hear the sliding doors slide open. And where is my family? Did he enter Ma's without being invited and see me on the back deck?

I sit up, swing my legs off the lounge chair, and get to my feet. I walk to the umbrella table and grab my glass of iced tea. Ginger chamomile to be exact. Stacey Anne sent the deli a care package. I think it's due to her guilt in contributing to Emma's death. If she hadn't given Emma roofied jam, the poor clown may have been lucid and strong enough to ward off Danielle's attack. She at least would've been able to scream and alert Wesley.

Stacey Anne confessed to the drugs, stating Naomi and Fawn were in on it too. They each tried to take Emma down. First, Fawn pushed her on the escalator at the mall, and then Naomi rented a car and tried to run her down. Just as I believed. According to Stacey Anne, when neither worked, Naomi got the drug and Stacey Anne mixed it into the jam. They didn't know what would happen to Emma after she ate it, but they were serious about keeping her away from their husbands. They've turned on one another, each blaming another for who came up with the ideas.

"What are you doing here?" I ask Julian.

It's been three days since the truth was revealed. Three hectic days of police interrogations, hospitals, and Ma fussing over me to make sure I'm still alive. She and Pop haven't let me return to my apartment. At least, not to sleep. I've been bunking in my old room, beside Izzie. This is my last day here though.

I'm putting my foot down. As much as I love being waited on, I'm beginning to suffocate.

"I need to see you and talk to you," he says. This isn't his first visit. I've just declined all the others. Ma didn't fight me either. She just told Julian to give me time.

"You've become the talker, huh?"

"I guess so." He pulls out a seat for me at the table.

I sit down, not sure if I'm ready for this conversation, but I'm tired of running from things, so maybe it's best.

He sits beside me. "How are you?"

"Better. The charges against Izzie have been dropped."

"I know. That's wonderful," he says, but happiness doesn't reach his eyes. I assume his guilt in all of this is high. It should be. I'm still not happy the charges ever existed.

Danielle suffered a concussion like me. But after Sanchez heard my story and saw she was dressed in plaid, he reopened the case. According to Mr. Hamilton, the evidence against Danielle is more damning than the hair found on Izzie's clothes. No one wants to consider the hair was planted. So without proof, Kevin is off the hook and still a detective. I'm certain he'll eventually do something else stupid and will one day get caught. I'm hoping I'll be around to see it. Front row seats and extrabuttered popcorn sounds about right.

At first Danielle was held for questioning, but she wasn't talking. Not until Wesley visited her. Then suddenly she was full of remorse and confessing because he pleaded with her to be honest. I think she thought they still had a chance if she told the truth.

Even though he's hurt and confused, Wesley still cares about her, and he asked Mr. Hamilton to represent her. There has to be a conflict of interest there, but I don't care as long as she can't hurt anyone else. Now, however, my nightmares are of Danielle coming after me with a shovel. Right before she catches up to me, the shovel clanks to the ground, and she turns into Freezer Dude. I can't wait until the morning I wake up calm and rested rather than drenched in a cold sweat.

"Will Danielle be convicted?" I ask Julian.

He seems hesitant to answer. If he even thinks of keeping quiet about it and not telling me what he knows… "I think they're going for an insanity defense. Blame it on the mass amounts of hormones she'd been taking. Though, I'd guess the transgender community may have something to say about that tactic."

As it turns out, I was right the second time. There was no Daniel. Not anymore at least. Danielle is transgendered, preoperation. She kept putting off setting a wedding date because she needed to wait until she could afford the operation that would physically make her a woman. Falling in love with a man who wanted to wait to be intimate until his wedding night was a coincidence that ended up fitting perfectly with her plans.

She swears she still loves him, according to Wesley—who visited me yesterday. He wanted to make sure I was okay. The poor guy is so torn up. I asked if he minded Danielle is transgendered. Would he have married her if she wasn't a felon? He couldn't answer, but the engagement is definitely off. There's no surprise there.

Danielle admitted the secret wasn't the pills. She kept her hormone replacement therapy pills in the birth control box so no one would get suspicious. She'd been doing it for years, long before she met Wesley. But when Emma walked in on her in the bathroom, Danielle thought Emma saw her preoperation, still-male anatomy, and she didn't want to risk Wesley finding out the truth until after the operation. Danielle believed Wesley wouldn't care she used to be a man biologically once she became a woman physically. But she knew he'd hate the lying. She said so at her apartment. Yet she convinced herself that he'd get past the lies once he learned the truth. How? Did she really believe their love would conquer all? Poor Emma was drugged *and* killed over dick.

That should be funny, but it's not.

"Is your friend still around?" Julian asks.

"My friend? Oh, you mean, Emma? Yeah, for now. She's leaving soon."

He nods. "I'm glad it worked out. I'm glad you're okay. What about us though?"

Wow, selfish much?

To be honest though, he's all I've been thinking about. Him and us and if we have a future.

"I don't know if I can get past what you do for a living. I still think it's wrong. Plus, you put my family through hell. Izzie's arrest, the ten grand for bail. Even if I can find peace with your job, I'm not sure I can forgive you for the rest of it."

He grips my hand on top of the table. "I know this is hard for you. I cannot express how sorry I am. I plan on repaying everyone. First I've arranged for an anonymous donation to the deli to cover the fees your parents paid for the bail bond."

Well that's a start.

He's left half a dozen messages over the past few days too. He apologized in each of them. I know he means it, and this definitely helps, but I'm still hurt.

"I'd like to do something for Izzie too. Whatever you think is best. A spa day, shopping spree, start a college fund for Alice."

Wow, he's serious about making up for his shadiness. And generous. With a new baby on the way, Izzie can use the help. But…

"I'm not trying to pay you off. I don't know what else to do while remaining quiet about my job," he says, reading my mind.

I understand. I just wish I didn't. It would be easier to stay mad and keep my distance. Easier on my heart anyway.

He reaches into his jacket pocket. "And I was able to get this back for you." He pulls out a silver chain, and dangling off the end is my diamond pendant.

I smile and take it from him. Suddenly this piece holds more sentiment than I realized.

"How about we take it slow?" he asks. "If you can't make peace with it…"

I shut my eyes as he trails off, not wanting to think of my life without him, but not quite sure how to live with him either. I nod and open my eyes. "Okay. Super slow."

He smiles, and a part of me becomes gooey.

* * *

Later that night, Izzie turns onto Enzo's block and parks three houses before his. We sit in the car and breathe in the magnolia fragrance from someone's yard. Emma's in the back seat being especially quiet. She's leaving shortly.

Before we go inside, I want to know how Izzie's talk with Paulie went the previous night.

She shrugs. "I haven't told him about the baby yet. I will."

"And?"

She glances behind her. "She's here, right? I don't want her knowing my business."

I glance back and smile at Emma. "It won't matter in a bit anyway. She's moving on. She's only here to help us. You specifically, since you want this so badly."

Izzie takes a deep breath and grins. "I guess if she can pull this off, I can forgive her."

I know she's thinking but has the tact not to say, "Especially since she's dead."

"And you and Paulie?" I ask. "Are you forgiving him, too?"

"I told him I'll go to counseling."

That's big. "Did he wonder why the change of heart?"

"If he did, he didn't ask. Thing is, even before I found out about the baby I wanted to make this work. I love him. That hasn't changed. And I'm willing to admit I had a hand in pushing him away. That doesn't excuse his behavior, but I guess I could work on my fear that he'll walk out on us like Alice's father did."

Alice's jerkwad father did more damage than we all thought. Therapy will help my sister.

"And what about the late nights, showers, and lack of sex?" I ask, although they must've been having some sex since I'm getting a nephew or another niece.

She half smiles and glances out her side window. "He was taking extra shifts, saving up so we can go on a proper honeymoon."

Oh, how sweet.

I gasp. "The nerve of him."

She playfully smacks my arm. "Shut up. He's been so tired, and when he turned me down for sex one night, I guess I made a bigger deal out of it. It escalated in my mind. If I just trusted him."

Trust. So easy to expect but so hard to give. At least for the Mancini sisters.

"What about you and Julian?" Izzie asks. "Are you guys on or off?"

She doesn't know he's a fixer, and it sucks that I can't tell her. Boy, would that be a dramatic conversation. I'd love to get it off my chest, but I can't. I promised. And this secret really needs to remain quiet.

"I don't know yet. We're taking it slow." I nod my head toward Enzo's house. "Shall we?"

Izzie's smile grows wide. "Absolutely."

I look to Emma. "Ready? You know what to do, and you don't mind? You'll be using a lot of energy." Despite really wanting to do this, I also want to make sure she's okay.

She nods. A lock of her red hair falls into her eyes. "Let's do it."

Izzie and I get out of the car and gently shut the doors. Emma's ahead of us. I don't know why I hadn't thought of this a week ago. It's perfect. And I owe it all to Kevin. Guess I owe him twice now. Kneeing Danielle in the balls was thanks to him too. Not that I'll be thanking him. Ever.

Izzie and I go to the side of the house and the window of the spare room, and we wait. We don't have to go inside, no need for awkward landings, or fumbling in the dark for circuit breakers, and certainly no need to get our dear brother suspicious. I cross my fingers that this works. It's a brilliant plan.

Emma hovers into the room and looks from the bed to me. After I nod she flies into the blowup doll. In a couple of seconds Dolly starts to move.

Izzie covers her mouth to keep from laughing.

Dolly jumps off the bed and sways into the hall. Gosh, I really wish I was inside.

Izzie and I hurry to the side living room window, hoping to catch a glimpse.

Enzo's on the couch, watching TV, and as it turns out, we have a perfect vantage point for the scare of his life.

I whip out my cell and turn on the video recording. If all goes well, I'm uploading this sucker to Facebook. I just want to capture Enzo's reaction. I'll edit out Dolly's role.

Suddenly Dolly rounds the corner and waves. As best as a plastic doll without movable parts can wave.

Enzo makes a sound I've never heard before, and I bet no human could ever make again. He jumps onto the sofa, dropping his beer. The bottle hits the floor and miraculously stands upright. When she walks closer, Enzo leaps over the coffee table and grabs his gun, which was in the unlocked lock box on the bookshelf. He fires two rounds into Dolly before she falls limp.

Emma stands in her place. Her eyes are wide, and she glances down to make sure she doesn't have bullet holes, obviously forgetting she's already dead.

Izzie can't hold her giggles back anymore. She screams, "Gotcha."

Enzo jumps and turns to us. His eyes are huge. Fear is etched into every crevice of his face. I'd be surprised if he hasn't wet himself. Still clutching his gun, he points it right at us.

Izzie and I duck. Squatting against the house, we burst into laughter.

"I'm going to get you two back. Just wait," Enzo shouts. He sounds super pissed. And super scared.

Izzie and I fall onto our butts on the grass and laugh harder.

Finally!

* * *

When Izzie drops Emma and me off, I grab my key and unlock the deli. Pop reopened it this week, but he's gone now, locked up an hour ago. I'm so glad to be almost home. It's gonna suck having an empty apartment though—just when I got used to the company.

Emma is adamant about leaving through the freezer. She says she wants to see what the big deal is, but I think she simply wants me by her side. Like we were with Billy. I'm glad. I'm going to miss her, although I won't admit that to Izzie. Even with the thaw, Izzie and Paulie have a long road ahead of them, and reminding my sister of her husband's one unfaithful night won't get them healing any sooner.

I open the freezer door, wedge the stool in front of it, and step inside with her.

One day I'll figure out why the freezer is so important to crossing over.

She turns to me. "Thank you for everything. I'm so glad you were able to prove your sister didn't kill me and that Wesley and I really had as wonderful a friendship as I believed."

"Me, too."

"I'm sorry Wesley lost his fiancée though. He has no one now. Will you visit him and make sure he's okay?"

I smile. "I will."

She faces the back of the freezer. "Okay. Here I go."

I take a deep breath and hold it.

She steps forward then stops and looks back. "Give Julian a second chance. He loves you, and he's right. Not everything is black and white."

I nod, but I still don't quite believe that. Or maybe I don't want to.

She takes several more steps and glides through the back wall.

I expect some big *ta-da*. I don't know why. There wasn't one when Billy left either. But just in case I still wait. Aside from the cold, I feel numb, like I want to cry. I'm really going to miss her.

I let out my breath finally and realize how much I enjoyed helping Emma and Billy. Maybe sandwich maker isn't all I can do.

I turn to leave. There must be a way to let other ghosts know I can help them. But how? I can't very well hang a shingle on my door.

Laughter sounds behind me.

I face the noise, thinking Emma didn't leave after all. Excitement bubbles in me. I should be worried that she's coming back, but I'm super excited she is.

Emma doesn't come through though.

It's him. Wrinkly face, shock of white hair, piercing blue eyes.

Freezer Dude peeks his head out, then an arm and a leg, and before I can run out and slam the door on him, his entire body shimmies onto my side of the freezer.

What the hell!

Fear grips me so tightly I can't move. My breathing becomes fast and erratic, much like my pulse.

His grin is unnaturally wide. He floats over to me and stands right before me.

Please don't touch me.

Just as fast as he arrived, he flies out the freezer door.

I finally move and run out, fearful he'll manage to lock me in. I look around the kitchen, run up front, search the office, and even the restroom. The entire deli is empty.

Where did he go?

And more importantly, what is he up to?

It hits me. All these years, he hasn't been trying to pull me to his side. He's been trying to get to mine.

Well crap!

ABOUT THE AUTHOR

Jennifer Fischetto is the *National Bestselling Author* of the Jamie Bond Mysteries. *Unbreakable Bond*, her adult debut novel, has received a National Reader's Choice award nomination. She writes dead bodies for ages 13 to six-feet-under. When not writing, she enjoys reading, cooking, singing (off-key), and watching an obscene amount of TV. She also adores trees, thunderstorms, and horror movies—the scarier the better. She lives in Western Mass with her family and is currently working on her next project.

To learn more about Jennifer Fischetto, visit her online at www.jenniferfischetto.com

Enjoyed this book? Check out these other reads available in print now from Gemma Halliday Publishing:

www.GemmaHallidayPublishing.com

Printed in Great Britain
by Amazon